Anders Flagstad's

Bone
Sliding

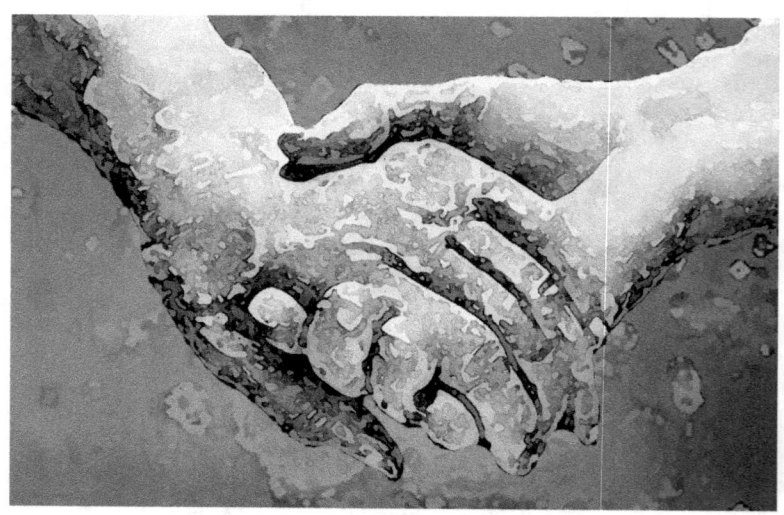

They stayed that way for some time. In a gold-white sack of light in the middle of the night, Jim standing, Daniel watching, his father breathing.

Jim stared at his father's hand, gripping his. It was beautiful. Clear pink skin, translucent over hard bone, it was a miracle of fragile unbreakability. That was his father's hand. His father used to look at his hands and ask Jim — how did I end up with an old man's hands? — these aren't my hands. But they were. He'd earned them. Year by year. Jim could feel all five fingers, the bones of his father's fingers, holding onto the bones of his. They weren't going to let go. None of them were. He looked and understood he couldn't tell where his father's hands left off and his own began. And that was fine. They were all the same hands, anyways. The same flesh. They always had been. They still were. They always would be. Nothing about that was going to change. Nothing ever changes.

It was good.

Jim blinked and thought and he was surprised again.

It was good.

He hadn't expected that.

from Chapter 62, Yearning, p. 116

Bone Sliding

A Novel by

Anders Flagstad

Bubble Eyes Publishing

www.BubbleEyesPublishing.com

Bubble Eyes Publishing

Library of Congress Catalogue Number: 2018931478

ISBN: 0-999-83850-4
ISBN-13: 978-0-999-83850-1

Illustrations and Design by K.P. Anderson

for
N.I.B.

Bone
Sliding

0
BEFORE

You know the feeling. It's a bad feeling.

Being.

It's confusing.

Then it gets worse.

Being.

Pleasures land on your front doorstep in fat, juicy parcels, so reliably, one after another, you don't even bother unwrapping them, let alone pick them up. Then, one day, you find steaming piles of pain and boredom deposited instead, and you wish you'd owned a different doorstep and you wonder, you have to ask – is there a reason behind all this?

Being.

There's no sense to it. What's the cause and effect of it? Where's the justice in it? How do its rewards and punishments work? And why? You ask why. Nobody gives you an answer.

There's no neat system of pluses and minuses. No equals sign giving you what you deserve. No tools. None that you can see. Or use. You end up un-asking the questions.

Being.

As long as you're here, and you are still here, maybe while you're asking and un-asking these questions, maybe you can practice something else. A new skill. A pastime. A kind of hobby. Like… Maybe… Love. It's something to do. As long as you're here. And you're still here. Who knows? Maybe questions weren't the reason we were here. Or answers.

It's confusing.

Being.

You know the feeling. It's a bad feeling.

1
CLICK

You know the feeling. It's a bad feeling. As if your flesh had come unhooked from your bones and your body was sliding right off your skeleton to fall – kerplunk! – as limp and shapeless on the floor as a shower curtain ripped off its rings. That's how Paul felt. All the time. He was tired of it. He hated it. First and foremost., as his dad would say.

A bad feeling.

It was almost as bad as when he felt his skin snapping back into place. Falling on top of his skeleton, draping over his skull, dropping over his shoulder blades, sliding onto his arm bones, cascading down around his leg bones... click! – click! – click! – fastening onto his many foot bones, everything almost hooking onto where it should be, flesh nearly back in its right place, but not quite, brother, not even close.

Almost normal.

You know, brother, that was an even worst feeling.

Then getting ripped off shapeless again. Falling on the floor.

No, brother, that was the worst feeling.

No, it was all bad. It was all the worst. It got so a guy even forgot his own name. Was he really Paul? Who was Paul? If he wasn't Paul, who was asking the question?

Feelings.

Why was it so complicated?

Then it would start again.

Those feelings.

Off. On. Off On. Anyways. You get it.

Paul hated it. If that's who he was. Paul? Paul? Yeah, it didn't sound right somehow. But that was crazy talk, right? Or does everyone feel that way? Anyways, whoever he was, his insides felt bunched and wrinkled. His mind felt as if it were an un-ironed shirt. And who wants a life as an un-ironed shirt?

Yeah, we've all been through it, right? Brother? Right? Well, Paul was sick of it. And he wasn't going to do it anymore.

When you can't even trust your own body, when you can't even feel comfortable in your own skin, well, brother, it's time for some serious thinking, some serious decision making. Enough is enough. And Paul had definitely had enough.

Paul was young. Maybe a little impetuous. Maybe he didn't think before he spoke sometimes. He was young – what could he say? He wished, he asked the Universe – get me out of this body – and sometimes brother, sometimes, you've got to be careful what you ask for.

2
ALMOST

Paul began coughing.

No, gagging, gasping was more like it.

He was lying down. In the snow. It had almost been peaceful. Until the car started up. The rusty exhaust pipe of the Model B he was lying beneath cleared its throat, then noisily belched woolly clouds of poisonous gas directly into his mouth and nose. He hadn't thought about that. You know, it had been all Paul could do to spit the gravel and ice out of his mouth when the car's rear tires started spinning. The tires chewed the powder up and cheerfully piled it, neat and tidy, onto his frost-bitten face. It was a pretty deep pile. It hurt. He hadn't thought about that either. Yeah, he blinked and spit a lot.

Paul was waiting for the car to slip and slide. It had been skating all over the road, all morning long, and of course, now that Paul was lying in back of it, it didn't want to slip an inch in any direction whatsoever. It stayed put and spun.

Paul was lying and waiting because he wanted the car to jump backwards and ride up on top of his body and roll all its ungainly, cast-iron heaviness over Paul's soft, squishy parts. He calculated the right rear tire would hit him in his head, above his nose, if he didn't move. Yup, that should do it. It should crush the life right out of him. The trick was not to move. He was more frightened than he thought he would be. You'd think he hadn't done this before. He was sure he had. Or had he? Did any of that make sense? He had another coughing fit. Maybe it was going to asphyxiate him first, instead. Well, brother, either way… Whatever it takes to get the job done. He coughed some more. Spit. He squinted his eyes. He kept on spitting. The car kept on shoveling snow at his face. Somebody kicked him. In the ribs. Right in the center of his heavy wool coat. Then he felt the sole of a shoe on his forehead.

He opened one eye. Not a shoe, a boot. It was Zeke's boot — well, one of Zeke's dad's boots, Zeke was in them now. Zeke had borrowed this pair since he didn't have a pair of his own. Another one of Zeke's brothers had borrowed Zeke's heavy leather boots a week ago, to help out an elderly uncle on an elderly farm out in the middle of nowhere, and they hadn't found their way home yet from North Dakota. These, the ones on Zeke's big oversized feet, they must have been made of even heavier leather, they were the Sherman Tanks of boots, military grade, and they surely had something akin to torpedo metal encasing the toes.

Yeah. All Paul knew was – they hurt. Yup. When used correctly. And the boots were being used by an expert. Zeke, at present. To be precise.

"Cut the engine Stan. Our boy here, he's asleep. You asleep, chump?"

"No."

"No? That's what you're telling me?"

"No."

"O.K., Paul, I give up. No, what? What do you think you're doing, you numbskull? Someone could get hurt lying in back of a car getting itself unstuck from a snowdrift. You pushing it with your nose?"

Paul didn't answer that.

But Zeke didn't go away.

After the engine slowed and the tires stopped, it got quiet, quick. Paul could see all this wasn't going to work, not as planned. He opened his other eye. He had a great view of worn rubber tread. You know, it never worked out the way you thought it would. It was never easy. It felt as if he'd done this before. Had he? The spitting, the boot tread and everything? How many times had he done this? How would he know? The bottom of the boot rubbed back and forth on Paul's forehead.

"Or didn't you think of that, Paul? Getting hurt? Getting killed? Or were you thinking at all? What's going on, brother?"

Zeke was giving Paul a strange look, halfway between a frown and a smile. The two expressions were fighting each other across his face. It was a fascinating battle to watch. The engine stopped. The frown won. The exhaust pipe wheezed, gave a final burp and settled into silence. He could hear a car door open, and Stan squeaking through the snow, plowing towards the two of them. It must be pretty cold out. The snow screamed it at every step. Yeah, even the icicles on his eyelashes had icicles. The engine exhaust had been warm though.

"What's he doing, Zeke?"

"No idea, brother."

"I'm checking the tires guys."

"He's checking the tires, Stan."

"Checking the tires. Now who woulda thought of that?"

Stan looked down at Paul. Zeke looked down at Paul. Paul looked up at Zeke and Stan. It hit Paul they were waiting for him to say something else. O.K. Great. Say something, Paully.

"C'mon guys. What did you think I was doing?"

Paul propped himself up on one of his elbows and turned his head around. This was ridiculous. He couldn't even get himself run over. In a blizzard. Behind a car. He coughed and blinked snow out of his eyes. His eyes had been aching, rolling them backwards to look up at his two best friends standing upside down in back of him. He hadn't been making much sense of the expressions on their upside-down faces. But, right-side up, the expressions became even stranger. Anger? Love? Betrayal? He almost laughed, they looked so comical. Then he felt like crying. Man! Why was it always so hard? In the end, Paul kept his face carefully blank. Or he thought he did. Who knew what was on his face? Who knew what was going on behind his face? Certainly not Paul. Life was a lot like riding a crazy merry-go-round, lately. Lots of motion... Always in a circle... Never getting anywhere... None of it meaning anything... The whole thing starting over... Around and around and...

Zeke and Stan looked at each other. Something unreadable passed between them. Or nothing passed between them. Paul could never tell. He could never figure out what they were thinking. They always surprised him.

"We don't know what you're doing, Paully" said Zeke.

There was a moment of silence for the three of them to take that in.

"And the truth of it is, brother," said Stan "we don't give a hoot anyways. So. Get the heck up and help us this time, the tires are fine. You get this bucket of bolts rolling forward again. O.K.? No more funny business, Paully, yes? *Entendu?*"

Stan looked over at Zeke again. They did that look/non-look thing again.

Stan grew up speaking French at home, he only mixed it up, speaking the Franglais, with his family and his best friends. He was trying to help Paul. He was treating Paul as family. Paul saw it. Paul understood it. Paul didn't want that kind of help though, just now. He didn't know what he wanted. This was all so wrong.

"Paully?"

"Paully?"

"Yeah. Sure."

Stan gave Paul his "I'm serious" look, wide eyes, raised eyebrows, the whole shebang.

Zeke looked at Stan. "He doesn't get it." Zeke acted as if he were going to kick Paul again. He smiled as he did it. But it wasn't a very convincing Zeke-smile. Zeke kicked the snow, and Paul danced up and out of the way, acting as if he'd expected to be kicked. Zeke pretended to kick Paul again, but at the last minute wrestled Paul down to his knees, not kidding, this time for real. Zeke was on the wrestling team. He was big. He knew how to get your cooperation, in a wrestling-way. Paul knew from experience. He was on the team too. Zeke easily and efficiently got Paul in his signature, inescapable head lock. Zeke was laughing. Now, this time, his smile was real. Paul was sure of it. Some hardness in Paul's chest slipped, melted into liquid, drained away through holes in his leaky soul, and suddenly Paul wanted to stay here. He wanted to stay. He didn't want to make his final exit. He wanted to be here. With these guys. Now. He wanted it. Where did all these feelings come from?

Stan went down on one knee and grabbed Paul's head-locked head with both of his well-mittened hands. He quickly ripped off Paul's cap, quickly tore off his own right mitten, and rapidly rubbed his knuckles painfully over Paul's head, back and forth, through Paul's thick red hair. It was freezing out, below freezing. Stan could only do it (mercifully) for a few seconds, before flesh would start getting frostbit. But it still hurt. Like a son-of-a-gun. It hurt. But it was a good kind of hurt. Did that make sense? If you were alive, you hurt.

"You're a crazy kid, Paully Olsen. You know that?"

3
CLICK

Out of the sides of his eye, Paul saw the penguins again.

Watching him. Silent as usual. Waist-high, silk-bright white torsos with lemon yellow mufflers and Fred Astaire formal coats, they usually stood politely to one side and surreptitiously followed Paul's movements with bored, expectant eyes and stoically hunched shoulders. The acted as if they were doing Paul a favor. At great personal cost to themselves.

Paul felt as if he were being scrutinized by any number of midget Winston Churchills. No pressure. Merely prime ministers watching you, Paully. Be yourself. Act natural. You know. As if they weren't here. So, Paul ignored them. Elaborately. He always did. Everyone else ignored them too, acted as if they weren't there. It seemed like the right thing to do.

Paul accidentally glanced at one, it caught Paul's attention between knuckle-rubbings, as it flapped its wings slightly and shuffled its big fluffy feet. Did he hear it sighing? Was that a yawn? Don't look, Paul. Look up. Look at Stan.

Why was it always so hard?

4
BURIED

Paul wanted to die.

Yeah. For as long as he could remember. Well, that wasn't true, not exactly. He couldn't remember very far back.

He felt as if he were a deck of cards, each card a life, and he could remember different people, guys, girls, different places, cities, farms, deserts, mountains, but nothing very clearly, nothing you could put your finger on and say – this happened to me, I was there, I know. He couldn't tell if he'd lived it, or if someone had told him about it, or if he'd read about it someplace. He was always looking at himself from somewhere way far away. Floating above it all. Where it was safe. Did everyone feel this way? He wanted to ask somebody if all that sounded strange. But he didn't. Did that make Paul a coward? He didn't know. He couldn't tell.

He had asked his gym teacher once though, about reincarnation.

Mr. Andrietti. A well-muscled fireplug of discipline and optimism. Paul liked him because he was short like Paul. At one point, during wrestling practice last fall, Mr. A. had shown the team something called "yoogah" and taught them how to tie themselves into pretzels. No one could. But they continued to try, pulling on their bones to make their teenage bodes as supple as rubber bands, imitating pigeons and dogs and frogs and plants. It felt good. And, yeah, it seemed to help in the wrestling department. But it was a crazy way to start practice.

Mr. A. was also a very inspiring speaker. He practiced endless variety in his motivational talks to the male teenagers under his wrestling supervision. Mr. A. had added smiling elephant-headed gods, and fourteen-armed dancers and remembering past lives to the rest of his encouraging banter as they huffed and groaned through their partially successful stretches and Paul had asked him once, after practice, if Mr. A. thought it was true – could you remember past lives? For real? Mr. A. had smiled and shook his head and slapped Paul on the back – "just you keep your weight down and concentrate on the Bakers Falls match next week. O.K., Mr. Olsen? That should be enough to handle."

Was that a yes?

Or a no?

But it didn't matter, because Paul would always end up hurting, in the end. Life hurt. And really, boy, did it, scout's honor. It hurt bad. But that meant you were alive, right?

Maybe. But he still wanted to kill himself. It hurt too much, he hurt other people too much, there were a lot of reasons. Good reasons too.

He'd thought about it. A lot. Anyone would say the same. It was common sense. If it got to be too much you made a change. Simple. He'd say so to anyone. If anyone would listen. Of course no one would. Well, Paul didn't ever bring it up. So, Paul supposed, they couldn't listen, right, if you never brought it up?

Wrong. They could bring it up. They could ask. No one asked Paul, did they? No, they didn't. No one asked him what was going on. No one asked him why he was so quiet. Time for a change, Paully. No more waiting. He was scared, yeah, who wouldn't be? He was scared but he'd decided. It was going to be today.

This was his last day on earth.

If this was his last day, why did it seem so familiar? How many last days can one guy have? Had he done this before? How could he know? Did he want to know? It was all so messed up.

Part of him was happy. Part was sad. Part needed to throw up. Would he be man enough to do it? And how would he do it?

Being polite and wanting to be a good Norwegian, he couldn't leave a mess, be loud, or draw too much attention to himself. That was a problem. The violence, the self-murder, that wasn't a problem. He lived in a violent age, if he didn't do it, the war probably would. No, it was a puzzle, wasn't it? Erasing yourself without causing a fuss. How did a guy do it?

And leaving all that love behind. People are the thing. People are important. Paul knew it as a certainty, as obvious to him as gravity, or his lazy, numbed fingers, or the ice in the wind trying to chap the face off his skull, or the knuckles grinding away at his hair. Yes, love was another problem. Love was obvious. You didn't question the obvious. It was love, stupid. It was why we're here. People. Love. People and love.

Yeah, love was the thing. It was it. And Paul wanted to forget all about it. How messed up was that? Paul was too messed up to be here. He needed to exit. Love made him want to stay. Paul wanted to go. Paul wanted love to let him go. But no. Love seemed to have a different opinion on the question. Love pulled on him. Love whispered to him. Promises. Lies were more like it. Why did love make things so complicated? It was always so hard.

And you didn't waste love. You spread it around. Paul had love around him, but he was really bad at giving love to others. He admitted it. Just ask his friends, his family. No one knew what to do with him.

It was time to go. And now, Paul wished he had more time. More time to learn to love better. Or to forget. To forget how to love at all. Forget love entirely. Yeah. Maybe he needed time to forget.

That didn't even make sense. Paul had no idea what he was talking about. None.

You know, brother, it all sounded so hokey when you tried to talk about it.

Yeah, Paul never tried to talk about it. How would a guy even start? He wouldn't. Not a normal guy. Paul was hollow inside. Other people had innards. He had empty space. Empty spaces didn't have much to talk about, did they? They were filled, these empty spaces, with all this junk about love. It wasn't his fault. He wasn't a normal guy. He wasn't. That was the thing. That was always the thing. Right?

5
CONSCIOUS

"Push, Paully. Now" said Zeke, yelling, passenger door open, leaning on the car frame, beating his big meaty left hand on the roof of the car and laughing, all in rhythm, all at the same time. That was Zeke. Paul would miss Zeke. Stan was back at the wheel. Pumping the gas like the wild man he was. Stan! He'd miss Stan too. Would they miss him? The car jerked in time to Zeke's pounding and Stan's pumping. Paul was behind the car, again, trying to encourage movement in the Model B, as it bounced and jittered in front of him. Snow fell in tight, self-important spirals around him. Even though he was the smallest of the three, they'd let him do the heaviest pushing. Same as any normal guy. They were being nice to him. That had to count for something, right? Right?

"You call that pushing, Paully?" said Zeke.

"Did you tell him to push, Zeke?"

"What do you think? I told him."

"Does he still have his skis on?"

"I don't see no skis."

"Well, we're not moving. Is he lying down again?"

"You lying down, Paully?"

"I think he's lying down, Zeke."

They could see him. They knew. Paul shook his head, pressed his shoulder to the boxy back of the Model B and grunted and pushed, let up and pushed again. Paul looked out over the silent fields. Snow flurries were a solid curtain now. Wind was blowing. Drifts were getting deep. He exhaled clouds of steam. He must look as if he were a Paul-sized musk ox. Butt-heading a black rock that refused to budge. A National Geographic photograph. Of deepest Alaska. Or furthest Siberia. The penguins were still observing him, huddled under a young pine tree by the side of the road, shuffling in the powdery snow and staring straight ahead through the branches. Paul looked up, shocked, when the car unexpectedly surged forwards and leaped up and out of the drift. Guess he could push after all. Oh. Wait. Zeke was beside him. He'd snuck back.

"That's how you push, Paully" said Zeke. "Use your big Swedish muscles and your superior Swedish brains. Like me. Oh. I forgot. You're Norwegian. My condolences."

It took a few minutes for Paul to find his skis. They were missing. Gone AWOL. Angled in a drainage culvert, completely covered in white, frozen fluff as if they were Christmas cookies and the snow powdered sugar. Cookies. Sugar. He heard noises way underneath his layers of jacket and sweater. Boy, that made a guy hungry. Paully! Why would you be hungry? You're not supposed to be coming home tonight. Ever. Never again. Hungry is for the living. Not for you. Not for the skiing dead.

Paul's stomach rumbled anyway, as if it didn't care. O.K., yeah, sure he was hungry, what the heck! And he knew exactly what to do. He reached inside his jacket pocket. Pulled out a brown and blue bottle. Liquid bread. Schmidt's best. The beer wasn't frozen. Yet. He found his can opener. He'd remembered to bring that along, at least. He wasn't entirely useless, huh? It took another minute or so to get himself set up, between chugs, and get the rope re-tied back onto the bumper. He jerked on the rope to let them know he was ready.

Now it was time to fly. Flying: it was the reason they were out here on a Saturday morning (afternoon actually), on January 1st, while everyone else was home eating aspirin and drinking seltzer and generally recuperating and recovering from last night's extravagances. O.K., yeah, sure, Minnesota was flat. Skiing should be horrible. But the way the three of them saw it, that was the point of it. Sure it was flat, but it was flat with ditches. It had flat roads which were for speeding, and drainage ditches which were for jumping, and any fool with half a brain could see where that argument was heading. Obviously, the point of all this flatness was flight. Skiing. Speeding. Jumping. Freedom. Flight.

So, Stan and Zeke had let him go again, a third time now, they'd let him ski even though it wasn't his turn. Yeah, they were being nice to him. He didn't know what to think about that.

Darn.

This was messed up.

Nope, he didn't want to think about it.

He waited with the rope in his hand. He jerked it again. They still didn't move. Zeke and Stan were deep in discussion, heads down, in the front seat of the Model B. What were they talking about? About him? A minute later, two more beers flew back over the top of the Model B. Oh. That's what they were talking about. The bottles barely missed his head. Paul smiled, for them, for the beer, for the extra turns at skiing, but they didn't see him doing it. Paul quickly found a place for the two bottles in his inside jacket pockets. He jerked the rope. The car roared into life. They inched forward. Paul looked up at the sky. So empty.

For a moment he'd felt excited. For a moment everything had made sense. He'd felt himself filling up a little. The hollowness relenting. His body settling back on his shoulders, skin settling back into place, all the wrinkles unwrinkling. Now he was empty again. Just a bony superstructure on skis. A space where there should have been a boy. It shouldn't be this hard, brother, it just shouldn't.

6
CLICK

His chest hurt.

Paul felt dizzy and he couldn't breathe, not correctly. He heard music in the wind, only there wasn't any wind. Paul could hear someone gasping, throat rasping, nearby. He blinked. He was lying down. On his face. Flat rocks a screaming candy corn orange, skies a rusty sugar red, and a blueberry sun floating on the horizon. He wasn't thirsty. He wasn't hungry. He wasn't cold. He wasn't warm either. He was scared, though. This had all happened a long, long time ago, right? It was hard to remember sometimes. He blinked again.

The cold hit his eyeballs as if it were trying to pry them out of his head, and he had to blink a couple of times before they were warm enough for him to see the Model B's bumper ahead of him. He looked around. The penguins were gone. He was moving across the snow. Slowly. His skis made creaking sounds in the snow. Yeah, way below zero. The tires weren't getting much to grip on either. They (Paul, the rope and the car) moved forwards in random jerks and tugs. Zeke hung out of the passenger window, beating the car top, trying to encourage the machine to sprint. It wasn't working. Zeke leaned further and further out. Anybody would say Zeke was crazy. Anybody would be right. Paul smiled.

No one saw. Not Zeke. Not Stan. Not the penguins. Nobody.

7
DISCOMFORT

His chest hurt.

That had started up six months ago. No, longer. Maybe the middle of his Junior year. It was hard to remember sometimes. Maybe after the penguins came. Maybe before.

So. Yeah, there was this ache in his chest. He wasn't complaining. He hurt. Why? No idea, brother. Did it matter? He hurt in a gentle, bittersweet, both-arms-and-legs-ripped-off-and-your-intestines-pulled-inside-out-through-your-butthole kind of way. He hated himself. He was such a disappointment to everyone and everything. His father, his teachers, his family, his friends. A big zero. He hurt all the time. He'd like to meet the guy who would want to live this way. He wondered why no one else noticed it, him dragging his raw insides outside, trailing them behind him, moist and bleeding and caked with filth, pulling them behind him everywhere he went. Did they really see him when they saw him? The important thing, apparently, was to act normal. Normal was a problem for Paul. It was a big problem.

He'd planned on doing himself in before Christmas, but Christmas day had come and gone and here he was. Still here. Still hopeless. Man! His chest hurt. It kind of felt good, though. At least it was familiar. It was constant. He could count on it. He was twisted, he was a mess, huh? Afraid of death. Afraid of life. Being a teenager wasn't supposed to hurt this hard. It wasn't fair. And Paul hadn't asked for any of this. Stop whining Paul. It doesn't help. Think about something else. Think about something pleasant. Look at the snow Paul. Look at the trees. You should be grateful, Paul. Lots of people have it worse than you, Paul.

The car bounded forwards. Slid left. Slid right. Zeke banged on the roof. Paul blinked a lot and clenched and clutched at the rope. You could walk faster than they were moving.

The blackness hit especially hard in the evening. It fell on him, more and more, a physical blanket thing, a feeling, maybe how a sodden, rubberized Hudson Bay blanket would feel if it were an emotion – wildly heavy, puncture-proof, watertight and insupportable. Blackness came for him and covered and smothered him. It dizzied him. It competed with him for air, it seeped into his head and his lungs and heart and solidified, cement-hard. Paul was tired of it He was helpless. Paul hated that. He was a little kid again, a toddler, locked in a broken-down basement, maybe under an abandoned church, windowless, broken glass, rusty nails, dark, cold, wet, stinking with mold, full of so many sharp, unpleasant things that cunningly sought his soft unprotected parts and cut him when he wasn't looking.

Nice Paul.

Now, is that any way to live?

Don't even answer.

He was alone. Well, he and the blackness, they were alone together.

And he knew. He and the blackness both knew. The blackness, it wanted to shut him up. Forever. It would never let him win, it would never fight fair, it would never give up. Never.

Never.

Remember that, Paul.

So it had to be today.

Yeah, he'd decided.

There weren't any cliffs near his home. He didn't have a gun. But he did have an automobile handy. Kind of. Zeke's dad's. He'd get himself run over. Have an accident. Minimum fuss. Maximum effect. He'd decided. He only hoped, looking at his friends in the front seat of the Model B, that he didn't get them into any trouble. He was a Minnesotan after all. You don't cause trouble. You don't cause a fuss. People's lives were hard enough as it is. There was a depression on, for Pete's sake. No need to make it worse, huh?

You know, he'd miss them both, Stan and Zeke. Had he ever told them that?

8

EXHALE

Yeah, the blackness always won.

Except, when it didn't.

Sometimes doors unlocked, windows unlatched, fevers broke and sunrises rose, lights flooded, sunsets flashed, horizons folded and nights opened, they widened, spread and sang, and stars sprinkled and sparked above Paul's head, and yeah, galaxies and nebulae bloomed bright over his bright hair as would tightly wound buds of a night-blooming flowers, and Paul's mind would shred in pleasure beneath it all and Paul would change. Those were the good times, brother, they were the best times. The darkness? It was a joke, he couldn't even remember it. The soft night burned, everything shifted, melted, flowed and Paul exhaled himself upwards, through his own ears, through his own nostrils, blown softly about on soft winds upwards, drifting into expanding nights, soaring through humid, blood-hot skies, enjoying his soul's summer shamelessly, and Paul would also find, trembling and amazed and somewhat disgusted, that he was happy. He was himself again. He was Paul. Just Paul.

And he was happy.

Again.

Nothing like that feeling, brother.

That was how it felt. Sometimes.

Maybe a Minnesotan boy wouldn't describe it exactly that way to another Minnesotan boy. But who cared? It still felt good. When the blackness lifted, he admitted it, it felt good.

The experience made it very hard to plan your own suicide, though.

Life and love are strong things. They didn't fight fair. And they fought back when you hit them. They'd punch you when you weren't looking. Love wasn't polite. Paul was learning that. Yup.

The car had by now, picked up a little speed. It still jerked. It still slipped. But it went forwards more than any other direction. Faster. And faster. And faster.

Almost like…

Flying.

Paul saw Zeke and Stan look back at him, one on each side of the car, laughing and hooting as the three of them hot-footed it through more and deeper drifts in their B-mobile and Paul loved those guys. Yeah, he loved them. Suddenly his face felt hot. He felt full. He felt the opposite of empty.

And he was here again. He was Paul again.

When it happened, like now, he was Paul Olsen, average guy, first trumpet in the band, red-haired, small for his age, a tortoise-shell-eyeglass-wearing, decent-tennis-playing, wannabe wrestler, girl-dating, brother of four sisters, typical modern Minnesotan Red River High School senior, Class of 1944. He was himself. Once again. He could breathe. He could walk. He could talk. It was glorious. It was heaven. He could move about as if the blackness didn't exist, because, brother, believe this, it didn't. Not for Paul Olsen. Not then. Not now. Not in any manner, shape or form, brother.

He didn't care. About blackness, about anything. He couldn't help it. He just didn't. He was seventeen, he was alive, and he didn't give a fig what anyone thought of him, or what the rotten future might hold for him, or even that he was trying to off himself today. He was here. He knew who he was. He was himself. He didn't care. That was all that mattered.

Remember this, Paul, remember this feeling. This one time, remember.

But he never did.

9
FLOATING

"Yeah! Fly, boys, fly!"

Paul war-whooped upwards, yelled at low-hanging masses of snow-clouds, howled his lungs out into cautious, lurking flurries and hesitating, curious squalls. He wasn't suspicious. He wasn't hesitating. He wanted to mark this afternoon. It was his. All his. He wanted people to know Paul Olsen was alive and Paul Olsen was here and he owned this.

The Model B ahead of him jumped its tracks, spun its wheels in the powder, fishtailed, sprayed snow at Paul's face. Paul laughed, he ducked. The car fought Paul. He fought back. It tried to get free of him – a big, fat, black lake trout caught on a hook and unhappy about it – but Paul wouldn't let it. It was his. He'd landed it. Or maybe it had landed him. Yes, Paul was tied to the car's rear bumper (well, holding the rope, tied to the bumper). He was strapped in on Stan's old cross-country skis. He was being pulled at a ridiculous rate of speed, and, as a result, screaming his hot breath out at all of Minnesota and everything this morning. But it was his choice. He was here. He was doing it. No one else.

"Yeah! Gun it, boys. Floor it!"

He bent his knees, balanced himself, the car accelerated. He didn't care. He didn't care what he felt like or what he looked like. Yeah he had a cold. His nose dripped. It had frozen all over his face already (it was January what did he expect?) and managed to cover his fuzzily frozen, green wool muffler too. Didn't matter. Paul was busy, man. His skis whispered to him, guaranteeing him speed, frenzy, peril. Yeah, maybe he'd get hurt. What of it, brother? Winter Minnesota (not to be confused with its gorgeous twin sister, Summer Minnesota) flew by him, on both sides of his head – too beautiful to explain, too deep an emotion to talk about. If you were trying to describe it, you weren't feeling it. Paul was definitely feeling it, brother. Almost. He felt something. He felt.

"Yeah!"

That was a start, wasn't it? He was in the middle of it. It was here. It was now. Paul was in the center. Of something. Of what, though? What had really changed, Paul? Just stop it, Paul. Let go. Get your kicks. While you're here. Be here. Be.

He could see every single needle on every single pine tree. The snow had stopped for a minute. The air was so clear and so cold, the light was a uniform, fluorescent, phosphorescent white, and he was skiing in the center of it, over a pearl, bobbing in cream, inside a white marble bowl, sliding on a cloud. It was clean and it was pure, and his body knew it. Paul wanted his body to know. He could feel every hair on his faint, but manly, red moustache standing erect on his upper lip in the frost. He could feel his life inside of him, erect, aware, watching. He could feel Paul Olsen being alive. He could feel it. He was alive.

"Yeah! Faster, Stan, faster!"

Stan couldn't hear him over the motor. But what the heck! Nothing mattered. Zeke was still hanging out of the car. Banging on the top. Face in the wind. A dog out for a car ride. Zeke was crazy.

Paul tried to forget, then he did forget, then he forgot he was forgetting.

"Yeah! Yeah, brother!"

Paul flew across the deep, long-waved snow the way a jap Zero flies over the deep, long-waved Pacific – barreling, skimming, strafing, climbing, stalling, dropping, turning, dipping, diving. He crashed up the side of drainage ditches, slammed down the other side of entrance roads, pounded the ground and burst snowbanks.

He dodged fence posts, grazed mailboxes and floated over snow-drifted lumps of various sizes and shapes, lumps that could've been anything and everything and easily could've ripped him apart. But did he care? Dumb question. He was Paul Olsen. And Paul was free.

The responsible voices in his head were too appalled, too disgusted watching from the inside of his eyeballs to protest as the landscape peeled by them at dive-bomber speeds. That was the price they paid. For being residents of Paul's head.

"Yippee-tai-yay!"

10
GRAVITY

The rope felt stiff and moody. He pulled on it, but it didn't want to do much of anything. It sure didn't want to bend anymore. It was getting colder. Paul was turning into a guy-sized ice cube frozen onto the end of a frozen rope. His feet were icy lumps. He could use some heat right about now. He tried jumping up and down on his skis as he whooshed through the Minnesota landscape.

Paul was moving, moving pretty good now. The wind was brutal. He chanced it one-handed to pull his scarf tighter around his head and nearly flipped head over heels. Not the smartest move, Paully. The car was plowing ahead. Paul was plowing behind. They were on a straightaway. He could see two ski caps leaning towards each other through the frost-covered windows of the car. Were they laughing? Was that music he heard? Why did he feel so scared? He kept his eyes on Stan and Zeke and missed the intersection they were crossing.

"Guys! Hey fatheads!"

He jumped the road, which was fun. When he hit the snow again, on the other side, Paul whipped the rope over an approaching stop sign with one casual, masterful flick. When that didn't work, Paul jerked it, then he wiggled it, then he threw it, upwards over his head, frantic, sweating, pretty much disengaging his entire shoulder from its socket. The rope disregarded him, then lazily snapped at Paul, explosively shedding ice and snow, and lifted itself, unenthusiastically, out of harm's way at the very last minute, at the very last possible second. Paul watched the stop sign disappearing in his peripheral vision. The rope felt less like a rope now and more and more like a woven two-by-four. The bottles in his jacket pockets clinked together. Well, it was more like crashed together. He felt them, more than a little compulsively, to see if they'd smashed and broken. This was feeling more and more like work and less and less like fun

"Guys! Hey Stan! Zeke! Guys!?"

The car locomotived onwards through a drift across the road, the deep powder exploded left and right as if they were motoring through land mines. Bam! Pow! The world was white. Everywhere. He couldn't tell if he was in the air or on the ground. When the clouds of snow thinned a bit. Paul realized he was sliding sideways. He jumped back into the Model B's wheel tracks, which wasn't easy because Paul was a sliding snowdrift at this point. Pinned to the ground. Blankets and drifts of snow attached to his coat and pants. Paul's eyeglasses boasted miniature drifts. He shook his head to clear them. Nothing happened. He wiped his glasses off with quick jerky movements, bending over, as he didn't want to let go of the rope, and he slid sideways again. He couldn't see a thing, for the love of Pete. he let go with one hand. Wiped his face. Smudged his glasses, and the rope saw its chance. It lunged at him, repeatedly. Paul could swear he heard it snarling at him.

11
HEAVY

From somewhere, Paul heard music, definitely, this time, it was a swing band, it was clearer than any radio he'd ever heard before. It was coming from the right. Must be an echo from the car. In the snow? Well, when it got really cold, sound got funny, didn't it? Sure. How cold was it out here? Jeez! No wonder they couldn't hear him. They weren't even listening for him. They were singing along with the radio. Zeke had said the radio was broke. Guess not.

Why would Zeke lie to him?

Was Stan in on it? Of course he was. They did things like that. Without him.

Stop it Paul.

From out of nowhere Paul smelled orange blossoms. His stomach did flip-flops. It was sickening. As if a whole field of orange trees had died in mid-blossom and been stacked upwind from him to rot. The two of them were spritzing perfume all over Zeke's dad's Model B? Why? What kind of a party were they having in there? Without Paul? Always without Paul?

Paul's heart sped way up. Paul's breathing slowed way down and got shallow. Don't do this to yourself Paul. Do what? You know what. No, what? Don't do this Paul.

This wasn't the blackness. No. It wasn't going to happen.

The car swerved, slowed down. To avoid what? Paul never knew. Paul jumped out of the way and into another drainage ditch. He moved his lumber-like rope to the left, then to the right. He missed a fence post. Barely. The car sped up. Paul sped up. The music got louder. His eyeglasses were collecting snow again. Dang! He bent his knees to jump back out of the ditch. He pulled back on the petrified rope. He wasn't sure if he was having fun or not. Was he?

12
CLICK

"Ah! C'mon!"

For a second, Paul heard rain hitting a pane of glass. His forehead was pressed to it. And it was dark. And he was sitting down. Dry. Warm. It smelled dusty. A sharp, tangy tickle in his nostrils. He was crying. A low murmuring rolled under his feet. Bright colored lights blinked next to him. He could hear breathing. In the shadows. At his feet, he thought he could see black beaks and black and white feathers shining back up at him, feathers and matching shiny black-button eyes. The eyes looked amused.

13
INTERMISSION

"Ah! C'mon, guys!"

The car bucked right and threw Paul left into the ditch again. He was O.K, yeah. It was easier to ski here. What were they thinking? The orange junk was still in his nostrils. If it had been a noise it would've been deafening. He breathed through his mouth.

Don't throw up. Don't throw up. He was a little dizzy. No. He was a lot dizzy. The orange was everywhere. Was he going to start seeing orange again too?

Paul's stomach was in knots. Not any simple set of slip knots either. A big mother-lovin' rat's nest of Stevedore knots. The navy kind, the kind you'd tie a destroyer to a pier with. It was all wrong. He didn't know what or why. Or even how. But it was wrong. Jeez, it came out of nowhere, brother, all this wacky fear. Not again. Not here. Not now. He was sweating it. He was drowning in it. He was going bonkers, nuts. Was he crying? For the love of Mike! He looked down at his hands, gripping the knotted rope.

The car bounced forwards and slid in front of him, to the left. Paul tried to ease to the right. The rope, frosted and slippery as all get out, bucked and jerked left, in his gloves, again and again and again. It was annoyed – a twisted, kinked up, frozen, irritated anaconda of hemp and it wanted him dead.

Well, he and the rope had that in common. Paul grunted and smiled, to himself, deep behind his muffler and with his neck hunched deeper into his jacket collar. The rope jerked left again and again. Each time, Paul pulled to the right.

Oof da! Paul leaned and put all his weight into it.

He wrestled the rope into temporary submission, and as he did, he asked himself, for the twentieth time – am I having fun? Are you, Paully? Are you?

He thought he saw tuxedoed torpedoes (penguins?) sliding on their bellies in formation on either side of him. The music was deafening. The orange smell wasn't mixing with his beery breath very well.

Are you having fun, Paully?

He started to glance to his right, to reconnoiter a passing squadron of tuxedoes. Just for a split second. That was all. Just to get a glimpse. To make absolutely sure that he, Paul was going completely and utterly nuts. Although he'd, pretty much, figured that out already. Big mistake. He never even got to turn his head.

The rope flipped upwards. It hit him in the face and flew out of his hands. Paul slowed, then came to a stop. The car sped on, rope flying every which way. It was free! Free! The music died down. The stench of decaying orange grove corpses dissipated in the freezing cold, and Paul stood still. It got very, very quiet where Paul was.

He stood in the ditch, stamping his skis to stay warm and clapping his hands and staring straight forward at nothing in particular. He stared for quite a while. O.K. Now what? He pulled a shirt three layers down beneath his jacket to try and clean off his eyeglasses. This time it worked. His eyeglasses had regained their transparency. He could see. He could also wait. So, he waited.

He could feel a big bruise forming on his forehead. Ouch. That hurt. Paul got it. He was alive.

The snow picked up. Then it was all over him. Paul was the only spot of color in his world. And he wasn't much of a spot of color, as spots go, now was he? No. Snow was attracted to Paul, right out of the air and attached itself quickly and efficiently to Paul's body as if Paul were a lint brush and the world was a suit coat covered in dog hair. Paul was being erased. He was disappointing as well as disappearing, just another snow-colored object in a snow-colored storm, in a universe of snow. Paul was alone. Paul and universal white and his brand-spanking-new bruise.

14
JUGGLING

He was calm. It surprised him. It frightened him.

They better not lose me out here. They better come back.

Of course they'll come back. They just have to turn around first. Have to find a wide enough spot in the road to back in and out of. Follow their tire ruts back to me. Follow them and they'll find me. Easy. Easy as pie. Get to me in no time.

Paul looked down, looked up at the road, watched the wind scour and smooth the snow, erasing the tire tracks, pretty much erasing the road. Stan's battered, old skis began to disappear under blowing white stuff that tornadoed around him in every direction. The skis were there. Paul saw them. And then they weren't. It was as if Paul were foot-less, legs ending in stumps in a shallow river of drifting flurries.

They'll find me. They'll turn back.

You know, Paul, people disappeared in blizzards. Re-appeared (in a manner of speaking) when drifts melted in the spring.

Then, as his stomach performed a particularly painful contraction, Paul squinted his eyes shut, and in the process realized something. Something obvious. Something important.

Maybe this is my opportunity.

All you have to do is ski into a field, take your clothes off, and lie down. You'll be gone in minutes. Twenty minutes tops. It was way below zero out here today. Easy. Easy as pie.

O.K.

All you need to do is do it. Get going. Go on Paully. Start skiing. There's a field. There are your skis.

For some reason, he immediately could see his dad's face, coming out of the snow. Walking towards him. That couldn't be right.

"Dad?"

Then it was nothing but white on white sheets of snow and more snow. Vortexing at him. Nothing else.

"Dad?"

This was getting him nowhere, quick.

You know, for the most part, his father was cheerful, soft-spoken, few-worded. People liked him, liked him a lot, he was popular, apparently. Paul wouldn't know. Paul hardly knew his father. Paul wasn't complaining. His dad was one of the most responsible men Paul knew about. The Olsens had a roof over their heads, food on the table, gifts under the Christmas tree, all through the depression. They'd even had cars and vacations. But dad was never home. He was a hypothetical. All kinds of things happened that pointed towards a dad existing somewhere near Paul's house. But his chair at the head of the dining room table was (almost) never sat in. The garage was (usually) empty. His mom had raised the Olsens, all five of them, pretty much on her own. Not that Paul was complaining. No.

And when his father was there, he wasn't. It was as if his mom had a guest in the house. Whatever room his dad was in, they had to stay out of. And the few times Paul and his father occupied the same physical space, Paul never knew what would get a reaction in his dad. He had no idea. Paul had no idea what his father wanted to teach him about life. Paul would say something, his dad would nod, reading the newspaper, that was that. Then Paul would say something else, the frown lines would manifest on his father's forehead. His face would fill with a new energy. A puzzled expression would float, pass over his eyes, then his face, eyebrows would lower, lips would twist into a half-smile – a thunder cloud briefly eclipsing the sun – then all of it, all the puzzlement, the eyebrow, lip, forehead motion, all of it would be gone, it would all vanish, and his father's eyes would be glancing at him again, friendly, but now, empty. He'd be listening to Paul, but Paul wasn't touching him exactly. Not in a way that counted as touching. Not on the inside. Not anymore. Maybe not ever.

Paul, apparently, was on his own.

Maybe, that's what his dad was trying to teach him.

15
KAOS

Shouldn't you be skiing somewhere, Paully?

Shut up, you.

Paul rocked back and forth on his skis, staring upwards at the cone of flakes targeting his face as if they were tracer bullets.

Vaguely he wondered where the penguins were. They seemed to like it when he was upset. They liked to watch.

What kind of bird liked to watch people suffer? That wasn't right.

Flakes pelted his face.

He closed his eyes. Pointed his face up at the sky anyways.

Dad confused Paul.

Yeah, take, say, that morning, at breakfast.

Paul had told dad, mom, and the girls, he'd joined the Navy. He'd done it, enlisted, months ago, in a fit of responsibility. He figured he'd better say something. At some point. So they didn't find out later. After he was dead. Since he was going to off himself. He'd better clean things up. It was the responsible thing to do.

Yeah, Paul had been waiting, carefully, cautiously, for the perfect time to break the news to everyone, mom, dad, the sisters, everyone. That time had never come. And then, this morning, it had just slipped out of his mouth, between the oatmeal and the scrambled eggs, before he'd realized he was going to say it. Maybe because it was his Exit Day. Maybe not. Who could tell?

Conversation had stopped, coffee cups had remained suspended in mid-air. Stupidly, Paul had thought people would be proud, pleased. But no. They were silent. Paul didn't know why. All the guys in his class in High School were doing it. No one had a choice. Everyone knew, everyone understood – you had to enlist or get drafted, that was the way things were – but brother, what a scene! Everyone looked at dad. Dad looked at Paul. Paul felt his face getting red. Dad's face went blank. A rigid, stony blank. The look of a man getting his legs sawed off with no anesthesia. Then his face went empty. He was encouraging. He was excruciatingly fair. Dad wanted Paul to be happy. If the Navy was what would do it, then Paul should do it. Paul should do what he thinks is right.

Was Paul doing right? Was he? Was he being patriotic and brave? Was he being selfish? Should he be in the army? Like dad was in World War I? In the trenches? Getting gassed? Cutting the dead skin off the soles of his feet with a knife? Or was it a bayonet? Not that his dad ever talked about it. No. He'd learned all about the war, and his dad's years in it, his losing his nurse sister in France and not even knowing it – all of it – Paul had learned all his dad's war stories from his uncles. His dad was a big mystery. An absence. Sometimes Paul felt as if he were pretending he had a dad. O.K. Maybe that wasn't fair to dad. But it wasn't fair to Paul, either. It wasn't fair. Paul hated it. He hated himself for hating it. You know, it hurt to think of it, all around, all that hating, and he didn't want to do it, but Paul couldn't stop, he couldn't stop himself.

His dad was never there. O.K. Sure. Paul had to accept that. That was dad. Dad travelled. The state of Minnesota was a big place. Paul's dad was all over it. Deciding, managing, delegating, impressing, he was a big man in the boardrooms of the Minnesota Dairy Cooperative. Paul was proud of him They all were. All the Olsens. Paul felt guilty about that too. Paul was the only son, but that didn't mean Paul wanted to go into the dairy coop business himself. Dad never mentioned it. But Paul felt it.

O.K. Sure. Fine. Paul liked butter and milk and all, like any guy would, heck, nothing wrong with that, they were O.K., it was food, dairy coops helped people, they made life better for others, farmers, families, little kids that needed milk, sure, all right, that was all true, Paul couldn't deny it. But… even so… dad… Paul… well, the truth was… Paul wanted… he wanted… he wanted more.

That was his dirty secret. He wasn't proud of it. Paul always wanted more. Yeah, that was his problem. He wanted more and more, and even then it was never enough. Getting more made you want more. Wanting more made you get more Then the more you got, the more you wanted. And then you wanted something else too, something else instead. And you got that. And then, more of that. And more and more. And then it all started over again, and you went on and on, and it never stopped, did it? – it was a kind of disease, wasn't it?

Wanting more? Sure it was. It was a sickness. It wasn't something a Minnesotan did. You were happy with what you had. You were grateful. A guy should be grateful. But Paul wasn't.

Paul wished he knew exactly what it was he was wanting so much more of.

And why.

He wanted to know that too.

And he wished he could get enough of it, so he could stop.

This wanting, it was making him crazy. He wanted to stop wanting. Just stop it, Paul. Stop.

Be like dad. His dad wasn't mooning about, always wanting junk he didn't have. Paul needed to be like him, like his father.

No.

No, he didn't want that.

Not like his father.

Paul didn't want to end up being like his father.

That was another dirty secret of Paul's. Paul was a mess. An ungrateful bastard. A bad son. A poor friend. An empty boy.

Still, no matter what he was, he didn't want to be like his father.

No, never that.

Never.

Not like dad.

So what were his choices?

That's when he'd decided. That's when he knew. Today was the day. Today he'd make his exit. It was simple, once you thought it through. Simple.

16
LION

He needed to go. Time to get off the road. Time to strip. Time to die.

He could see a row of trees in the distance. A lot of trees. That would be the place to do it. Hidden. Away from the road.

He caught his breath. Cleaned his glasses. This time it didn't work so well. More smear than clear.

Get out of the ditch, brother. Take the road for a bit. Head for the trees. The trees, Paul. O.K.? Can you do that, Paully?

He started pushing forward. Squinting. It wasn't easy. It looked flat. But it sure didn't feel flat. Must be on the upside of a hill here, Paully. The road was fighting against him. He had to chicken walk it, crossing his skis behind, pushing out ahead. Slow going and the wind picked up. It splashed around him, tickled his nostrils, slapped his chest, tried to get him to slow down. When that didn't work, the wind swung around, pushing him from behind, trying to knock him over, toss him onto his bumpy forehead, but Paul still didn't stop. He pushed on. He sweated and gasped. And as Paul's face unfroze a little bit, he felt how good it was to move his flesh, compress his bones, snap his tendons, pump his thighs. It felt good. His body worked. His lungs worked. They hurt. But it was a good hurt. He felt muscles he didn't know he had. On the sides of his legs. Down his calves. They hurt too. Every time he stepped forward on his crossed skis. Yeah. He was feeling something. He decided he liked travelling through the blizzard this way. Huffing. Squinting. Inching forward.

It was good.

As if he had a choice.

He stopped. Got his breath again. Blew his nose onto his glove.

O.K. Paul Bunyan time. Norwegian north woods strength and all that hullaballoo. Time to do it, Paully. Time to show a little backbone for Pete's sake! Just get to the woods. Get naked. Do what you have to do. Time to be a man, Paully.

17
MAMMOTH

Push. Lift. Glide. Push. Lift. Glide.

Clink! Clink! Those were the bottles in his coat.

Paul was sweating. Breath was coming in hoarse coughs. Nose was running. Snow wouldn't let up. Wind had switched on him a number of times now. Blowing from his left side. Then from the front. Had to keep on going. Luckily he could still see the Model B's tracks. He stayed on top of them. The shadows of them anyways, a slightly darker white on white. At least he wouldn't ski right off the road onto a lake, right? Right? You could be 10-15 miles out on a lake and not know it. Then it would be too late. Unless you skied into a colony of ice fisherman and their houses.

Well, a lake was just as good as some trees, right? Did it really matter where he died? No. It didn't. He should probably not be close to the road though, huh? Need to hide. Need not to be found. Go for the lake, Paul, the lake!

Clink! Clink!

His beer was calling to him.

Push. Lift. Glide. Push. Lift. Glide.

No, go for the trees. Follow the plan.

Push. Lift. Glide. Push. Lift. Glide.

O.K.

Push. Lift. Glide. Push. Lift. Glide.

Clink! Clink!

Was that the road?

Push. Lift. Glide. Push. Lift. Glide.

Hard to tell. It looked darker. Was it getting darker? Was that the sun going down?

Push. Lift. Glide. Push. Lift. Glide.

Yes.

Push. Lift. Glide. Push. Lift. Glide.

Yes, darker.

Clink! Clink!

The trees were still a ways off. Were they even trees? Or were they tree-like blurs? He looked behind him. The tire tracks were gone. More dark grey blurs behind.

18

CLICK

Paul could hear music in the wind. Again. He felt light. As if he were a kite. A kite whose string had snapped and twisted and spun now whichever way the wind pushed it. He thought about that as he sipped his beer. He felt his skin loosening, his bones unfastening. His eyes were closed. The sun was shining straight into his face. A warmer gray than the sky around it. He felt warm all of a sudden. Water flowing over his feet. He was barefooted.

Humid air pressed down on his face. His face was sunburned. No. His skin was very dark. No, his skin was a different color. He could hear birds calling, insects buzzing, a thunderstorm somewhere far off rumbling. It was loud. Nothing smelled of Minnesota. It smelled as if he'd broken a spice rack and poured it over his head. Sharp. Stinging smells. Dry, smoky smells. He felt lazy and quiet and his stomach was full. He had a stalk of something in his mouth, and he could smell fresh-cut hay, or grass, or whatever it was, all around him. He opened his…

No.

He shook his head.

No. Not here.

Not again. Not now. No.

He shook his head again, closed his eyes tighter. His face still felt warm. Then it was cold. Very cold. What was he afraid of? He wasn't sure. He couldn't remember. What was he trying to remember?

When he opened his eyes, all he could see was white. Which didn't make sense to Paul. Not for a very long time.

19
NOWHERE

Paul found himself standing in a snowstorm. O.K. He took a swig from one of the many beers he'd found in his many pockets. He remembered, they'd been calling out for attention for the last half hour. He better start moving. Why? He wasn't sure. But he needed to go somewhere, he was positive.

He brought his skis together (oh! I'm on skis) bent his knees, and started sliding backwards.

Well.

That didn't work out so well.

He stopped, made a "V" and started pushing forwards. Slowly. It was a lot of work.

Push. Lift. Glide. Push. Lift. Glide.

This seemed very familiar.

Push. Lift. Glide. Push. Lift. Glide.

He began to feel as if he were Paul again. If that made any sense. His thighs hurt like a son-of-a-gun, though.

And his calves.

Okey-dokey, Paully, let's see... – he should be thinking of something – something to get his mind off of his aching legs – let's see – how did he get here? – in the storm, on skis, roped to a bumper, messing around and having fun with my best buddies? Drinking? Lost in a snowstorm? Sad. Alone. Lost. And he still hadn't managed to do himself in. Oh yeah.

He was trying to kill himself.

That's it.

But why?

He couldn't remember.

Why, Paully, why did you screw-up like this again? This was stupid, Paully. For darned sure. Something a kid would do. A spoiled little kid. Decide. Do it. Do it, Paul.

He thought he heard a car coming. A low throbbing in the wind. He slowed down. Listened. Just his luck. They'd found him. He heard someone calling his name. Who had found him? Oh. Had to be Stan, huh?

"Paully! Paully!"

20
CLICK

Three penguins stood in his way. They were handsome beasts. Healthy, sleek, round and sassy. Their feathers gleamed, even in dim, mid-winter, Minnesotan daylight. Their yellow necks were nearly neon-bright. They stood in a line. The first one kept calling his name out – Paully! Paully!

"He doesn't know where he's going," said the second.

"You can call me Fred," said the third.

Paul took another crabwalk step forwards, pushed himself sideways and stopped. The wind died down. The snow fell in great dandelion puffs of flake all about him. It was very quiet. He tried to catch his breath. It took a while. The air was fresh and startling. As clean as a naked knife. The penguins couldn't look him in the eye. They flapped and shuffled and looked to the left and to the right. They looked at each other. But they didn't look at Paul.

"You're guys have names? And now you're talking to me?" said Paul. His voice was a little hoarse. He probably needed more beer.

"Call him Fred," said the second.

"You can call me Fred," said the third.

"Call him Fred," said the second.

"Paully!" said the first.

"What made you decide to talk all of a sudden?"

"You can call me Fred."

"Call him Fred."

"Paully!"

"He doesn't understand," said the second.

"You can call me Fred," said the third.

"Paully!"

"They never do. Understand that is. Que triste, no?" said the second.

"Paully!"

"You can call me Fred."

"We may as well call it a day, lads. He's not going to do it, is he? Not hardly. I'm afraid this affair is not a go."

"Are you talking to me?" said Paul.

"You can call me Fred."

There was a moment of expectant silence.

"Right. Most definitely a no-go."

A minute or so later, Paul was huffing and puffing, pushing his way up the road, and thinking about how nice it was going to be, sliding down the other side, giving his legs a rest. The woods should be right ahead. He'd get to rest. He'd have a lot of rest. Soon. Eternal rest, even.

He heard someone calling his name. He slowed down. Great. Just his luck. They'd found him.

"Paully! Paully!"

21
OUTRAGEOUS

Yeah, that was Stan. Only it wasn't. Because Stan wasn't here. Was he?

"Stan? Stan?"

Nope. Not here.

"Paully, Paully!"

He smiled at no one in particular. O.K. This was getting confusing. Stop it. Stop yelling at me.

"Paully, Paully!"

"Stan?"

This was getting nowhere fast.

Stan confused Paul.

Paul hated it when Stan called him "Paully." Only his mom called him "Paully."Stan could be a little on the irritated/irritating side himself sometimes. A knucklehead, if you let him get away with it. Stan wasn't a creep, nah. He was just a little opinionated. And high strung. Paul thought of him as a young dog trying to outgrow its big puppy paws. He'd never say that out loud though. Stan would flatten him. And Stan would be right.

Stan had a lot of people depending on him. What with his ma passing away years ago, and it only being his dad (who may have drank a little more than was strictly necessary, weekdays and weekends) and his five younger sisters at home. It was a life of being outnumbered by females. Paul had that in common with Stan.

So, yup, Stan was busy. With his dad on the sidelines, he was left being mom, oldest sister, oldest brother, star high school student, and multiple wage earner, on top of being an inductee into the army in the Spring.

Jeez! Yeah! Any guy would look dazed and be a little tense, a little irritated, with all that going on, huh?

"Paully?"

"Stan?"

Horsefeathers! Paul wished Stan would stop shouting his nickname up to high heaven and over most of Northern Minnesota. He took another swig from the beer. Stan didn't know when to stop sometimes. Yeah, Stan was being a knucklehead. Grade A, 100% Certified. And Paul would tell him so, if he saw him.

Throwing his head back, for a second and taking a last swig from this bottle, Paul lost his balance. A moment later he found himself sitting down. Unexpectedly. Legs spread-eagled. Skis pointing every which way. In the middle of the road. Laughing his head off.

Nice Paul. Well done, kid. Much better this way. Much better.

Stan was short (same height as Paul), but wiry, and explosive – a very un-Minnesotan stick of TNT that went off (kaboom!) when touched the wrong way. Yeah, a guy could never be sure with him.

Not with Stan. Paul's ma said that was his French showing. His folk weren't the quiet, calm and careful types, like Lutherans. No. They tended more towards the fiery, the impulsive.

They were Lutheran-opposites. They were French. A one syllable word packed with beaucoup de meaning up here, up in northern Minnesota. Paul thought Stan's family was loyal, fun and loud. Especially loud. That was more than O.K. by Paul. Paul liked a little loud sometimes after days of careful living in his very calm Scandihoovian home.

Stan's sisters (and very rarely, Stan) went to the big white Catholic church, St Francis, that woke up Paul and Paul's entire family every Sunday – it (the church) being on Elm street where Paul Olsen lived and diagonally across from all the Olsen bedrooms and equipped with the largest bell in Red River County. You couldn't ignore it, St. Francis got your attention, no matter how hard you tried to pretend otherwise

Ma said that was simply the point. It was French. There was that word again. Paul's ma could say a lot with such a little word: French. The church was French and filled with Frenchman. Enough said. Like the town St. Alfonse twenty miles north. In the same county. But in a different country.

Yeah, well… Stan's real name was Emile Jean something something something Boucher. Paul had to admit, that was pretty French. But you didn't call Stan by the name Emile. No. Not unless you wanted to fight him.

And Stan was always ready to fight. Fight with somebody, fight for somebody.

If he had to.

Sometimes he'd even fight for Paul.

22
CLICK

It was calm. Windless. Paul's behind was getting pretty numb. Sitting on the road, in a drifted-over, tire track from the Model B. The snow was packed. It was hard. It was cold.

Well, it really wasn't all that bad, brother.

In fact, it was fine. Just fine.

He was fine. The road was fine. Everything was fine, brother.

Paul sipped some more beer, pouring it into his mouth and onto his muffler. He slipped the bottle back in his coat to keep it warm-ish. And pour-able.

Yeah, the wind had disappeared. Snow was piling on his head and legs. And yeah, fine or not, he'd have to get a move on soon. Get up, right? Real soon. Any minute now. He had things to do. Move around. Get the blood circulating. Get off the road. Get to the trees. Get warm.

That or drink some more beer.

Paul reached into his pocket, feeling for a bottle.

The bottle, a bitter disappointment, turned out to be only a quarter full. Paul made short work of that. Then he threw it over his shoulder, laughing. He scrounged around for another, in the pocket on the other side of his jacket. Paul was a walking refrigerator. Or a sitting one. He couldn't stop laughing. Yeah. That was a good one. Zeke and Stan would laugh too, when he told them.

But he'd never get a chance to tell them, would he?

In a flash, Paul felt like crying. He snuffled as he drank.

Pouring the last of it into his waiting mouth, Paul finished that one, threw it over his shoulder again, into the snowstorm, and brother, it was crazy. He was laughing, it was so crazy. It was as if the bottles were dematerializing, vanishing – the second they left his hand. Zapped by a space gun. You couldn't see them to save your life, just swallowed by the white, swallowed by the flakes, and whenever they landed, wherever that was, the bottles made no sound. Not a clink. Not a ping. Not ever. From Paul's perspective, they were ceasing to exist. The moment they left his hands.

Crazy, huh? Crazy.

He liked throwing them.

You know, he could do this all day. He felt for more bottles.

Darn. He was out of empty bottles. He sure wasn't going to throw away a full one. And maybe he should slow down. His view of the road kept being obstructed by these moving trees. Orange. Spotted with black. On the thin side, though. Sickly trees. They swayed in the now, non-existent wind. They bent and flew upwards, (whoosh!) pulled up by the root and disappeared. Then they'd blow back down (whoosh!). Right in front of his face. It was really annoying. Paul cocked his head to one side. A tree moved. Blocked his view of the snowstorm. He cocked his head to the other side. More trees appeared. More blocking. They huddled in front of him. They swayed and taunted him. He was surrounded! Now, he couldn't see a thing.

Darn! Couldn't see the road. Couldn't see the sky. All the darned trees! For Pete's sake!. His head felt fuzzy inside, and dizzy. He blinked. And did it again. And again. But all he saw was blurry orange and white and brown stripes in front of his (surely) bloodshot baby blues.

Paul leaned back and closed his eyes. He felt the air whoosh beside him. Nope. Wasn't going to look. Wasn't biting. He felt another whoosh. Then another. And another. And... O.K. Fine. He opened one eye. The trees were still there. Hiding behind them were the penguins. Boy! What a surprise! He hadn't seen them in... what? five whole minutes? The penguins hunched. And they stared. Not at him. At some point above his head. Paul had to admit, their eyes were deep and wise. He turned his head and an eyeball the size of a fist with extravagant lashes floated past his face. An optical dirigible.

That was new. That was a surprise. He hadn't been expecting that. It took him a few moments to get his thoughts in order again.

All right. Paul figured it was time to open both his eyes.

He was surrounded, yes. Surrounded by giraffes.

Yeah. Of course.

Very funny, guys.

"They promised me pink elephants. Pink. Elephants. I'm drunk guys, remember?"

The penguins were shaking their heads and looking away. The giraffes were batting their Rockettes eyes at him and kicking their Rockettes knees at him and milling about. They seemed a lot happier than the penguins. The penguins could learn a thing or three from those giraffes.

Paul's head was spinning. He leaned back and lay down on the road. Closed his eyes. It didn't help. He went around and around and around. His knees started to hurt – they didn't appreciate being bent at a funny angle and accommodating the skis still strapped securely to his feet. Was he starting to have a headache?

Yeah. Maybe all those beers hadn't been such a good idea. He could swear he was on a roller coaster. Up. Down. Sideways. Left. Right. Up. Down... Paul squinched his eyes more firmly shut, and frowned up blindly at all the loitering giraffes and penguins, and he groaned. He thought to himself – Paul, let's just stay horizontal for a few more minutes, huh? Yeah. Just a few more. Rest a little. Good idea, Paul. Now you're thinking, now you're cooking with gas.

23
PEACE

"Paully!"

"Stan?" Was that Stan? Again?

Paul listened. Heard nothing. Let himself sink deeper into the snow on the road.

Stan couldn't wait for the army. Stan wanted out of Minnesota. Not that he hated Minnesota – who could? – who would? – this was God's country, for sure, but Stan wanted something else. He wanted bigger. He wanted freer. He wanted more. More. All three of them wanted it – Zeke, Stan, Paul. More. With a capital "M".

It wasn't that they hated Minnesota. No. It was they wanted to love something else too. And there was nothing wrong with that. You could love two things at once. Lots of people did. Despite what people might think in Red River County, Minnesota.

Paul asked Stan last fall – when the three of them went on their big, annual canoeing trip up near Lake of the Woods, way up north, by the border, hiking up and down those low granite hills, clothes smelling of wood smoke, heads upside down under Paul's dad's ancient, monster canoe, traversing portages they'd done a hundred times – they could hoof it here blindfolded even, they almost were, under those canoes, heck! – well, anyways... Paul asked Stan how they'd manage – Stan's family that is – how they would all manage when Stan went off to Basic Training come June? What would his sisters and dad do without Stan around? Didn't they want him to stay? Didn't Stan want to stay?

Stan had laughed, maybe too loudly, maybe too quickly, it was hard to tell with Stan. Was he sore? At Paul? For asking? Paul had no idea.

"Why you asking me that, now, Paully?"

Paul couldn't see Stan, but he knew Stan's eyes would be a little too bright, his smile a little too big. O.K. Maybe a mistake. Yeah,

Stan confused him sometimes. Paul braced himself. He tensed his shoulders (Stan was in back of him in the upside down canoe).

"What are you trying to say Paully?"

"Nothing Stan. Nothing. I was just wondering."

"Wondering. Oh. Yeah. Of course. Wondering."

Paul expected the unexpected. Something was up. Paul was about to tell him to forget it, when Stan started yelling at the back of his head. He could tell, from the big breath Stan took at the beginning, that this was going to be a long speech.

"Well, you see, Paully, this is how it is. You gotta understand, Helen's only a year younger than me. The twins are just two years younger. And the rest... well... there's plenty of Bouchers to go around. I love them, Paul. You gotta understand. But I also have to get out of here, before I drown."

Stan took in a big breath and continued. Even more loudly.

"You see, I'm sinking, Paully."

Then he stopped. Paul waited a moment. Was this a trick?

"You're sinking, Stan?"

He heard Stan pull in another couple gallons of oxygen in back of him. Then he heard his big voice echoing again under the canoe, painfully, right into both his ears.

"Yeah, Paully. I'm going down. For the last time. I'm not getting any younger. I want to see something other than these damn forests and corn and lakes and cows. There's a whole, big, wide world out there, Paully, just waiting for me to grab. It's just waiting."

There was a pause. Was he wanting Paul to say something?

"For you too, Paully, for you too. If you just reach out and take it. Take it, Paully! Take it."

They were huffing, slogging up a little hill, Stan's voice getting louder and louder. He pushed the canoe forwards a smidgeon, making Paul stumble. Stan laughed – a little too quickly – yeah, he was sore – and Stan edged his hand closer and closer to Paul's, along the edge of the canoe, finally, his big ham of a hand wrapped easily around Paul's right hand, squeezing it without mercy, waiting to see when Paul would cry uncle.

Paul didn't move. Paul didn't say anything. He struggled silently to break free, waited for Stan to stop horsing around. Stan didn't stop. Paul moved his hand all over the place. Stan kept gripping.

Paul's knuckles ached. The canoe was gouging his hand. Then Paul had had enough.

Paul shook his hand free. He really shook it. That took a moment or two. The canoe bounced off their heads and slithered down a rocky slope knee-deep in pine needles. It scurried and skipped and floundered around some tree roots and rolled to a noisy stop, sticking backwards out of a bush, pointing straight up into the air. Paddles, cushions went everywhere. Leaves flew. Squirrels scolded. Birds winged it, up into the clear, blue sky, where it was more peaceful. Random stray branches broke off and fell down around them.

As the air cleared, Paul looked back over his pack, and he saw Stan's face lit, eyebrows up, mouth wriggling in a straight line, him trying very hard not to laugh, and at the same time look absolutely and purely innocent. Paul didn't know what to say or what to think. Why did Stan do stuff like that? What had Paul said? Why was Stan so angry?

Zeke, carrying his own canoe behind them on his head, bumped into the two of them standing still, staring at each other. He looked at Stan, looked at Paul, looked back at Stan, tilting his canoe up one way and then the other to see each of them clearly. Then he searched for the location of their huge, old war canoe, finding it perched below the three of them, nesting in a big patch of dogwood, and he looked back over at the both of them, shaking his head.

"Why'd you two throw your canoe down the gully?"

"Don't ask me, Zeke, ask Paully here. Why'd you do it, Paully?"

"You're fighting again, aren't you guys? You guys promised. No fighting this trip."

"We're not fighting, are we Paully?"

Paul didn't say anything for a moment. He looked up at the sky. Blue. Deep. Peaceful. Then he cleared his throat.

"Nah, I'm not fighting, Stan."

"See, Zeke. No fighting."

"Good. Because you promised."

"Not this trip. Nope. No fighting."

Zeke did not look convinced.

"Look, Zeke, I promised already, but I'll do it again. I promise. You promise Paully?"

Paul sighed. Cleared his throat. He must be coming down with a cold.

"Yeah. Sure. No fighting. I promise."

"Sure. See? Zeke?"

"O.K. you guys. We have a couple of miles to hike, then a lake to get across before dark. You doofuses remember that at least? Huh? Stan? Paul?"

"Yah, Zeke."

"Stan?"

"You know, I think I may remember something about that, Zacharias, I just might."

"Good. Let's get your canoe, fellas. Hey! Watch out for this! I think it's poison sumac. Remember what happened last year."

"Yeah, sure, Zacharias. Sure."

Once back under the canoe, and hiking uphill, Paul had hissed a whisper back to Stan.

"Well, if you're in such a hurry to leave, Stan, why are you re-shingling your dad's roof, and saving to get the twins into Concordia College, asking Mary out every Saturday? Huh? Why? Huh? That sounds like a guy who's coming back and staying. I think you're a big talker. I think you might not know what you want."

Paul didn't know what came over him. It was as if someone else were talking with his mouth. He waited for the certain explosion.

But, no. Stan was quiet. He stayed quiet for the rest of the day after that. Both under the canoe walking and inside of the canoe paddling. Paul thought — I can't ever win — either it's silence or fighting — isn't there something else? Don't I ever get a break?

24
QUIET

That night, from under his blankets, Stan whispered back to Paul (well, Stan had definitely thought it was a whisper, but it came out more of a breathy yell). Paul had been trying to get some shut-eye and ended up watching the stars instead, nestled deep in his blankets, and then, from out of nowhere, he heard Stan, talking causally, as if they'd been talking all day and Stan had just stopped a minute before to take another breath and organize his thoughts.

Paul twitched and jumped a few inches in the air when Stan's voice exploded over him.

Now, Stan was what you might call a conversationalist. He loved to talk. And he had a silky rich voice. And yeah, it was a strong one too, for sure. It was good at expressing opinions in an earnest way, and making its points clear. And, it could sing. Sing up a storm, in fact. Father Patrick at St. Francis had tried and tried to trap Stan into joining his choir for years (St. Francis' choir being famous in Red River Falls, especially for the Christmas Carol Pageant and its festival midnight masses). This summer was no exception. Father Patrick had pretty nearly trapped Stan, on the sidewalk in front of the drugstore downtown, just last week. Stan had escaped, claiming a toothache. That was one reason they'd made this canoeing trip last over 3 Sundays this year. To give Stan a break from being hinted at and enticed and also give him a fighting chance at freedom, since a guy can have only so many toothaches before people begin to wonder.

Father Patrick had been hunting Stan ever since Stan's voice broke. Good tenors were hard to come by. Stan was a beaut, a trophy tenor. Father Patrick sensed success in the near future, he could just about taste it. Years before, he'd captured three of Stan's sisters for the alto section and the sopranos. Stan's father already sang bass (when singing was a possibility for Stan's dad on a Sunday, usually it was a recovery day) and Father Patrick had figured he'd round out the Boucher family's service to God with the donation of a substantial tenor — Stan, to be exact. So far, as has been explained, Stan had dodged the bullet (barely), fending off all priestly requests. But he had eleven long months left in town before he was safe forever and off serving in the army who-knew-where. And who knew what might happen in eleven long months? Especially since the Father had God on his side. Right? Stan just had Zeke and Paul. It didn't seem a fair fight.

In any case, Paul heard Stan's melodious tenor, unexpectedly and suddenly, filling the soft night air of their camp, right next to his left ear. It wasn't an entirely unpleasant experience. One moment the night was quiet as death. Only the buzz and whir of the insect world. The next moment it was alive and filled to overflowing with Stan.

"You're right, Paul. I don't know what I want. Sometimes I'm just a big mouth. No brain. You're right."

Paul didn't know what to say.

Zeke yelled out of his blankets "Guys!, it's late."

Paul still didn't know what to say.

People surprised Paul. All the time. After he gave up on figuring people out, he'd decided – after thinking about it for quite some time – that rather than working on figuring them out, maybe Paul was better off working on liking being surprised.

And you know, it really did work out better that way.

As if Paul had a choice!

The stars rippled. The sky was broad and deep. The stinging sweet smoke of the pine fire drifted back and forth over the three of them. Paul coughed and blinked his burning eyes and he smiled. Paul loved this stuff. It was why he went camping. With his two best friends. This was why they were Minnesotans. This was why anybody was a Minnesotan. He cleared his throat to get enough of the smoke out of the way to tell Stan he understood. Not that he did. But he was trying. He cleared his throat again, maybe a little louder than he'd realized.

Before Paul could mouth a single syllable, Zeke beat him to it and bellowed straight up into the black night. You couldn't see him. It was almost as if the ghost of Zeke were yelling.

"C'mon guys! For the love of Pete! You promised!"

Paul cleared his throat. Opened his mouth. Started to reply to both Stan and, now, Zeke. Zeke talked right through all the throat-clearing.

"C'mon. You promised. How could you fight out here in all this beautiful nature? C'mon! Time to sleep! You're done fighting!"

Paul cleared his throat again. But, again, before he could say word one, someone else jumped in and took over – it was Stan this time – and Stan was laughing and yelling loud enough to wake the stars. Paul laughed too.

"Done? Zacharias?"

Stan knew that Zeke hated that name as much as Stan hated Emile – so he used it, judiciously, to spice up his conversations with Zeke, mixing in a little pain with the pleasure of his company. It was just something Stan did. You got used to it.

"Done? Why, Zacharias, we ain't even got started yet."

25
REVELATION

Paul's head still spun. He flexed one knee, then flexed the other, tried to get the blood flowing. He ought to get up off his keister and do something. Yup. He ought to take all his clothes off. Go in the ditch. Get it over with. The sooner you start… Man! He was dizzy. He didn't know if he could walk. He ought to… He heard music again. Heard the voices. No orange smell this time. Wait. No. There it was. That sick smell. He didn't even look up. He knew he was alone. The orange smell was haunting him. His head hurt. Man! He should…

All of a sudden, Paul jerked himself into a sitting position and vomited all over the road in front of him.

A few moments of heaving, and then of cleaning his face in the snow, and Paul collapsed back onto the tire tracks he'd been laying on. He felt better. That was strange. But he was thirsty.

He gulped some more beer. His stomach settled down. His headache got a little better. He belched. Then he threw up again.

This time he lay himself down for a few extra moments of motionlessness.

It's time.

Need to get up.

C'mon.

Maybe ten minutes later, he pulled himself to his knees.

He put his gloves up to his muffler and began to take it off. He went to grab his heavy wool winter cap with the bright red pom pom to expose his bright red head when he stopped. His glove brushed his pocket, he heard a happy clink! clink! sound and Paul suddenly wanted more beer.

Don't you ever learn, Paul? No. I don't. He may as well die happy, huh. Not again. Yes, again. And you don't go wasting perfectly good alcohol. That wasn't right. The first bottle he found, he pulled out and it was frozen. He threw that one over his shoulder. It dematerialized in mid-air, like all the rest. Paul laughed. The second one was full. He opened it by gently rapping it against his ski. Then, when that didn't work, by not-so-gently rapping it. Some beer spilled out. Yeah, a little slushy. He caught part of it in his gloves. Slurped it. The rest he drank in one long gulp. Burping heroically, Paul threw this empty over his shoulders too. Poof! It disappeared.

Paul waited to throw up again. Nothing happened.

All right, Paully. So far, so good. That meant he only had one beer left. He was a little dizzy again, had a little headache. Now what? Now maybe you should lie down. So he did.

Snow immediately started to cover his face. He let it.

26
SYNCOPATION

Cut to earlier that morning – no it was already afternoon, no it was morning. Whatever it was, it was New Year's Day. Today. The same day, gosh darn it! Paul wasn't that drunk, brother!

So. Today. Earlier. Paul had been leaning on Zeke's pa's Model B, foot up on the front bumper, poking away at his wavy red-blond hair, which was poking right back at him, protruding out of his head at the oddest, darn angles you could ever imagine. Paul pushed clumps of it away, self-consciously, this way and that, so he could see out of his tortoise shells. Sometimes he blew up at it, when he was too lazy to brush at it. Stan was with Paul, and the two of them were in Zeke's garage. It was so cold, his glasses frosted solid every time he breathed. He couldn't keep them clear.

Paul hiked his foot up and waited. He had to reach up high with his foot. Seventeen year old Paul was, yes, short for his age (stop reminding him of it), looked as if he were twelve (though he'd never admit it) and even though girls called him a dreamboat, he felt as if he were every girl's kid brother when he went out on a date.

Paul was sensitive. About being short. About a lot of things. He was shy and he knew it, but what could a guy do? At least the girls said he was cute, right? He was on the wrestling team. They wanted him for the 92 pound class. That was going O.K. He played tennis, (decently, he was quick, and he could slam the ball when he had to), he played hockey, (O.K., sure, sometimes he got bounced around more than the hockey puck), and he played baseball like everyone else did in Red River Falls. He figured if he did enough sports, at some point his body wouldn't smarten up and give him a few more inches. So far it hadn't worked.

Yeah, he wasn't crazy about wrestling, or hockey, but a guy didn't like to hear all the time that he was cute. Sometimes a guy wanted to be a guy. He liked to hear he was a man. Even from his date. Especially from his date. Paul wanted to be a plain joe, the same as everyone else. What was wrong with that? His mom said he was waiting on his last growth spurt. No one could say Paul wasn't patient.

And just because you were small, it didn't mean you were scared as a mouse all the time, it didn't mean you needed protecting. He'd been standing there in the garage, when out of nowhere, Stan had bellowed at him. Like he always did.

"You scared, Paully?"

Paul looked up. It took a second for Paul to try and figure out what Stan meant. He tried. He had no idea.

"Why would I be scared?"

"You done this before, Paully?"

"Have I skied before roped to a car? What difference does that make? Look, it was my idea. And call me Paul, Stan."

"Even the guys with the ideas get scared sometimes, Paul."

Zeke and Stan always made out as if Paul were some kind of boy genius. Paul didn't know why. His grades weren't all that good.

"Not this one, Stan. I'm not afraid."

Stan squinted at Paul. He looked down. Kicked some gravel on the garage floor with his shoe. Then he looked up, smiled.

"Swell."

Stan could be a wise guy sometimes. And be confusing.

It was about two o'clock. Yeah, it was late, so it was the afternoon. They'd been waiting on Zeke, in Zeke's garage, out in back of Zeke's house, for an hour. It was gray, solid gray out. And it was cold. The kind of cold that asked for and got your attention. The world was smell-less. It was cold, and you couldn't smell a thing, not the oil and not the gasoline, not the red-painted wood of the garage peeling and flaking. Nothing. That meant it was cold. No-ifs-ands-or-buts cold.

They were polishing the Model B. It was something to do – polishing the rust. Paul was rubbing the front fender with his sleeve, looking at his reflection in between the orange-black rust-blooms on the chrome, on the long curving black metal of the car, frowning at it. He didn't like his new round glasses. It had been his ma's idea. She said he looked scholarly. He thought he looked cute. He hated it. Stan was lying down, balanced on the running board, watching Paul frown at himself. Stan draped himself all over the running board as if here were a corduroy-covered, man-sized pretzel. He assumed more and more gymnastic positions, trying to get Paully to look at him. Brother, it was freezing in Zeke's garage! Most people didn't spend January Sunday afternoons in a garage. But that's where the Three Musketeers (their name for themselves) had always met. To plan their mayhem. After church. So here they were. Except Stan hadn't gone to church. Neither had Paul. Zeke had, though.

Finally, Zeke got there, last (as usual), banged the garage side-door madly, furiously (on purpose), pushed it open on its sagging hinges, and appeared, in a cloud of snow falling off the roof. Stan flipped off the car bumper spectacularly, into the frozen oil and sand, feigning he did it on purpose. He looked at Paully out of the side of his eyes. Paul (without looking up) duly smirked. That got a smile out of Stan.

Zeke cleared his throat, authoritatively and with great ceremony. The Three Musketeers were big on ceremony.

"Gentlemen, what's the difference between a duck?"

Zeke said it in his best general-addressing-the-troops-the night-before-the-big-push voice, keeping his feet spread wide, his hands held in back of his waist, managing to smile and frown ferociously at the same time. He looked like a younger General Patton when he did that, and Zeke knew it.

Stan rolled his eyes and winked at Paul. Paul looked up, just in time to catch it.

In unison Paul and Stan replied.

"One of its legs is both the same."

"One if its legs is both the same, what?"

"One of its legs is both the same, sir."

"Very good. At ease men."

Stan remained lying on the ground, Paul's foot didn't leave the bumper. Zeke's eyes met both of theirs. Paul loved this. He loved these guys. He loved this garage. He even loved his green muffler, the one he'd got from Auntie Helen for Christmas. He'd wanted canoe paddles. He'd gotten knitting. But, strange to say, he loved it, in all of its lumpy, warm imperfection. It made him feel invulnerable. And noticed.

Fits of love and sentimentality fell on Paul at times. He was used to it.

But it didn't make his Exit Day easier, did it? You know, when Paul had no chance to off himself, no opportunity whatsoever, he was wild to do it. And when Paul did have the opportunity to off himself, when it would be easy, as easy as falling off a log, he fell in love with life all over again.

Boy!

Was he a mess, or what?

He hated it. He hated all this.

He loved it. He loved all of this.

Hold onto this, Paul. Hold on to this. Will you hold onto this Paul? For once? Remember. Remember this.

"Gentlemen?"

"Shall we?"

"We shall."

27

TESTIMONY

Maybe it was time.

Paul rolled over in the snow. Avoiding the vomit. He closed his eyes. Paul reached up and took off his hat. That was easy enough. The hat stuck to his glove. He didn't try and get it off. He let his hair and head fall back down into the snow.

Next he took off his muffler. Brother! It was freezing. The tips of his ears went numb and he couldn't feel his face anymore. It was going to be fast, huh? He didn't know where to put his muffler. He couldn't feel his neck, but he didn't feel cold. Not exactly. He pulled off his coat. The last beer bottle rolled out. Yeah. This was North Pole cold. This was going to be quick. He heard those voices again, the music. When was this going to stop? He didn't want to open his eyes again. Why was someone making him open his eyes?

At least the penguins were leaving him alone for once. And their long-necked friends with the false eyelashes. Jeez! Why'd the Universe make everything so difficult for him? Why?

Paul twisted his neck, opened his eyes, pulled himself up on his elbows, looked behind, focused his eyes, he looked left, right – all he saw was virgin, untracked snow, piles of it. A faint, almost phantom line of tire tracks stretched out behind him. They led under his butt and under his feet and emerged from under his skis (still attached to his shoes) to smack right up against the fat tires of the big, black car idling and chugging in a good natured way in front of him, as if it were a big, mangy, friendly dog. Paul was next to it, so he patted it in a companionable way, on its rusty bumper, as it bounced and growled to itself. Good car. Nice car. Yeah. So far, so good.

The hood of the car was warm. It felt good.

"What you think you're doing, huh? You acting crazy, Paully? You're going to get run over, lying down in the road. Get your hat on mister, before you lose that head. Where's your coat? Oh Jeez! You been sick, huh? Had too much? Or maybe not enough?"

Paul nodded twice. And blinked. He tried to get his hat on. It wouldn't come off his glove. Stan was yelling at him from the open window, from the far side of the car. After Paul kept on smiling at him and slapping at his hat frozen onto his glove, Stan jumped out of the car and ran up to him, smiling. The smile was tense and wild, even for Stan. Zeke looked over his shoulder from the driver's seat.

"You didn't hear us calling, Paul" – that was Zeke. He sounded strange. Worried? Angry?

"Sure you didn't Paully. How could you? In the storm?" Stan was pulling Paul's arms through his coat sleeves, re-arranging his muffler, pulling his hat down tight. He knocked the pompom around with his fist a couple of times as if he were boxing it. Smiling into Paul's face. Looking into his eyes.

"There. All tucked in. Ready for bed."

Stan patted down Paul's side. He looked down. Saw the bottle.

"Hey, I think one got away, huh, Paul?"

Paul nodded. It seemed the right thing to do at the time. Then he belched. And he smiled.

"Guess I don't have to ask where the rest of 'em went, huh? Brother?"

Stan smiled, a little bit easier, a little bit more relaxed and turned back towards the car. Put his hands in the shape of a megaphone. Yelled at Zeke (who was all of three feet away). Stan. When he bellowed you could hear him for miles. What'd he need to use his hands for? Paul laughed to himself. Using his hands... ha!

"I think we're almost empty out here. Toss us back a few, huh, Zacharias? Fill 'er up."

After hesitating a moment, looking at Stan, Zeke nodded once and disappeared for the shortest of times in back in the car. Two brown bottles erupted from open rear window. Stan effortlessly snatched them, spiraling towards the two of them, out of mid-air. If those bottles had been wanting to escape, they hadn't had a chance. None. Zilch. Stan packed them away in the now-empty pockets of Paul's jacket.

"I got to re-tie this rope, Paully. You wait here, huh? This time nothing comes loose, huh?"

Paul nodded. He was dizzy. He wondered why. He was standing up again. He looked down at his glove. He had a beer in his right hand. The beer was opened already. He brought it up to his face, dribbled it in. He looked over Stan's ox-shoulders, over the car ahead of him. He couldn't see much, Stan was throwing off thunderheads of steam as re-knotted the frozen rope. His big arms flashed back and forth, his red-checked coat shone bright as a flame in front of the black car.

The snow, which had been dumping on Paul for hours as if it were Niagara Falls, let up for a second. To one side, a long row of stubby telephone poles leaned in various angles of inebriated helpfulness towards each other and disappeared into white eddies of whiter snow flurries. They got smaller, and smaller, until they were barely dots. Dark smears of pine trees huddled together here and there on the horizon, trying to keep warm. Oh. His trees. There they were. Let's see. What else? White sky. White ground. Snow. More snow. A white, blasted, mathematical flatness yawned open, spreading out to Paul's left, flooding and fusing in the distance with the exact same shade of white sky itself. It was so flat. So perfect. It was too perfect. You could lose your soul in it if you weren't careful. That was a lake, right? Pine Lake maybe? Zeke would know (or hopefully Stan), and , let's see... what else was there? Nope. That was it. Nothing. Nothing else.

28
UMBRELLAS

They were alone.

In a big, white, flat nowhere.

He could've done it. He could be dead, By now. Or mostly so. No one would've interfered. No one would've noticed. There wouldn't have been any disappointed fathers. No. No police cars. No farms. No farmers. No farmers with shotguns. Well, Minnesota farmers didn't shoot people just for skiing on their land. Or dying on their land, naked. At least not in modern times, not in 1944. Wait. Did they? Stop making a fuss, Paul. You're not so darned important someone's going to shoot you, now, are you? Stop. Just stop.

He could've done it. He would've done it. He'd literally been doing it, darn it all. He could still hear singing. He could still smell those durned oranges. He was probably sick. Pneumonia. Something.

The stinging snow had now let up, completely. Everything was quiet, except for Stan cursing the rope in French. For a moment he could see a patch-let of purple-blue sky straight overhead. Were those stars coming out? Yes they were. Were they making the music? Singing to him. He'd like that. Stars singing to him. Singing his way home. But which home? Paul knew which home. This was his Exit Day.

The stars disagreed. He could feel it. They wanted him alive.

Darn.

Always the hard way, huh? Paul?

"O.K.," said Paul to the stars, in a whisper, "I'll stay. I'll stay for a little while longer. A few hours more. A few days. But not longer. O.K.? This has got to stop. There's got to be an end sometime. O.K.? I want out. You listening? Up there? Where you never have worries or are cause for disappointment? I want out."

It was so quiet. Except for the music. But the music made him feel calm. He felt calm. It had been a long time since he'd felt that. Why had he been so upset before? Nothing to get upset about. He hiccupped. Automatically reached for his beer. Everything was

O.K., brother, everything was fine, just fine. Even his head didn't hurt so much anymore. He looked up to find Stan looking at him.

"Whatcha looking at Paul?"

"The stars."

"Oh yeah. They're pretty."

Paul nodded.

Stan nodded back.

"Paully, wait a second. I'm going to get Zeke to help."

"Sure, Stan, anything, Stan."

"And Paully?"

"Yeah, Stan?"

"Calvaire! Don't do crazy stunts like that again, huh? Talk to me first, O.K.? What! Do you think you're alone, huh? No one's alone, not with Stan around. O.K.?"

Stan slapped his hand against the back of Paul's head. But was a gentle slap. Paul nodded. He wasn't sure he'd heard everything Stan had just said. But it seemed like a good idea to nod. Stan seemed so serious.

Stan leapt away. He came back in a few seconds with Zeke.

"You still want to ski, Paul?" said Zeke.

"If you don't want to, yeah. You want to, Stan?"

"Sure. But you go first, Paully. You have fun, O.K.?"

"Sure, Stan, sure. Whatever you say."

Zeke and Stan looked at each other. Then they beat on the rope until they could retie it. They handed the rope to Paul. They looked at each other again. Stan shrugged. Zeke did too. Then they turned and tackled Paul. The three of them were in the ditch rolling for a few minutes. Somehow Paul ended up on top of the two of them, legs, knees, elbows twisted into pretzels around theirs, laughing his head off. He still had his skis on. Zeke and Stan were laughing too. He didn't feel cold at all. That was strange, huh? He turned on his back and got to see the sky for a moment, before the two of them threw him off and onto the road. He slid down off again on his skis into the ditch. They pushed him back up.

Unlikely large snowflakes began to appear, flocking towards the three of them in their thousands. They fell as if they were a revelation in physical form. O.K. I get it. Yes. I am content. Paul wanted to remember this moment. For later. He never did, but he wanted to try especially hard this time. When he went into the Navy, he'd want to remember. No he wasn't going into the Navy.

This was going to be it. This was his Exit Day. This was Minnesota. This is where he started and this is where he ended. He was going to end here. He was to end with his best friends. This was who he was. This was why and how he was.

Maybe it was a good time to stop.

While he was ahead, huh?

He stood up in his skis. Stan and Zeke pounded him on his shoulder. They headed back to the car. The car was still huffing and puffing. Clouds of monoxide rolled in cotton-gray waves around Paul. It was a friendly monoxide. He was immersed in it, a sickly-sweet ocean of fuzzy poisonous warmth, and you know what?

Paul was fine. It was all fine.

29
CLICK

It was fine.

And then it wasn't.

Paul plunged back into inner ear hell – dizzy and nauseous and unhappy. He heard an unlikely clear and loud swing band strike up a snappy number. It was militantly cheerful. He couldn't see. Which possibly was a blessing – less nausea, right? – his world turned pitch black. Well, mostly black. Black, except for this bright, painful light poking its needle sharp photons directly into his irises… Paul swayed in his skis, doing a sort of hula dance (he hoped his friends weren't watching) and stamped and jiggled and danced to stay upright in the deep wheel tracks in the deeper snow and not throw up all over himself in the process.

Then he didn't feel the need to do any of those things.

He was lying down. He felt warm. Then warmer. Then he was toasty. It would have been great except Paul was in a lot of pain. And numbness. He hurt. And where he didn't hurt, he couldn't feel. Couldn't move his left hand. His face felt wooden on the left side. Had a headache again. That was an understatement. It was bad this time. Not a hangover. More like his head, his skull, had split into pieces, a walnut in a nutcracker, or, no, more likely, Paul was a cartoon skyscraper, and an evil wrecking ball had crashed into him, his upper floors were gone and the wrecker had shattered him, and Paul had been smashed and his Paul-rafters splintered to Paul-bits and Paul-smithereens. It didn't look good for Paul-the-Building.

He was going down. He started to fold in on himself, it hurt so much. He bent forward. He crumpled and caved in and the pain got worse and worse and he was falling, he was in pieces and he was falling, falling…

A snowball hit him in the face. Well, in the green muffler.

"Hi-de-ho! I didn't know you could jitterbug, brother. Trying to stay warm?"

A voice. In the dark. It sounded familiar. A familiar voice. Yes, Paul could use one of those right about now. But whose was it? Where was it? Where am I? What am I doing? What should I do? All his brain gears and levers were loose and flopping this way and that, all over the place, in a very un-brain-like way. He could see again. But not very well. Somehow this feeling was familiar. He'd done this before. Many, many times. And he was tired of it.

I'm… I'm…

"Paul? You're dancing right? Are you smashed?"

Oh yeah. I'm Paul. That's Stan.

That's right.

Yeah.

Now, what do I do?

Answer dummy. Paul, answer.

"Uh, yeah, uh, what if I am? Dancing, I mean?"

"Dancing? Smashed? What if you are? Just checking, brother. Get ready, cuz, cousin, we're about to blast!"

30
VANISH

They started slow. Stan was driving. Paul could walk faster than they were moving.

Something slipped behind his eyeballs. It slipped sideways and everything made sense – of course – Paul, Minnesota, skis, Zeke, Stan, Model B, everything. How stupid, Paul. Stop fooling around. Then it slipped sideways again, another direction, and all his thinking apparatus went skidding and sliding off the edge of something. All his memories rotated. Cleanly. Out of sight. He looked. They were gone. He felt blank. He felt new.

Paul had never been up this road before. He'd never seen this car before. He didn't know why he was skiing. Zeke and Stan were both of them leaning out the car windows. They were watching him. Why?

Something was wrong.

No, nothing was wrong.

No. Something was very wrong.

Zeke looked so young. Impossibly young. No laugh wrinkles when he laughed, and his scar, the one over his left eye was gone. Where was his wife? They were inseparable. Paul always kidded him about... Now, when had Zeke finished his Engineering degree again? Wait, Zeke was retired. Building his cabin on Evers Lake. Living in their garage while they framed and finished it out. He and his boys were... Right? Right? Two years ago last summer Paul and Susan had visited them and they had... Had... What had they done? What? What? And Stan... Stan... wasn't Stan in California? Tanned and desperate to squeeze money out of his crazy mountainside avocado groves? Who farmed a mountain? Only Stan would. Only Stan. Crazy Stan. Goofball Stan. Stan hated winter. So what in the heck would Stan be doing out in this? It was colder than a witch's... Wait. Wait just a minute. Wasn't Zeke dead? Dead? He was right here. No, they'd had to move back to Minnesota. And Stan Boucher was dead. Something with his heart. No one knew he'd been having pain, Stan never complained, then out of the blue... and... Paul had been a pall bearer. Yeah, it had been so sudden and Joyce, his second wife had been dry-eyed all day until she saw them carrying Stan over the grass towards that open hole and then they'd had to let her sit down before she fell down. Her kitchen had been buried chin-deep in casseroles and hot dishes when she'd got home. And... And... Paul had helped her walk up the steps, she'd dropped her keys, Susan had... He'd never forget it. Susan had... She'd... What had Susan done? Their two little boys and three girls were out in the rental car watching, not fighting for once, and Susan had...

Something was wrong.

No, nothing was wrong.

Wasn't it? Was it? What was wrong? What was he doing here? What were any of them doing here? What was... Then Paul felt the world crack a new sideways, a new direction, and Paul was blinking into the sun, where the sun should be, it was only a brighter shade of grey – he blinked – eyes watering, nose dripping, feet stamping in his skis, one foot at a time, as he slid evenly over the freshly fallen snow. He could walk faster than they were moving. Paul needed to keep his feet warm and the car was slowing down, and he could see two heads moving blurrily through the iced-over rear car window. His chest hurt a little bit. His heart beat in an odd rhythm He felt numb, his left arm, his whole body was scrunched into a letter "C" and he heard a swing band playing on the car radio. No. None of that was true. He wheezed through his filthy muffler. Wait, he was on a pair of skis. Why was he skiing?

Horsefeathers! What in the name of Pete?

He swung sideways again, in yet another direction. There was a big open space in his head. Where something used to be. Just a second ago. It was moving away. Slowly. He could feel it. He could catch up with it. Hold onto it, Paul. Hold on. Grab it. Dig your fingers in, Paully. You can do it. Hold on.

Nope. It got away. It flipped, did a hand-stand, and disappeared. Laughing at him. Punching him in the gut. Dancing just out of reach. He couldn't hit back. Paully was scared.

Why? Why should he be scared?

Paul couldn't remember. Couldn't be important. His muffler came undone and flapped, greenly and stiffly, in the wind. His nose kept on running. His head was a little dizzy. The muffler was new. How did he know that? Zeke was leaning out of the car again. He was a wild man, brother, a wild sonofagun. What if he fell out? What if he got hurt? Whose car was that?

I'm skiing.

They were in the middle of nowhere, out in the boondocks. Paul had never been up this road before.

But he didn't care.

I'm skiing.

31
WORRY

His skis hissed. The wind burned. His throat hurt. Paul loved it. Hold onto this Paul. Hold on. The sun hurt his eyes. What there was of it. His nose was running again. Dagnabbit!

I'm skiing.

Almost bought the farm with that last one.

You know, Paully, only a goof would croak the day before the night of his big date with Rose Sorenson, now wouldn't he? Paul hated being a goof. Who would?

Wait. He wasn't going to be here in few days. That was the plan. Wasn't it?

Paul's lungs accordioned oxygen deep into his body. His heart pumped its four-way beat strong and clean. His bones compressed and sprang back regularly. His muscles tensed and relaxed in a well-known rhythm. He was a tightly-knit, tightly-organized structure, a wet, flesh machine, a Norwegian boy (with a dash of Irish) built for hell-raising this morning. He knew it. And his body knew it. It was a thing he and his body had going on.

His body felt young. He felt great. Better than he had in years.

Paul's battered skis slipped, then abruptly bit the snow with their raggedy edges and Paul jerked right and skywards. Dang! Here we go, 'round the barn, one more time. He'd been skiing the ditch, but he was skiing it no more.

Wet gray clouds of sick-smelling, honey-sweet exhaust filled his lungs. He breathed in deep. He swung up and over toward the road. Then he bent his knees, leaned back and slingshotted his way heavenwards, slicing the cold air in two, winging it three feet above some grade-AAA, iron-hard, frozen farm road – all sweet Minnesota gravel and rich Minnesota dirt and deep Minnesota powder. Wow! Take a gander fellas! The car in front of him roared. It thundered and bellowed its deep-throated pleasure at him and Paul, boy, Paul thundered and bellowed just as loud right back at it.

Paul uncurled his legs and tip-toed his skis across the tops of the wheel tracks in the snow as he flew across. He landed just in time for Stan to let up on the gas. Then the car jerked forwards, Stan honked some crazy syncopated beat hammering it into the bottomless blue skies and started singing to it. Zeke jumped in, with his off-key baritone. Stan wanted Paul to join in. He knew Paul would. Paul always did. Paul's throat was hoarse but he croaked it out anyways.

Until he got hit. Zeke pumped out a curveball, a hard-packed ice-ball of snow he'd been scraping off the top of the car- leaning backwards out of the front passenger's window and looping his feet around Stan's thigh, he closed one eye and aimed. He peered over the top of the car unexpectedly, raised his eyebrows, and fired. Bam! It hit Paul in the chest. His skis skipped over something rectangular and metallic in the ditch. A shed or something had collapsed into it.

Bam!

That didn't sound good.

The three of them called these things "umbrellas." Things that hid in a ditch and popped up and flattened the inattentive ditch skier.

Inattentive. That pretty much described Paul right about now.

He needed to get out. Out of this ditch. Before something happened.

32
X-CITEMENT

As if on cue, the point of his ski grazed, scratched, then bumped across (bam! bam! bam!) another something under the powdery surface. An object. A mystery object. Downed branches from trees felled by this storm? Maybe. Corrugated iron from a snow-collapsed roof? Could be.

Well, what did it matter? It had been happening all afternoon. Paul could handle it. Usually Paul just gripped the darned rope. Tighter. And looser. Both at the same time. That was the trick. He held it in both hands, grabbing the knots as if he wanted to push them into his forearms and lace them through his muscles, then, he gave it some slack and Paul yelled himself hoarse. It was a new year. It was 1944. There was a war on. There had always been a war on. Life was short. He was one of the living. He was alive. He was free. He was flying. He was young. He was immortal (for the present moment). What else could there be?

To cap it off, Paul heard the radio in the car again. Loud music. It was right in his ear. The Andrews Sisters? Never heard this one before. It was right there. It was really loud. It was so loud he couldn't remember where he was.

He couldn't remember what he was doing.

He couldn't remember his name.

It was a wacky feeling.

But it was a feeling.

And it was a sweet feeling and it was his and he wanted it. Boy, did he want it!

Then Stan's long cross-country skis were whispering and spitting through Minnesota winter again, and thumping noises were happening under the snow. A lot more of them. Unhappy noises. Bad noises.

All this happened really, really quickly. And it happened really, really slowly. Yeah, it was wacky. Yeah, a strange feeling.

So, the mystery object hit Paul as if it were a torpedo, the snow the wide waters of the South Pacific and Paul a lone (doomed) destroyer out on reconnaissance maneuvers. It hit when Paul was moving, brother, really going, maybe 30, maybe 40 miles an hour. For dumb. For stupid. Should've been watching. Paul knew he was in trouble. Big trouble. He knew it. The ski point shuddered, dug in, hesitated, then it stuck and it held. He clearly heard it shatter. The pain in his ankle was immediate and urgent.

A part of him, calm and observant, bored in a way, as if he were back in class at Washington High School during a long, long December afternoon of American History listening to Mr Swanson lecture them on Valley Forge one more time – well, a piece of him saw the whole scene: Model B, bumper, rope, farm road, lake, drainage ditch, spraying snow, breaking ski, it saw all of it, and it was only an illustration in a book. Not a particularly good illustration. And not a particularly interesting book. It was tiring and tedious. It was happening so often. It was happening so slowly. It was happening so long ago. And it was happening to someone else. Paul tried to care as he tumbled forwards. He wondered what would happen next. What would happen, Paully? Guess you're about to find out, huh, boy? Good thing you're so short, you don't have so far to fall.

He looked up. He shot forward. And he toppled. It was easier than he'd thought.

Snowed a foot and a half last night. Dry snow. And at least a good two, two-and-a-half feet, solid and packed, already on the ground from early December. It was the 1st of January, it was 25 below and it was northern Minnesota, to boot, for crying out loud. You could hide a car under the powder piling up in these big drainage ditches Anything could be under four feet of snow by now. Anything, Paul.

Keep calm, Paully. You can do this, Paully.

The moment before his ski stopped moving forward, the blur that was the black Model B in front of him fishtailed again, and for a moment Paul couldn't see a thing. Sprays of snow spinning out of the rear wheel wells swept a curtain of snow crystals across him, splashing ice and crystalline rainbows across his tortoiseshell glasses. Previously, he could barely breathe through the phlegm-encrusted scarf engulfing his whole head. Now he couldn't breathe and he couldn't see either.

And he couldn't be seen.

You're on your own Paully.

Paul's shattered ski stuck. It stuck hard. Paul expected panic. But it didn't come. Paul was proud of himself. He felt rational and cool. Is this how you feel as you're about to die? Probably. It probably never was like the novels or the comics. It wasn't going to be heroic. It was just going to hurt. This was going to hurt a lot, for sure.

Yes, it was the end of his right ski, and as if he were seeing it from a great height above (as he'd already mentioned), all the motion slowed way down, and he saw his left knee bending in a way that shouldn't have been possible. He saw his right leg crossing the back of his left ski lifting both legs easily out of the snow and pirouetting backwards off to the side (never a good sign) taking him with it. He saw himself letting go of the rope (another not-good sign), as his face fell forward.

He'd had to let go of the rope. The rope was being jerked right out of his hand. He'd missed flipping it over a mailbox, in fact, a whole row of mailboxes. The rope was busy now lassoing all of them, mailboxes, skier, all of them as if it were a baler bailing exceptionally unmanageable hay. The rope began whipping around in front of Paul's face, trying to find an eye to gouge out while it was at it That would've concerned him. A lot. If he hadn't already seen the barbed wire fence approaching him rapidly from the opposite direction.

Instead of cutting a graceful, wild, whooping arc in the air above the driveway they were speeding past (as he'd been doing all afternoon) Paul was doing somersaults and impromptu handstands towards it. He slammed into the gate on the driveway and slid, tumbling, head-over-heels, along its barbed wire, shredding his wool coat, then his sweater, then his shirt, then his skin as he slid and bounced his way down towards the rest of the fence. He missed the other corner post. But he hit the next post. Upside down. The beer bottle in his jacket shattered. His right ski was broken off again, down to a stub. His long left ski somehow managed to entwine itself between the top two rows of the fence's barbed wire. And that slowed him down.

Which was a lucky thing, huh? Well, maybe. It also slashed his pants to ribbons and twisted his left knee nearly backwards and off (at least it felt like it). His forehead bashed into the second wooden fence post, effectively stopping his face, head, and neck, but allowing the rest of his body to rotate and twirl into an impromptu naval knot (the "Paully Hospitalization Knot # 27 – Paul knew knots – he was going into the Navy for cripe's sake). He was a messy ball of Paul, barbed wire and splintering wood. Then as if things couldn't get any worse, the end of the rope whipped downwards and to the left and found him and his body. Things got real confusing after that.

33
YONDER

The last thing he remembered was wondering if the rope would yank the fender off of Zeke's dad's car. It was either the mailboxes or the bumper. Paul didn't want to know. He didn't want Zeke to get in trouble. Zeke's dad was strict. They were poor. There was a depression and a war on, for crying out loud. Could Zeke's family pay for it? Hah! With what? Maybe a farmer, maybe Stan's dad could weld the old one back on. Whatever might be left of it that is. Stan's dad was not going to be happy. Zeke's dad was going to be mad as all get out.

He could still hear the Andrews sisters singing their hearts out, somewhere, somehow. What radio station could be that strong? Why had he never heard this song before?

Fixing the wrecked car? – that just left Paul and Paul's dad (who travelled – all the time – who was more absence than presence – who was pretty much invisible), which really meant Paul and Paul's mom (who's Irish anger was legendary), which really meant – that just left Paul. Yes, brother, Paul alone and Paul in trouble. Over and out. Amen.

But it didn't really matter.

Did it?

Nah. It didn't matter all that much, not to Paul. Not when you thought about it for any length of time. Paul was certainly going to be dead, Very soon. Anyway he looked at it.

Dead.

Finally.

There was a certain peace in that.

Finally.

Not that he wanted peace. He didn't. He wanted life. Yeah, he was swinging back again to loving life. Typical huh? But life was over. Death hadn't stumbled upon him slogging through a jungle or storming a beach or drowning in a monsoon-swamped ship or being methodically punctured by dive-bombing Zeros. No. Nor did it find him, as he'd planned this afernoon, freezing naked in a deserted corn field, or squashed flat as a bug by a sliding car. Nope. None of that was going to happen. Death had been waiting for

Paul, for years, despite all his angst and pain – it had been waiting for Paul all along, in a ditch, under a snowdrift, underneath a corrugated iron roof alongside a highway by a lake next to a forest. It had always been here. It had always been waiting for Paul – waiting for Paul and his green wool scarf that should've been laminated canoe paddles but wasn't. Always. It had always been here.

Man! He wish he would've known. Darn. His life could've been a lot easier.

Paul came to rest in the snow. It felt clean. It felt cool. And it felt warm. Which should've surprised him. But it didn't. He only wanted to sleep. Nothing wrong with that. It was peaceful here.

The sky was bluer than any blue had any right to be. He could see a tree in the distance (upside down). A turquoise blue pine tree. More than one. A handful. Dappled with pillows of snow. They didn't look real. Wrong ways up. Looked as if they were a hokey Christmas card. That was Minnesota for you. Too perfect. Had to be hokey. Paul had to admit – he liked hokey. It wasn't so bad.

The Minnesota air smelled bright and clean and amused to find a boy doing a headstand and bleeding into the snow. Could air smell amused? The sky was so bright. And so loud. And soft. And the music was still there. And the trees were so soft. The air was soft too. The snow was soft. You know, if you had to be someplace, the Red River valley in winter in the snow was a good place to be. If he had one word to describe his situation right now – he'd have to, he'd be forced to describe it as, yes, "soft."

And soft, well, it wasn't all that bad, was it?

And you know, it was kind of like being killed by family – one of his own, it was a Red River valley ditch that did him in. One of his own. Like one of his family.

And it's better when you're killed by family, right?

Someone you know?

Right?

Didn't that make sense?

Did it matter?

He wasn't sure. Well, one thing was for sure – there hadn't been any fuss. There hadn't been any noise. He'd done it right. In the end.

Right?

Where was he going with this?

Paully? Guy?

You there?

You're not making sense.

But dying guys don't have to make sense, do they?

No, Paully, they don't.

The truth was — life didn't make sense. Life didn't have to make sense. In Minnesota, it's not the meaning, it's the doing. You play the hand you're dealt. Summer ends. Winter settles in. You don't whine. You don't complain. You get on with it. That's what you do. You've got six, maybe seven, cold, sunless months to get through. So go on and start getting on! For the love of Pete, it's not that hard to figure out, people. It's not that hard.

Paul thought he could hear Zeke yelling. He thought he could hear Stan calling out his name. And he heard another voice. It was familiar, but with a funny accent, flat and thin in all the wrong places. Not a Minnesotan, then. Probably an Iowan. It was a deep voice too. Ma? Ma must have a cold. It was saying "Dad." But that didn't make any sense, did it? Ma's dad had been dead for five years.

Makes no sense.

Paully, none of it has to make any sense.

None of it?

None of it.

There's only one "have to" here.

Oh yeah. Sorry. I forgot.

Paul grabbed himself by the metaphorical suspenders. His own, his actual suspenders were wrapped around a nearby fence post, along with other parts of his body, so Paul grabbed those figurative suspenders and Paul got on with the exacting business of dying. He was turning from Paul to ex-Paul. He hoped it wouldn't take a long time. He was pretty tired.

34
ZOMBIE

The call came unexpectedly.

That's exactly what people always say. But it's not exactly true, is it?

No.

It's not unexpected. Your body knows. It feels ahead with its own toolbox of secret sensory instruments, as unspecified as they are innumerable, and it judges, estimates, plots, lists, cogitates, puzzles, extrapolates, erases and re-extrapolates with compulsive affection.

It worries. It panics. Your body agonizes, while you're doing more important things – having sex, sleeping, defecating, eating, being employed, getting drunk – your body runs its fleshy sense-fingers along the many-dimensioned shapes of its futures and its futures' futures and it whispers importantly to itself. It nods, notes, and it considers. It hesitates. Then it progresses forwards.

It's slow going. It's hard, exacting work. Your body can't be too careful. Bodies are fragile things. Futures break bodies as easily as avalanches mow down alpine forests. Futures hurt. It's what futures do. Your body knows that. It wants to pick the least painful future it can.

But which future to choose?

Hesitantly, your body moves ahead. It explores. It pulls back drapes better left un-pulled. It scuttles down dark basement stairs. It opens locked doors barred for good reason. It gets hurt. It heals. Gets hurt again. It cuts itself on knife-edges while running. It endures sleepless nights with bloodshot eyes, pleading and arguing. It paints itself into corners. It jellifies its hands reaching under moving truck tires. It leans over the side of improbably tall buildings, fingering the undersides of cornices, feeling for clues, for answers, slips, and feels its spine snap and face implode as it impacts sidewalks. It does this over and over again.

You realize, of course, your body doesn't want to do these things.

But it does them nevertheless.

It does all these things so you don't have to do them. It does them because it wants to know the truth. It wants to know the future, however pleasant or unpleasant that may be. It wants to know, it has to know. For you.

But your body's not happy. Knowing's not peaceful. Knowing doesn't bring it much hope, much less any rest. But what's a body to do? Bodies are very cautious constructions. They're prudent, risk-adverse. It's their business to find out, then cry out. It's your business to listen, then act. That's the contract.

It's exhausting to have a body.

It's even more exhausting to be a body.

35
AUTOMOBILE

So yes, the call came unexpectedly.

And, no, the call was not unexpected.

Jim looked down at his cellphone warbling back up at him and his life changed. In less than a minute. It turned. On a fucking dime.

Jim's dad was dying.

Shit. Fuck. Now what?

He didn't remember ending the call. He didn't even remember where he put his phone down. His hand was empty. Where was his fucking phone? Did he drop it? Dropping, now that would be very much out of character for Jim Olsen. Jim loved him his shiny new cell phones. That he did. He got a new one every year. Or every other year, minimum. His excuse was he needed them for business. Yeah. Maybe. The truth was – they were practically his pets, part of the family. He gave them names. They had special charging shelves built into the wall near the front door. He attended to their every need, their every app, update, patch, memory/battery upgrade. They never got scratched. They never had to be repaired. They were cherished, for better or worse. So, if Jim may have destroyed a cellphone that evening, well then mister, it was a sign. Definitely a sign. Jim had become, as they say, unhinged. His door was swinging off the friggin' frame. It was sailing, free and untethered, out into the wild blue yonder and taking Jim with it, whether Jim wanted to sail along or not.

Jim thought (or pretended to do what passed for thinking) and thought and thought about this, about all of this shit, and a lot of other shit, in much detail, and for much longer than he thought he really should have, all through the night in fact, for starters. He thought as Daniel Alvarez and Jim Olsen barreled north on I-5 up, down, and between unnaturally steep California mountains. He thought as they shot in and out of heroically-sized groves of pecan trees. He thought as they crawled across vast valley floors under unblinking stars. What else was there to do? Jim was a thinker. But that night his thinker was broken. It was "thinking lite." You did it, but it didn't get you anywhere at all, and you took a hell of a long time doing it.

"I should've been up there" said Jim, after twenty minutes of silence.

Daniel was shaking his head.

"No one plans these things, Jimbles."

Their battered Corolla wasn't quiet. Once it was top of the line, brand new, but that was 200,000 miles ago. Now, it shimmied and shaked and complained about the road every trip it took. Tonight was no exception. The gears ground. The heater whined. The radio belched static and talk shows. Its tires hissed. It was raining, so its roof drummed.

And that wasn't all, Jim was doing his bit too. Being cacaphonically creative. Adding to the general Corolla hubbub. Rocking his seat. Sighing. Talking to himself. Snapping his fingers. Squeaking that damned damaged back seat cushion back and forth every few seconds (gotta get that fixed). Biting his nails Staring. Peering, intently, eyes blank, out the passenger window through smeary Jim-forehead marks Jim had made when he bumped his head against the cool glass (bump – bump – bump – he did that a lot). Yeah, you couldn't exactly describe the trip as quiet or peaceful.

Fifteen minutes later…

"I would've been up there, if they'd told me sooner. Even if sis isn't talking to me. She could've texted. She could've… Sent a carrier pigeon. Some shit like that. Smoke signals even. She could've done that."

"Maybe. You're probably right. But, Jimbles, it's never easy, these things."

Then, more silence, more squeaking, more nail-biting.

It was noisy, yeah. But that was O.K. Jim didn't notice – why would he? – he was the one making most of the noise. And the other person in the car, the driver, Daniel, well, he didn't notice either, it was all very familiar to Daniel. Too familiar, sometimes. Welcomingly familiar others.

Daniel half-listened to Jim, half-listened to the radio, half-listened to himself, (yeah, he was multi-tasking, that was 1-1/2 Daniels on the job tonight), thinking, concluding, wondering how seriously Jim was going to unglue himself in the next couple of weeks and what it would take for him, Daniel, to put Jim back together, keep him pasted together, have him look as if he'd never been not-together, have him appear outwardly joined, all the Jim-parts in one Jim-piece, presentable, polite, showered, clothed and moving vaguely in a forward direction. How was Daniel going to manage all that? How?

Daniel worried. Daniel fussed. One thing, the two of them were definitely going to avoid alcohol for the duration. If you're sitting on an unexploded bomb, you don't light the fuse just for the fun of trying to put it out, just in time to save your life. At least, Daniel didn't. And guess what? Jim wasn't going to do it either.

Daniel looked over at Jim, bumping his head against the window and shook his head. It was going to be a long night.

Daniel didn't call it worrying. Daniel called it planning. It was something he did. And he did it well. Besides, it kept Daniel awake. He drove better that way. And after 38 years of Jim-experience, Daniel was used to it. He'd better be used to it. He was, in actual fact, the planet's number one expert in Jim-ology. Daniel was a pro. He knew it. And he had the scars to prove it.

36
BENT

Daniel checked on Jim, checked on the gas tank, passed long lines of trucks, avoided road debris, fought the slow drivers in the left lane and frowned a lot.

Jim had been acting odd even before tonight. Sometimes it felt as if Jim were letting go of Daniel. Or Jim wanted Daniel to let go of him. He'd stopped arguing. Always a bad sign. Jim drifted through their mutual life now, fidgeting, irritated, jumpy and touchy. And silent. Nothing Daniel said or did helped. Daniel felt... superfluous. A strange feeling. Not one he was going to put up with. Daniel was going to have to fight his way back into the center of Jim's life. Something he'd had to do a couple of times before. No one could say it was fun. But it was necessary.

They'd been through rough patches before. Some of the patches being so rough a person couldn't even have called them patches, really. More like long moments of pure terror and chaos. Such is married life. Daniel sighed. Checked Jim out again out of the corner of his eye. And Jim had left dirty dishes in the sink last night. He'd left dirty shoe tracks across the kitchen floor and dirty blankets on the floor and all over the couch and that glass on the floor in the living room… Jim knew that drove Daniel crazy. But there was something different… Something else… Swept into a corner someplace, somewhere. Something bent and wrong, maybe broken… Something… Daniel checked on Jim one more time. He was rocking that seat and resting his head again. Ah well. At least he was talking to Daniel this trip. They jetted northwards through rainy California darkness.

37
CONVERSATION

Jim was not having a good night. He was talking to himself. He knew it. And he wasn't bothering to hide it.

"Fuck."

"Fuck. Fuck. Fuck. Fuck. Fuck."

"What did you say, Jimbles? Do we need to stop? Here's a rest area. Button-something. In a mile."

"Nope. Uh… Not saying… uh nothing, Dan, nothing. Don't need anything, Danny boy. Nothing. Nope."

"Really?"

"Fine. I'm good. Really."

"Really?"

"Didn't I just say that?"

He'd said that a little too loud. Jim forced himself to keep his lips zipped. Fuck Jim. Fuck. Shut the fuck up. You don't need to get Daniel mad at you. Enough people mad at you as it is. Fucking Jim. He had a headache. His lungs hurt. Probably had pneumonia.

Fuck. Fuck. Fuck.

So, tell me, why are you so angry, James? Be as honest as you're able. Just Jim and James here, you know. Just us two. Talking to ourselves. Same as always. Why so angry?

Uh…

What? James? What? I can't hear you, James. What?

No idea, Jim. Not a fucking clue. Leave me alone.

You want to know what I think, James?

Do I have a fucking choice, Jim?

You've never had a fucking choice, James.

Don't I know it, Jim

So. What do you suppose I'm thinking, James, right this minute?

What are you thinking, Jim?

I think you're a shit, James.

That would explain a lot, Jim.

But you already knew that, James.

I already knew. It's true.

And there's more, James.

There always is, Jim.

Dad's death doesn't mean shit.

Oh. Is that all?

Not hardly. Dad's life didn't mean shit either. Our life doesn't mean shit. It's all shit. Nothing makes sense, it's never O.K., it's never over, You never win. You never lose. Life just goes on. On and on and on and on and... Experience sucks. It's all overrated, James. Life is overrated.

You're just figuring this out?

I'm just figuring it out.

And?

You want more? All right. Look, James, it's all over for dad. His book is written. Last page done. Cover closed. And what did it mean? What was the meaning of it all? He worked like a dog his whole life and for what? What? I'll tell you, James. Shit. Nothing. Fuck-all. It's all nothing. It's all shit. All of it. It's all shit. Fuck. Fuck. Fuck. Fuck. Fuck.

Are you through, Jim?

No. Fuck. Fuck. Fuck. Are you deaf, James? I'm revealing the fucking secret of life, the innermost secrets of the entire fucking Universe, and as usual, you're not even fucking trying to fucking listen. Or fucking think. I'm agonizing here. And what do I get? You, Jim. You. Wallowing in self-pity. Thinking of your fucking self. You're a shit, James. A shit. Open and shut case. How did I ever get stuck with you?

I'm thinking, Jim, maybe, just maybe, you need some alone-time, big guy.

Whatever you say, James, whatever you fucking say. You're always fucking right.

Jim was a fucking prick, but nobody could say he wasn't an interesting prick, huh? Don't answer that. Yeah, not exactly the funnest guy to be around right now. Jim wished he could slam a door in his face and walk out on himself

38
DESTROY

Jim looked over at Daniel.

Daniel had a tight-lipped look about him. His eyes were squinted and he was focusing intently, entirely on the road ahead. He wouldn't look at Jim. No matter how much Jim cleared his throat.

Oh.

Yeah.

Jim tried to take a deep breath, but that didn't pull much oxygen in. His lungs still hurt. That hadn't changed in the last five minutes. He looked out the window, through the grease marks, into the rain. Looked back at Daniel. Daniel still wasn't looking at him. Jim either wanted to cry or punch a hole in the windshield with his bare fist. Or maybe both. Yeah, that would do it. Fuck.

O.K. Jim. You know what you need to do. No, I don't. Yes, you do. You need to make this right. Jim? Jim? You listening? He looked at Daniel, looked out to his right at the rain again. Then he rested his forehead against the exquisitely cool glass, blinked out at all that black and rain. Why was it so hard to admit you'd made a mistake? He was tired of people holding him accountable. He should be free. Didn't everyone want to be free? Didn't they deserve it? Didn't he deserve it?

He looked at Daniel, looked away. Sighed. O.K. All right. I'm doing it.

"Look. I'm sorry Daniel. I'm sorry. I'm sorry. I really am."

He peeked out of the side of his eye. Daniel wasn't looking at him.

"I'm sorry. I'm sorry."

Daniel didn't respond.

"I'm sorry, Danny, sorry. What more can I say?"

Daniel still didn't say anything, still looked straight ahead. Jim put his hand on Daniel's leg. Daniel flinched. For a moment. Then Daniel sighed. Bit his lip. Sighed again. Daniel looked over at Jim. Jim turned his head and looked back. Jim realized his own face was wet, his eyes were bubbling, they were a pair of blue-irised fountains. His chest felt tight, tighter than before. He slobbered all over himself as he wiped his face dry with his right hand. He was a mess.

But Jim's lips were smiling. Jim was surprised at how ridiculously happy he was to get a glance from Daniel. Jim was scared. He had no idea how much he needed to be seen.

And noticed.

And forgiven.

No idea. His emotions were flapping about all over the place. Nothing made sense. Jim was flying blind. That made him even more scared. And, in a strange way, it felt good. If you were already totally out of control, how much worse could it get?

"I know, Jim. I know. I know. Relax. Try and sleep. We have a couple of hours. We have gas. We have time. I'm fine. I'm not sleepy at all. Just rest. O.K? Will you do that for me? Huh? Just close your eyes."

39
ERUPTION

The Corolla's gears thrummed down awkwardly. It started to climb a long hill. Spread in front of him, all Jim could see, for what looked like miles in the bleached out moonlight, were zebras. Who would need so many zebras? And why? He rested his head against the glass. He stared, dumbfounded. He kept his hand on Daniel's thigh and stared out into the night.

No. Not zebras, cows. Oh. Tens of thousands of cows, standing on mountains of their own excrement, mostly motionless, huddled sociably in groups, in rows, a few loners wandering off by themselves on inexplicable, but important errands. What were they doing out here? What? Why?

Oh.

Yeah.

Waiting to be slaughtered.

Jim smiled. He smiled out at them. Welcome to the club, my bovine brothers. This is life. Knee deep in your own shit, worrying about the future, but in reality, the whole time, moments away from a miserable death.

Wake up! Get out! Escape! Shoo! Get out of here. Run! Run for your lives you stupid cows!

He watched. Fascinated. They kept driving uphill. They kept passing cows. He expected the endless, square stockades full of steaming cows standing in the rain to run out at some point. They had to have a terminus, right? A boundary? Sometime? They weren't infinite, were they? An infinity of cows in each square in an infinity of square stockades. The infinite slaughterhouse. That couldn't be right. They had to end. But they didn't. The Corolla grumbled and growled its way up the long uphill stretch, and the cow-crowds stretched right along with it. On and on and on.

Why?

Why is the Universe showing me this? Tonight of all nights?

Jim closed his eyes. I won't look. It's not there. He tried to think sleepy thoughts. But all he could see were cow faces, patient, wise, soft cow eyes, big cow mouths carefully chewing their cud, muscular cow nostrils geysering hot breath into cold night air.

Jim was breathing in short, hyperventilating breaths, talking quietly to himself.

Incurious, dull eyes looking up at an incurious, dull sky, a sky black and pitiless as death, no, it was death itself, death himself, hanging above them all, amused blackness, a watching, a clever waiting, a...

Jim felt a hand on his. It was familiar. Then it was under his. It pushed his hand upwards. It nestled beneath it and floated Jim's hand over to his Jim's own thigh. The hand pulled out from underneath and settled on top of Jim's hand. Strong fingers rested themselves there, covering Jim's more slender, ink-stained hands, and a strong grip squeezed Jim's hand a couple of times. It patted and caressed the hand underneath it. Then the hand was still. It stayed on his hand, pinning his hand to his leg. But it was still. It felt like a kind of anchor. A thing a guy would stay tied to and hold onto.

And now the Universe is showing me this?

I can't believe how fucking strange the universe is.

Jim was silent. Daniel was silent.

"They could've told me dad was really sick this time. They never tell me anything."

Jim's leg got squeezed.

"I ask, but they never remember. What am I? The invisible brother? What's up with that?"

Jim's leg got another squeeze.

Daniel kept his hand on Jim's left thigh, the two of them tunneled, Bay-Area-wards, through the night together. The hand kept Jim tethered, kept him nearby, kept him relatively safe for now, as safe as Daniel could manage.

It was enough.

Well, it had to be enough.

For now.

40

FUMBLING

So rewind back a couple of hours.

The call came unexpectedly.

Yeah, let's just stick with that.

Jim got home from work, same as always that night, same old, same old. So far, nothing to report. But his stomach, his guts were uneasy, they weren't comfortable.

Now, Jim listened to his stomach (and his stomach's intestinal friends). They usually picked up on things way ahead of time. Bad things, catastrophic things, things about to unload their dump-trucks-full of shit on his head, disastrous shit-hurricanes rotating their way towards him – you know, the normal, malevolent weirdnesses of daily life – his stomach knew all about that stuff winging its way Jim-wards, and it tried to give Jim the heads-up. As best it knew how. In a friendly way. With stabbing pain.

Jim's stomach knew from disaster. It was, in fact, a disaster compass. It knew, with absolute certainty, long before his happy-go-lucky brain even glanced in the direction of a panic button, that, this time, Jim was going down. It was all falling apart. Hope was not an option. There was, to be exact, no hope available. Jim was hope-less. It was time to run screaming into the night. Now. Right now. Before it was too late. His stomach cared. It was a thing that it did. A kindness to the guy lugging it around in his torso all day.

So, Jim perked his ears up and listened when his stomach churned. His guts were clearly and reliably paranoid. Jim had learned to rely on them. Only a fool didn't listen to his gut. Especially when it stabbed you. Repeatedly. Confidently.

Jim checked for texts on his cell. None. Fuck. Gotta stop this. Getting compulsive. He checked again, just to make sure. Then one more time.

Stop it, Jimmy-boy, just say no.

Jimmy-boy was a nickname his first boyfriend – Sean-from-Dublin-and-don't-you-be-forgetting-it-now – it was a name Sean had, in a fit of princely generosity, bequeathed and bestowed on Jim on the occasion of Sean buying his Jimmy-boy his first ever Guinness and Jim liking it. It had been a proud moment. Sean took it so seriously. Guinness was not merely a beer. Beer was not merely beer. It was a sacrament. It was a process. It was a ceremony. Jim could never mouth the syllables "Jimmy-boy" to himself without imagining a pair of bright eyes hovering over a cloud of white foam smiling out at Jim from underneath an overgrown bramble of red hair. Jim liked being stared at by eyes like those. Shit! So long ago. Yeah, it was a good memory – it was a good beer – it was a good name – it had been a good year, that year with Sean. When was the last time he'd kissed Sean? His mouth tasting like hot and sour soup? And plum wine? It had to be that night, shit yeah, Jim had been so stupid and stubborn, Sean had caught him…

Some internal organ, probably his stomach, did a backflip. Yeah, Jim's stomach was not happy.

Oh. Yeah.

Disaster loomed.

Either disaster or the aftershocks of the grande sushi burrito he'd crammed into his pie-hole in 4 minutes flat as he worked through lunch at his desk today, dripping soy sauce onto his keyboard and shorting it out. Jim felt a wild, throbbing pain. He stopped where he was. He looked up at the ceiling above his front door. His stomach twisted and turned. He looked, he waited, he watched. As if the answers were up there. Hiding in the stucco-covered cornice. They weren't. He sighed. Breathed through his mouth to clear his head. Not good, Jimbo, not good. His intestines sucker-punched him once more, just for the hell of it, and Jim stood and breathed for a moment more, breathing through his nose, trying not to move his diaphragm. After a tense minute or two, he pushed forwards and closed the front door.

Only seven steps up to their condo door and Jim was already breathing hard. He patted his spare tire lovingly – something a construction vehicle would be proud to carry as a spare. It was massive. Heroic. Epic even. How long had it been? Since he'd seen his waistline? Since he'd glanced at his genitalia without a lot of folding and re-arranging? A while. O.K., more than a while. Shit. He couldn't remember how long.

Jeez. He was sweating too. He wiped his forehead with his sleeve.

And Jim kept on hearing – what? What was he hearing? This annoying whooshing sound tickling his ears, flexing his eardrums the wrong way, making his throat feel hollow and echoing (a very odd feeling). And he felt cold. And his hands were stiff. And yeah his left leg was starting to hurt. Literally throb. Yada, yada, yada.

Heart attack? How would he tell? He was always aching. There was always something out of kilter in this ageing fossil of a body he walked his mind around in day to day. So Jim didn't think too hard or too long about the crowd of aches and pains yelling and waving their hands this way and that, trying to get Jim's attention. He blinked a couple of times. Put his hand to his chest. Felt a beat. All-righty then. He closed the front door. He got on with his life. Whatever was left of it.

Besides, his friggin' body was usually a wreck when he got home from the office anyway. Most people's bodies were 98% water. Jim's was 98% stress. He was used to it.

Jim could take it.

He was strong, right?

Right. Damn right.

41
GUY

He checked his phone one last time for texts. None.

Gotta stop. Gotta stop this.

O.K.

He was an Olsen. Olsen's poured stress on their pancakes for breakfast. Not that Jim usually had time for breakfast in the morning. He was usually late. When they were passing out the punctuality genes, Jim must've been AWOL. Or in the wrong line. Or maybe, he was just late. Ha ha ha.

Speaking of which, he was, in fact, late. As usual. But unusually, he was very late tonight, indeed. Thankfully, Daniel was even later. So it didn't count, did it?

He checked one last time for texts. Stared at the screen. Are you going to stop, Jim?

He and Daniel had been in the same routine for so long, Jim couldn't remember who he was without it. He was the routine. He was an assortment of self-perpetuating behaviors. They walked and talked in his body, but Jim wasn't there anymore. His body was home, but Jim wasn't home. He hated it.

So, there was this guy at work, Benny. Younger than Jim, O.K., a lot younger, just starting out as a Junior Engineer, and Jim and Benny and a handful of other guys went out to lunch a lot because all of them had been dragooned into rescuing the same doomed project and they couldn't stop talking about it. The team had to spend so much time together, building, arguing, bitching, complaining, that they unconsciously got hungry simultaneously and exited for nourishment in a depressed, excited herd every friggin' day, and a guy, well, a guy just couldn't not do it. You had to go. It was a reflex action. Not voluntary. It came from the subconscious. It wasn't Jim's fault. None of it was. You'll see.

Yeah. So that was Jim's life at present. So far, the same old IT work environment. Nothing new. Every company was like that. Every project was like that. Intense. Condemned. Soon-to-be-forgotten. It was a process. Young engineers being put through the software-writing-development meat grinder, turning them into… what? Into Jims. Senior Engineers. Burnt out, overweight, opinionated husks of formerly energetic Juniors. Same old same old. Yup. So, yeah, Jim hadn't thought much about it.

But this time it was going to be different.

Benny was goofy. Benny was fun. He was smart. Benny laughed at Jim's corny sense of humor. He especially commiserated with Jim's constantly changing, internally conflicting and irredeemably conflated design specs for the new database. Benny got it. Benny had good ideas, good suggestions. And Benny liked hearing Jim explain why Benny's ideas/suggestions wouldn't work. He didn't get mad. He got more interested. Benny understood Jim. He got Jim. And he was easy on the eyes. Very easy on the eyes. He had these lips… well… It was nice. It was nice having him nearby. Within visual range.

Jim started looking forward to lunch, he started looking forward to Benny. Last week, the usual gang that went out for lunch was reduced to only Jim and Benny, due to some last minute QA rush on an admittedly nasty bug they'd been working on over the whole weekend – another doomed project – and… well… there they were. Just the two of them. Jim and Benny, yucking it up with brightly-colored paper bibs tucked into their collars. Benny had put his hand on Jim's leg, in the middle of the all-you-can-eat barbecue place they liked to hit on Wednesdays – Fat Frank's Flavor Planet and the infamous Half Price Humpday. The two of them were on their usual back bench sitting at a picnic table discreetly covered with a long, plasticized, red-check table-cloth that hung down nearly to floor level. You couldn't see a thing below a guy's chin. It was all hidden. And Jim had just grabbed a new spare rib after washing his hands off from the last one when… time stopped.

Yes, they'd been tucked away in a shadowy, barbecue-splotched corner. Yes, they'd been arguing about the necessity of foreign keys in the new lookup tables in the database. All normal. It had all been so innocent. Suddenly Benny had, quite out of the blue, put his hand on Jim's upper thigh. Benny had put it there and Benny had left it there. Jim, after a second or two of looking Benny straight in the face, well, he'd let him. Partly because he hadn't been hit on in God knows how long, partly because he was choking to death on the spare rib he'd been industriously gnawing on as a bunch of hot Benny-fingers hit his unprotected Jim-kneecap. Benny jumped up. Benny pounded on his back. Said soothing words. Gave him a quick, microsecond, shoulder massage-let. Sat down. Put his hand back on Jim's thigh. Started eating again with his free hand.

Huh. Well. All righty then.

They kept going out for lunch. They began to avoid the gang. The hand kept finding its way to Jim's leg. Then, one day, Benny sent a text with a photo of himself, from the waist down, nude (a very nice photo, in fact), and that had been yesterday, and now it was today, and that had been why Jim had eaten alone at his desk at noon. He didn't trust himself. With good reason. Who would trust himself in a situation like that?

42
HERO

Yes. Jim had, what was commonly called, a situation.

He had it and he had it bad and he knew it.

And of course, knowing Jim's luck, it had rapidly escalated from situation to problem to obsession to… well, God knows what it was now.

Benny had put his hand on Jim's shoulder when he left work last night, a friendly touch, on the way out. Jim could still feel Benny's hand up there, on the slabs of Jim's stiff, sore and unyielding-as-steel-cables shoulder muscles. Jim could feel them. He swore he could. The handprints were burned through his shirt into his skin. Benny had massaged Jim's battered excuse for upper back musculature for a second or two, then patted it, then moved on. It was brief. It was nice. Nothing wrong with that, right? Nice is human. It was human interaction. Nothing to write home about. No harm, no foul. Nice is nice.

O.K. It was more than nice. Jim was sweating afterwards. Jim's old life here with Daniel was killing him, slowly but surely. O.K. Jim wanted a new life. A more human life. Fine. Before it was too late. He wasn't dead yet. He wasn't a mechanical man. He was flesh, right? Again, fine. He wasn't getting any younger. And… What? Jimmy, what?

And is Benny a new life? Is Benny all that? Is Benny what you want? What you need? Do you need him?

So many questions.

No?

Yes?

Maybe?

Pick one, Jim. Pick something. Do something, Jim.

There was more. With Jim, there always was.

Then, Benny had cornered Jim in the stairwell. That had been tonight. That had been a surprise. Jim usually walked down a couple of dozen floors when he left the building at night – it wasn't running the bleachers, crazy aerobic, heart-rate-bending effort like he used to do at college – but it was something, right? – better than nothing? Right? He didn't exactly love it, but he did it. A guy had to try, at any rate. Like flossing. You didn't have to like it. You did it so pieces of you didn't decay and fall off your body.

And Jim was a creature of habit. So, as usual, lately, Jim sent a last InterDev text to Benny (a corny Programmer joke), and he was busy doing his normal exiting behavior, hiking down the infinite office building staircase, squinting to see because the staircase was painted this iris-widening, fluorescent white, and all the while Jim was shaking his head, talking to himself, regretting every minute of it. All in all, the usual nightly routine. He couldn't see, it was so bright. He blinked a lot. And he was gasping. And he was late. Yeah, so far, the same routine as every other night.

It was always the same for Jim, always. His life was caught in a 4-D loop. Every day like every other friggin' day. When was it ever going to change for him? When?

Well, maybe tonight. Why tonight? Because tonight, Jim was also pulling a rolling suitcase behind him (plunk! plunk! plunk! – softly Jim, better pick that up Jim), he was pulling it down the stairs and shifting his shit from hand to hand and trying not to miss a step and then ending up stepping down three steps at once by accident and almost killing himself in the process. That was different, right?

So he started again, going much more slowly. So sue him. After missing another step he decided he'd better pick up the suitcase, and rest at the next landing. He picked it up. But he still missed the next step.

One floor down, he was taking a breather. He was also seriously considering the elevator as the only viable alternative for a rational Software Engineer such as himself. He waited a moment. All right. He'd reached a decision (yes, time to bail) and he'd reached out his elbow at the same time, to bump the bar and pop the door open to get to the hallway, juggling all his office paraphernalia at the same time, when the stairwell door exploded and whooshed open and swung away from his arm, and there was Benny, all six feet of him, in the flesh, right in front of Jim. Right. O.K. Benny. Standing there. With a shit-eating grin on his face. Jim stared, he couldn't keep his own smile off his own face. It's as if his face had developed a life of its own.

All right. What next?

Benny, not missing a beat, stepped into the stairwell, pulled the door closed behind him, reached out with his left hand, cupped

Jim's neck, and pulled Jim's face into his. So, there was Jim, one hand on the railing, the other fumbling in the open air going down twenty stories, suitcases, briefcases, papers (Jim's and Benny's), scattered on the concrete landing in front of him, and Jim found himself necking in public.

Benny had grabbed Jim's crotch with the other hand and kissed Jim thoroughly and strenuously as he explored Jim's private regions with the same painstaking completeness. Then the two of them had spent 2 hours talking about it, people passing them, hiking up and down the stairs, the emergency doors clicking and banging and echoing and voices distorting and floating back up and down at them – you could hear whispers ten floors away. Neither of them wanted to leave. They were trapped in the stairwell. By each other.

It didn't seem like two hours. It seemed like two minutes. Mostly they pretended to discuss code and roll-outs and quality control (had they? – Jim for the life of him couldn't recall a single sentence of their conversation, it was office-speak, whatever it was). They stared deep into each other's eyes as they spoke. People hiked down past them. They rubbed their bodies against each other as if by accident. The door next to them would open and close. At one point, Benny bent over to pick up a file and bit Jim on the ankle. Jim loved it. All of it. Every five minutes or so they got a break – perfect silence, perfect solitude – and they giggled and panted for thirty seconds as they tried to choke each other with their tongues and massage every available inch of the other guy's body with hungry, unashamed hands.

Jim was blushing furiously the whole time. And he was hard as a rock. It was teenage life again. It was awful. And it wasn't so bad. It was as if his body had staged a coup d'état. It demanded more. It wouldn't take no for an answer. It had decided to live! – live! – live! No more Jim being a poor sucker. Jim was free.

Between kissing sessions, Jim figured he'd made a decision, somewhere, somehow. He'd had a problem. He'd made a decision. He'd come up with a solution.

He'd made a decision, right? He had, hadn't he? But he didn't remember making one. Did it matter? He wasn't sure. He really didn't care.

He'd somehow found his car (psychic powers? echolocation? – he had no idea). The two of them had wandered in and out of elevators, drifted through lobbies and hallways. All this after Benny had finally released Jim from the lip-lock he'd had him in. O.K., maybe the lip-lock had been mutual. It had been a mutual release. He didn't remember much. It was all a kind of testosterone fog. The best kind to be in. It was all new for Jim. Office romance and such.

Jim. Romance. What a strange pair of words to pair together.

They'd shook hands goodbye in the parking lot, giggling, again. Jim had unlocked his car door. Thrown all his shit into the back seat. Made his way to the front of his car. Then he'd thrown up in the bushes, right next to his front bumper.

After that, Jim had driven home. Smiling and whistling to himself. He'd snapped his fingers. He'd done drum rolls on the steering wheel. He'd played the radio too loud. He'd thought of Daniel, and crammed chewing gum in his mouth between songs to get his breath smelling of something other than Benny's mouth and Benny's body. Yup. He'd have to take a shower when he got home. He'd smelled his hands. And his shoulder. And his shirt. He reeked as if he'd run a marathon.

What had he been thinking?

Well, he hadn't been.

And that was all that mattered.

43
INTERIOR

Jim was home. Jim was alone. Jim was free.

He whistled. Then did it some more. Winked at the ceiling. Locked the front door.

Jim positioned Albert IV, his cellphone, on its cell-shelf, checked for texts, messages (none), and waited to hear it gurgle and burp. It was happily charging. He patted it a couple of times. Then, on a whim, he pulled a tiny felt rectangle of cloth from a hidden holder on the shelf and wiped down Albert IV completely and thoroughly until Albert gleamed in the gloaming of the hallway light as if he were a precious jewel. He checked for texts. None. Wait. Wasn't that a text? No. Shit. He put Albert back on his perch.

The rest of the condo was pitch black. Jim yelled out to turn the lights on. The condo complied. He asked the time and a voice responded. He yelled at the thermostat and a voice made a suggestion and turned up the heat. He had the condo throw in some music while it was at it (he liked Smooth Jazz, and the voice knew it) and obligingly, something slow and funky filled the empty, echoing rooms.

Jim loved him his gadgets.

Especially when they did as they were told. Not always the case. He was a programmer. He knew. They often did whatever the fuck they wanted. But not tonight.

Yes, Daniel wasn't home yet. No Dictator of Antisepsis watching his every move. So Jim was still off-duty. Jim was free. Technically no. But practically, yes. Household rules and regs? He didn't have to pretend to care. Hygiene? Cleanliness? They were only words, they were, after all, merely social constructs. He could pick his nose, pass gas and eat potato chips off the floor if he felt like it. Simultaneously. He could and he did. Given the chance. When he was off-duty. Sans King Daniel.

This was the real Jim. Living his savage, solitary Mad Max, post-apocalyptic life.

Daniel was high order. Jim was high entropy. Polar opposites.

It was a relationship. It had worked. Yeah. For a long time. A very long time. Maybe longer than it should have. Maybe? No? Yes?

He checked his phone for texts again.

I'm not going to keep doing this.

Why didn't Benny say something?

Stop it, Jim, just stop it.

Jim wiped down Albert and left him charging again. He bopped and bounced his way down the hallway, dancing and bumping against the walls. His ample posterior followed behind him, a beat later than the front of him. He checked, looking over his shoulder, to be sure he hadn't knocked any pictures to the floor. He hadn't. Good. Great. A knot of intestine spasmed and Jim momentarily paused, bending over, breathing through his nose (which did not help this time), closing his eyes. It went away quickly enough. He was up and dancing again in no time. He still had it. Yup. Still had what it takes.

44
CLICK

Every so often, lately, as Jim wandered about the condo, living his life, Jim thought he caught a streak of fuzzy, furry motion in the extreme sides of his peripheral vision. It rolled around, spun, sped by and disappeared. Like... There. Right then. Off to the left.

Almost as if it were an animal. Or almost as if stuff (surplus light?) were squeezing out of the sides of his eye sockets and spurting into the air. It was that far off to the side, you know, way, way over, barely still in his vision. Yeah. Way, way, way over. Hard to see, but once you saw it, it was hard not to notice it. It was even harder not to be concerned.

Dust in the air?

Floaters in his eyes?

Rats?

Also, his left arm would feel cold and stiff. Then his left eyelid would sag.

Then he'd be fine.

Did everyone have problems like this?

And his ears. Jim couldn't be sure. But he thought he'd hear a voice. A high-pitched, whistle of a voice. Always behind him, or way to the side, where he couldn't see anything. It would start up, and if he turned around, it would stop. A high-pitched squeak. Like, maybe...

Yeah, rats.

Fuck.

Jim hated rats.

And probably he had a cold coming on.

Fuck.

Always something.

45
JABBER

So, Jim was free.

For now.

He could leave his clothes in the middle of the floor. Including his dirty t-shirt and socks. He could dump his briefcase open all over the dining room table. He could leave dirty dishes in the sink.

He could do all this, he liked to do all of this, luxuriously, ostentatiously, until the sound of Daniel's key clicking and clacking in the back door deadbolt began to echo throughout the first story of this, their over-priced, California colonial, brightly-colored stucco-pile of Los Angeles condo they called home.

Jim would hear, and then Jim would have 9 seconds (he'd timed it) to save himself from most certain destruction. In an orgy of tidying, grabbing and retreating, he'd spin around the condo, as if he were a slightly-overweight, crazed tornado, and suck everything up and hightail it back to the master bedroom barely milliseconds ahead of Daniel. And Daniel would follow. He'd be calm, always encountering Jim, nearly every night, red-faced and panting, getting undressed under their harsh, usually-never-used, ceiling bedroom light, looking innocent and harmless and sweet as pie. Always.

Well, mostly always. It was a routine. That was how their evenings started. That was the pattern. Jim did it nearly unconsciously now. He didn't remember doing it usually. It just happened. By itself.

Daniel wasn't stupid. He knew exactly what was going on. As long as he didn't have to experience it, he was fine. The condo was clean when he saw it. He didn't want to know what happened when he wasn't around.

And Jim did not do well with a lot of complaining.

And Daniel wasn't shy about announcing his opinions

So, yeah, you might say, Jim walked a fine line.

He balanced on the knife edge between slavery and torture. His only two choices.

Was that right? Jim wasn't sure what he thought about it. Some might say he thought he was a guest in his own home. Others might say he had no backbone. Jim might agree with both. But, no matter what people might think, it worked.

Yeah. It worked. It did. It had worked for a long time.

Only some of the many, many compromises of married life that prevented nightly homicides.

And that was what really counted.

Right?

Right?

46
KVETCH

So, Jim was free.

Tonight things would be different. Jim was absolutely free. For a while, at least. Daniel was going to be very late tonight. Something about a conference call. And some new construction Daniel was contracting on. Daniel was a plumber. He seemed to have a lot of conference calls. But he did a lot of business, and he was always bidding. Daniel did (apparently) more paperwork-ing then he did plumb-work-ing lately (to hear Daniel tell it), but the plumbing Daniel was responsible for turned out... gorgeous. That's what everybody said. Jim had to believe it.

Daniel was respected. He was honest. And he created a sort of Renaissance tapestry of hydro-dynamics, an artist's version of valves, a symphony of... well, Jim had no idea what Daniel would do symphonies of, in the plumbing line of things. Daniel was good. Jim knew it firsthand. Yeah, he'd re-done the condo, and the pipes in their place (Jim had seen them) were squeaky clean and perfectly joined and a geometric wonder. Daniel was meticulous. A perfectionist. Yeah, he was friggin' famous. In plumbing circles. He was an artist – working in copper and permits. Daniel never had to go begging for jobs. Jim was proud of him. The money was decent too. More than decent.

Daniel was a keeper. Husband material.

You didn't let a man like that go, did you?

Right? Right?

Fuck. He thought he heard his cell ring. Went to check. Nada. Fuck.

So Jim was free and Jim had time. He prestidigitated his keys, from one hand to the other, stepped through the double doors into the living room backwards – bouncing them open with his bouncing butt – balanced his laptop stacked on top of his briefcase in one hand, and danced and sorted his keys and wallet and mail he'd picked up in the other hand. Sort of a fan dance. There. Perfect.

He was pulling his metal suitcase thingy also, since he'd had to bring home a server from work to mimic dropping an image onto it tonight. Fun, fun, fun. That was going to take a couple of hours. He was going to have to run it five times, under different conditions that made no sense and would prove nothing, but did they listen to him? No. He was only the Team Lead. Why should they listen to him? But Jorge had said… Ah. Fuck Jorge. So, yeah, Jim hadn't been happy about it. But what could you do? Nothing. That's what you could do. You could waste your evening imaging. And doing nothing. And keep your job.

Jim walked backwards all the way to the laundry room, dropping off the mail, balancing, tip-toeing, tap-dancing and nudged the laundry room door open with his elbows, backing up towards the back door without dropping a thing, not a single friggin' thing, and with the silver suitcase trundling along behind him, obediently. Was he good? Yeah. He was. He was very good.

He smiled. He was sweating, again. Sweat was dripping into his eyes. His shoulder hurt. He had a headache. But he hadn't gouged a wall or trashed a laptop or burst a blood vessel in his head on this heavily-laden voyage from front door to back door. Yeah. He still had it. He could go toe to toe, with all the twenty-somethings he worked with in Data Applications back at good old CDZ of the LLC. Toe to toe. Head to head. He could do it.

Without thinking, he automatically thought of Benny. Now going head to head with Benny, well.. He blushed. That shocked him. He couldn't remember the last time he'd blushed. Well. Except for all this evening. He literally hadn't stopped blushing for…

Bam! Jim bumped into the back door. Bam! Again. Damn. Dented it. Fuckin' cheap metal doors!. Bam! He did it again. Shit. He twisted around, looked over his shoulder, and squinted one eye as he tossed his wallet onto the shelf above their washing machine. It was a reflex action, a thing he did, the usual thing, that's where he kept his wallet, he always did this tossing thing when he got home.

But his keys were stuck in the middle of his wallet – somehow the key ring found a hole in a seam in the leather and screwed itself solidly inside of it – and (why? why me?) as Jim watched, unbelievingly, both keys and wallet shot, meteor-like, out of his hand, arced in a flash across the space lit by the bare bulb here in the utility room, bounced off a bottle of fabric softener, spun against the wall, teetering, toppling and then they both slipped –

easily and efficiently – through a space between wall and shelf, disappearing forever into shadowy tangles of cords, pipes and dust bunnies that nestled way, way down behind the dryer – between the machine and the sheetrock – far, far out of reach of anyone who didn't have six foot long, double-jointed, very skinny arms. All of which Jim didn't have, by the way.

Shit.

They were gone.

Shit. Shit. Shit.

He couldn't have made that shot if he'd tried.

He stared at the washer and the dryer. Could the wallet maybe have bounced onto one of the pipes? And he couldn't see it? Maybe it was right in front of him, wedged, balanced, whatever – waiting, easy to grab. Maybe this wasn't so bad. Maybe.

A kind of wild, panicky piano duet, a war of sound, a shifting, kaleidoscopy jazz orgy was going on in the condo behind him. Jim couldn't think. He was sweating again. He bellowed out for the music to stop. The volume increased. He bellowed again. It got louder.

47
LOSER

O.K. He grunted and pulled himself onto the top of the washer. Now we're sweating. He wiped his face with his shirt collar. He may as well have tried to dry off his forehead with a sink full of water. The collar was mostly water now. Hardly any textile. It came back limp. And sopping. His face was wetter than when he'd started. Not good, Jim, not good.

He scanned the enameled metal, the bright chrome (Daniel liked to keep their laundry room as clean as the laundry that came out of it – i.e. surgically clean at a molecular level), and the mysterious, dark crevasse beyond it yawned provocatively. Jim inched forward. His hand slipped. His head hit the wall. His hand went down behind the washing machine. With his cheek wedged between the washer and the wall, Jim scanned the dusky depths below. Nope. And Nope.

Shit. Shit. Shit. They were gone. As if they'd never been. Shit. Was there a hole in the floor? Where would a hole go to if there wasn't a basement down there to go to? Shit. He couldn't even see them. He had no idea where they were. He should go move the dryer. He should. He'd get his weight belt on (where had Daniel put that thing?), wrestle/walk the dryer out of its corner, crawl in between all those pipes and electrical cords, find the keys, retrieve his wallet. He should. He should do it. His forehead started to hurt, pressed against a nail in the sheetrock. He should try and get them back. He really should. He should.

Five minutes later, defeated, Jim kicked the laundry door closed behind him, ricocheted through the kitchen and stumbled through the dining room, shedding layers of clothing, briefcases, computers, in various unobtrusive spots, the whole way. Of course, as usual, Jim grazed his leg on the corner of the most devious and vicious piece of furniture they owned – the ancient oak dining room table they'd bought together some 30 years before, their first big purchase, full of medieval-looking serrated corners and knife-like leaves – Jim's bruises had bruises to prove it – and of course, as usual, Jim wandered, stumbled and collapsed and crawled up onto their nearly-as-ancient, but wholly immaculate (thanks to Daniel) Italian, motorized, red leather coach, and it was there that Jim stopped. He fumbled his fingers at some buttons on the arm of the couch and a headrest appeared. A few moments later a footrest followed. Jim spread out.

Textiles draped every which way on the couch, covering an unknown number of the many remotes that Jim needed at that moment. Daniel must not have seen them. He hated "storing" blankets out in the open on the couch. Jim'd better move them. But first, Jim needed the TV on. So he could turn his gray matter off. Shit. It would be so nice to talk to the air, and seconds later have the TV on. So nice. He had to get those friggin' remotes linked up with voice commands. He needed to. He did. Someday. When he had time.

Fuck.

Jim's brain sputtered, backfired, sputtered again, then lurched to a painful halt. He stared at the blank ginormous video screen that dominated their living room and pushed his fingers blindly through cotton comforters and brightly colored afghans on the couch, over and over again. Searching, searching, always searching. Many remotes were buried. Many weren't. None were the right one. His knuckles hurt for some reason. Especially on his left hand.

He searched. But he kept one ear pointing towards the front of the house. He realized what he truly was doing, what he truly was listening for – his cell. Aching for it. Hurting to hear it ring.

Jim, let it go.

Jim!

All right. All right.

Remotes. O.K.

Remotes. As long as a few were visible and reachable, Jim wasn't all that concerned. He could work his way through all of them eventually. Statistically, you'd think he'd have hit the right one about halfway through, wouldn't you? But no. He'd been through most of them already. He'd fumbled. He'd searched.

He sighed. He could barely blink. Hell, he was lucky he could even sit.

Then he felt something poking him in the underwear.

Score! Jim 1, Remotes 0. He flipped the sought-after remote right-side up with aching fingers (yes! – the right one – finally) and massaged their familiar buttons. Things started to happen.

48
MEDICATE

Mostly naked, one sock on, one sock off, arms akimbo, brown-gray hair matted and cowlicked, Jim remote-controlled the TV on and the floor heater roared into life, dimming all the lights. Wrong one. He turned it off. He yelled at the condo to turn the music off. It couldn't hear him. The music was too loud. He yelled and yelled (he refused to get up off the couch). It finally complied. He remote-controlled the TV on, with what he was sure was the heater's remote. This time it worked. The TV convulsed into digital life. Couldn't tell you what he was watching, something loud, jerky and streaming, and he downed a tumbler of gin (which he'd poured as he'd navigated the kitchen), ran his fingers up and down the smooth leather of their Italian couch, following the seam over and over and over with the fingernail on his thumb and he closed his eyes and breathed.

O.K., Jim.

It was a start.

Time to let go.

Unwind.

He'd found the tumbler on its side in the sink – how it got there was anybody's guess, Daniel would never have allowed it to stay there overnight. How late had Daniel come home last night anyways? Jim had already been asleep when he felt the right side of the bed depress and the covers jerk to one side which woke him up, barely long enough, to massage Daniel's shoulder, kiss it and roll over to his side of the bed.

Yeah, the lukewarm gin felt good – anesthetizing his vocal cords – the ones he'd been arguing with all morning long during that stupid team-building exercise they'd had at work – no time to test, only time to talk – so here he was, bringing his work home with him, like a fool. If he'd had any balls he would've said no. Daniel hated Jim working at home. Jim could never explain, in a way that Daniel could understand, how and why he ended up working from the couch, in their bedroom, all over the condo. Why bring your work home with you? Why? Well… Coding wasn't plumbing. They were different things. Anybody would know that. Anybody would understand that. Anybody but Daniel.

Like… Well… For instance… Benny would understand that.

His lungs felt tight and cramped – bronchitis?, pneumonia? So what else is new? His throat hurt. Jim sighed. That hurt too. Sighing shouldn't hurt. He yodeled a long (painful) despairing cry into the injustice of an empty condo filled with throat pain and waited to feel better. He didn't.

Jim had a flair, no, a genuine talent for the dramatic. Drama was second nature to him. He secretly craved emotional uproar. Sometimes, he even admitted to it.

And, you know, he got better at it, the more he drank. Time for more gin, boy.

He thought he heard the phone in the hall beep out it's text-just-arrived noise, as he got up off the couch. It was beeping something out. It was beeping to get attention. Jim let it beep. Why? He didn't know. He didn't want to answer.

It was nice, though. Finally. Someone noticing him.

Benny?

Daniel?

Who do you want it to be?

Jim, what a stupid question.

Is it? But I noticed, you didn't answer. Who, or whom, do you want?

I...

See? You can't even say it.

I...

Do you even know what you want, boy?

I...

49
NOTHING

It was a couple of hours later.

Yes, he had the usual headache. Yes, he had to squint his itchy bloodshot eyes shut and try (and fail) to squeeze out the pain through his ears. Yes, he had to crack his knuckles and his neck and his spine and jerk and squeeze some flexibility back into his joints. Jim pushed his sore knuckles into his bloodshot eyes. Worked them around. Get some of the red out at least. His headache was much worse than usual. He better not be getting migraines again. Was he seeing flashing sparks in the corners of his eyes? Yes? No? Was that the T.V.? Was it lightning outside?

In Southern California? In the winter? C'mon...

All right.

O.K. Jim.

You can do this.

Let go.

Meditate.

Right...

No. Do it. Do you want to be in pain for the rest of your life? Do it.

But...

Shut up!

Nope.

Be here.

Be here now.

Now, Jim, now!

Ooooom. Oooooooooom.

He tried to empty his mind. He genuinely did. He tried. But instead he did a data dump of the last 10 hours of mind-pretzeling, cranium-crushing meetings, the indecipherable requirements, the terrifying, clueless questions, the even-more-terrifying lack of questions, the useless sprint of computer coding he'd attempted (his build had failed) – the look on his boss's face when the fail was announced – all of it, the whole fucking endless day of it, it disgorged into his short-term memory and he relived it all, moment by painful moment by painful moment.

This was not meditating.

OOOOOOMMMMM.

Was it working? Tomorrow was not going to be a good day. In fact it would almost certainly be up there in the top 10 of Jim's list of D.O.F.B's – Days Of Furious-Backstabbing. If QC didn't make up its mind soon, they'd all be there, doing 24 hour shifts, all weekend and next week and then his boss would…

Jim's head was expanding and contracting in rhythm to his heartbeat. He was sure he could make out the first faint traces of rainbow electric streaks starting to appear in his peripheral vision.

Nope. Not doing this again.

He sighed. Not a yodeling sigh. More of a bagpipe-poked-through-and-through-and-bleeding-its-air-out kind of sigh.

Shit, his left foot was ice-cold.

He tried moving his big toe. It moved. He would live.

Felt like fucking Minnesota in here. The portable heater wasn't worth a damn. Oh. It wasn't on. The heater down the hall, it wheezed at him, emitting a vague, listless puffs of almost-warmth in his direction. Then it sighed. That's just what it did, sometimes, this sighing thing, at random intervals. A lot of sighing went on in this room. Not a lot of heating, though.

Are we still trying to meditate?

Ooooooooommmm!

No, we're not.

Jim stared at the distant heater. He couldn't take his eyes off of it. Then he stared at the empty glass in his hand. He was too neuron-depleted to figure out how to refill it. Besides, it was covered in wispy fingerprints, ghosts of fingerprints, covered in them, everywhere. In different colors. Strange, intersecting patterns. They twinkled in the jittery colored light from the TV.

He spun the sticky glass in his sticky fingers following the pretty colors. Good thing Daniel hadn't found this in the sink. He'd have had a fit. Better sneak it into the dishwasher. Get up. Do it, Jimmy. Do it now. All right. Doing it. Getting up. Now.

Jim moved, but not up. Instead, Jim fluffed the two pillows behind his back, collapsed back against them, and tried to concentrate on the TV through the reddish haze of his worsening headache.

50
CLICK

That's when he heard it. In between each blood-soaked heartbeat malleting his brain into mush, Jim heard a voice. Or voices. It (or they) spoke. Cheerfully. Hopefully. Earnestly As if Jim were back at Comicon and a random someone he barely knew was introducing Jim to an even more random acquaintance he would probably never remember in a noisy and participant-clogged hallway and Jim was frantically looking for a restroom. In other words, Jim wasn't listening at all no matter how much warm sincerity was ladled his way, and furthermore, he wasn't ever intending to listen.

"You can call me Fred."

Jim didn't open his eyes.

"You know that never works, Halvalvesterston."

"And your better idea, Pediduggles, that would be… what exactly?"

"Get a giraffe on the job, that'll get him talking. They always do the trick, Halvy."

"You can call me Fred."

"You can stop that anytime, you know. Utterly useless. It's crap, actually. Yup. Giraffe's the ticket, Hal."

"What? A giraffe? Are you mad? Giraffe's don't talk."

"Well. Maybe not to you."

"Call him Fred."

"You can call me Fred."

"Not to me? What are you implying?"

"I don't know. What am I implying Lewis?"

"Lewis? Is Lewis here?"

"Behind you. I think you might be implying. Peddy, that while your average giraffe will talk to most any pika, she or he, will most assuredly remain silent in the presence of a penguin. Is that about right, sir?"

"I couldn't have said it…"

"Well, of all the…"

At that point, Jim pressed two pillows to his ears and moaned into the living room. He continued moaning for a while. It felt good to moan. He should do it more often. One hundred twenty seconds later he experimentally lowered a much-smooshed pillow from one ear. The voices had exited. He sighed. He let the other pillow fall from his other ear. His head was a ring of fire.

51
OBVIOUS

He smiled into the darkness. It wasn't helping. It wasn't much of a smile. He must've had a strong family resemblance to a gargoyle. He tried to smile wider, brighter, better – and you know what? – it still didn't help. Smiling was a notoriously bad analgesic. His head hurt. His stomach hurt. Flotsam and jetsam. It was all flotsamming and jetsamming inside. And outside. All of it. Everywhere.

How much other sad shit floated and bobbed in his polluted internal ocean, waiting to wash up on the trashed-out beaches of his abused brain after a crazed day at work? James, Jimmy my boy, that was way too long a sentence to parse this late in the game, at this hour of the day, with this little gin inside of you. Let go. Give it a rest, Jim. Stop the madness. Stop.

Penguins?

Pikas?

He licked his fingers to get the sticky off. It made them stickier. Stop the madness. He wanted out. His left eye was twitching again. He wanted out of his head. He wanted out of his life. Was that so much to ask? Shit.

Where was Daniel? Jim wanted to talk.

So now you want Daniel, do you, Jimmy-boy?

Jim smiled up into his empty glass. Why? Why did Daniel put up with him? Why did Jim stick around? Habit? Reflex?

And Benny? Jim felt a guilty rush of electric something flash from his rotting brain down his spinal column into his waist and out his genitalia. Wow! Where had that come from?

Do you think it would be any better with Benny? A total stranger? He felt that rush again. Are you that dense, now, Jimmy-boy?

Are you?

Yeah. Guess I am.

Jim smiled to himself. It was all so wrong. But he couldn't help it. He didn't want help it. He didn't want help. He didn't want out. He wanted more.

Look. There had to be something more to life, right? Right? Marriage should be more than a habit. Shit! There should be more to… Shit. His head was a blast furnace. He carefully laid his head on the arm of the couch. Marriage. It should be… should be…

52

PENETRATE

Of course, that's when the call came.

Unexpectedly.

Except Jim had expected it.

Expecting it, not expecting it, Jim had been waiting, not-waiting for it for years. For years and years and years and years. Non-expecting/expecting hadn't changed anything, though. It still hurt. More than anything he'd thought likely or possible. One single phone call. Crazy. Painful. Angry. Helpless. Afraid. Crazy.

Yeah, it had all came crashing down on him again, it was as if he were a teenager, as if he were a kid, back home, hearing his folks argue late at night, terrified they'd leave, wondering how he'd make it as a kid, all alone, by himself

Only this time it was true. Jim was all alone. Jim was all by himself.

Shit.

Dad was dying.

Fuck.

Yeah. For Jim, nothing changed. Nothing.

Nothing changed anything, ever. It was always the same. Always.

Only more so.

At first he thought the phone call was from Benny. Idiot. How could Benny get the number to his land line? He'd almost not bothered to answer it. Then he'd stumbled all over himself to get to the phone before it rolled over to voice mail. It wasn't Benny.

Afterwards, he wished it had been Benny. Fuck! Why couldn't it have been Benny?

Then he forgot to wish anything at all. His mind shorted out. It emptied. Quietly. Efficiently. The emptiness rolled to a stop. It got very still and quiet in his aching head.

Of all the Olsens, Jim was most like his dad.

Maybe that's why they argued so much.

Screaming. Eyes closed. Waving hands. Pointing fingers. Red faces. They argued alike. More like brothers than fathers and sons. Or twins maybe, born 33 years apart.

And maybe that's why they apologized so much too. Arguments. Apologies. More arguments. More apologies. What's that saying about the broken bone mending stronger than the unbroken bone? Jim and his dad were a walking piles of broken bones, knitted back together again, clicking and clattering their way through life together. Being broken all the time is the same as being unbreakable.

Right?

Yeah.

And of all the Olsens, Jim was the least like his dad.

Jim was a dreamer. He liked being by himself, keeping his own company. Getting grounded in his room was never a punishment as a kid. Jim appreciated silence. He was like his mom that way. Jim was shy. Jim was a mess.

Jim's mom and dad didn't get along all that well. They never had. In fact, it was World War III, the Olsen Conflict, 365 and ¼ days a year in their house, growing up. Each parent was a general, marshalling the events of the past, marching armies of injustices at each other on a daily basis. It was a battlefield. The kids watched. The kids weren't involved, except as innocent by-watchers. And, yeah, it was brutal, and yeah, it was a battlefield, but it was the Olsen battlefield, so they were proud of it, in a twisted kind of way. They were unique. Or so they thought.

And yeah, to the extent Jim had both his mom and dad talking inside his head, giving him their "helpful" advice, Jim was a royal wreck. A walking, talking ball of mutually-contradictory pain.

Yay Olsens! Yay Jim!

53
QUICK

For years now, since his dad had gotten undoubtedly sick, they had talked every day on the phone. At night. When it was quiet for both of them.

Then Dad became very sick and moved to a series of rehab/assisted-living places up north. Near Jim's brother. Who was looking out for him.

Dad had been a metaphorical health-train-wreck in mid-crash for many years now. His body was the fleshy equivalent of a slow-motion detonation of metal and machinery. A break-down caught on high speed film. Hard to watch. Harder to live through, especially for his dad, most importantly for his dad. First, this railway car would get hit by a semi at a crossing, buckle and jackknife upwards right off the track. You'd have to get it fixed. Fine. You'd do it. Kind of. Then another would come undone, unlatch itself, and half the train would start rolling backwards. You'd take care of that. Sort of. You'd get the engine and all the cars back on the track and vaguely sitting in a row. You'd check the connections. Slap them on the back, get them rolling forward again, it would be great for a few minutes, then... Bam! – a wheel would fall off, Then two more. You'd get those half-on and the brakes would go out, and then before the breaks were working properly, the engine would throw a rod and you'd have to stop and rebuild the engine, slowly, and then before you could test it properly the... Well... You get the idea.

Jim's poor dad. What an existence!. His dad didn't deserve it. His dad had worked hard, his whole life. Never complained. Never looked back. Stable. Responsible. Friendly. Helpful. Towards the end, Jim had hoped his dad wouldn't have to suffer through all of this much longer. Strokes. Diabetes. Skin cancer. Strange bodily malfunctions. Odd symptoms that got worse, then better, then much worse. Incontinence. Fuck. His dad had been uncomplaining (mostly), and upbeat (certainly), through all of it, so why did he have to suffer so much like this in the end? What was the reason? There had to be a reason, huh? Ninety years of Stoic Scandinavian Cheerfulness – that had to count for something right?

Being cheerful wasn't all that bad (that would be his dad's response). His dad was from Minnesota. That's what you did. You didn't think about it. You got on with it. If you lost one leg, you used the other one. Ditto for the arms. Do you still have a head? Well, then use it and think. Figure it out. Get a move on. No dawdling. What was there to complain about? Complaining never solved a thing.

54
REVERSE

The call.

He remembered that.

Picking up the phone.

Listening for Benny's voice.

Hearing another voice, a familiar voice.

Then he was standing there.

Just standing there. He remembered he was smiling. Or at least places on his face were still trying to construct a smile.

Yeah, he remembered, in one hand was the phone.

In the other hand was his glass.

He remembered looking at it. Trying to see something in the reflections and tracing the greasy whorls of Jim-fingerprints all over it. Looked a little as if they were faces constructed of smudges. Or torn, topographic maps of the Sierras. Or sticky snowstorms of slime. Yes, his hands were still sticky. His head hurt. Shit. He was going to throw up.

He could smell flowers. Or maybe it was gin. Or maybe it was... He smelled under his arms. His armpits definitely did not smell flowery. His stomach was not happy.

He rolled balls of sticky stuff into bigger balls of sticky stuff between his fingertips, standing there, still holding onto his glass, still smiling, the T.V. in the distance babbling into the darkness of the living room. He looked for a place to put the glass down onto. No furniture in the hall. He had no idea what to do. He finally set the glass down on the floor. His stomach began to do backflips. Then somersaults. Words rolled in his head. But they were only sounds. He was blinking like crazy. His face was wet. His head hurt like a motherfucker.

What was he going to do?

What?

He ran to the bathroom. He got there just in time.

He heard his cell ring between retches.

Please not Benny.

Please not Daniel.

I mean… please… no…

No.

He didn't answer it.

He was busy.

55

SIBLINGS

The phone call had been succinct and admirably to the point. His older brother, Luke, the policeman, excuse me, the detective, had laid it out for Jim in his usual slightly aggressive, militantly business-like manner. Luke's motto was – the best offense was a good offense. He always initiated with overwhelming force. And finished with thorough subjugation. This phone call was no exception.

Jim pieced together more of the story later from his older sister Teddie, in between texting travel plans back and forth to her and his other sisters – but even then, Jim never found out very much of what had, in fact, happened to Dad – mostly because Teddie tended towards the uncommunicative at times, especially under Periods of Stress (P.O.S.) – as she put it – and Jim, well, he worked it out for himself that there was a high probability that this qualified as one of Teddie's P.O.S.'s and so that meant that Jim shouldn't expect much more in the way of details, and – guess what? – Jim was right.

So that, as they say, was the end of that.

Their second oldest sister, Amy already knew. She'd been the one to call Teddie. Teddie was still trying to get ahold of their youngest sister Lily (Jim was the baby of the family – youngest of all – something no one in the family ever forgot to remind him of). Jim got Amy's texts later. He never heard from Lily. Teddie was texting with one hand and layering (lasagna) with another, writing out lists with a third hand and washing and folding clothes with a fourth. She always seemed to be making dinners and managing life for her voracious, apparently helpless family. Teddie was good at doing a lot of things, all at the same time, quietly, quickly, and serially. Multi-tasking serially. That was Teddie. She did task number one, got as far as humanly possible on it, went on to task number two, and didn't look back. She didn't trust other people's work. She barely trusted her own. Which meant she was a very busy person with a perennially healthy to-do list. And it was a good thing she liked to work. She had four kids and no husband (or wife). She didn't get over-excited very easily (unlike Jim). She couldn't afford to. She was the family rock. A rock under pressure. But holding steady. A very Olsen woman. The most Minnesotan of all of them.

Lily was in South-East Asia. On a business trip. She said she'd try and make it back, but nobody honestly expected her any time soon. Amy was taking courses at a community college, in Des Moines Iowa, where she'd sort of washed up on shore after a long-distance relationship/marriage which had limped and stumbled along for a decade. Amy was trying to change careers after her divorce (husband-less women was a thing in the Olsen family) and not having much luck. Amy was poor as a church mouse. (her own words), and about as aggressive. Lily was sending Amy money to fly out to California, otherwise Amy wouldn't have been able to come, and she probably wouldn't have told anyone why she wasn't coming and there probably would have been a lot of hand-wringing and mutual recriminations as a result, so Jim was happy Lily was responding in some way. Lily and Amy were close.

Luke was putting everyone up. Everyone except Jim and Daniel. That was Jim's choice. And a very good choice it was.

But back to the briefing. Officer Luke had summarized the details as if he were reading from an Incident Report on the Olsen Case, an informative, but concise document he'd just typed up and been asked to read out to the squad as part of their routine morning briefing. That was Jim and Luke's relationship – Luke's leadership, Jim's subordination. The Report was short. Point one: Dad was dying. Point two: get your ass back here.

He and his brother, they didn't talk much. When they did talk, the little of it there was turned out to be chock-full, brimming with vital information, about everything and everyone else except, of course, Jim and Jim and Luke's fucked-up relationship. They never talked about that. Not a word was wasted on that. It was an unexploded missile, a time bomb lodged and ticking in the middle of their lives, ever-present, a constant danger, but something a normal person clearly would learn to live with. Think! What else would you do with an unexploded bomb? You certainly wouldn't try and defuse it. No. Not that. That's crazy talk.

The bomb had a long and rich history. It was there the whole time they were growing up, tip-toed around, dodged, ignored, poking up out of their mom and dad's living room, practically part of the furniture. Everyone acted as if Jim were the only one who could see it. And if only Jim saw it, then, it was only Jim's problem, right? So what was the bomb exactly? Jim really didn't know. All Jim could figure out was, that early on, Jim wasn't exactly the brother everyone had wanted. And it was true. He wasn't. But his siblings had put up a brave front and made do with whatever they'd got, and what they'd got was Jim, so mostly they ignored him. And when ignoring didn't work, they gave friendly, helpful criticism.

Silence. Then correction. Silence. Correction. Silence. Correction. It became a routine, another of Jim's many routines. It became a way of life.

But that was a long, long time ago, Jim. Back when there had been a family living room, back when there had been a family house containing a family living room. Except, remember Jimmy, the family had sold the living room, had sold the house, the family was sold now and erased, and all the past erased with it, right?

Let it go. Dad was in rehab. All his assets were cash. The bomb was gone. Long gone. Problem solved. Case closed. There was nothing to talk about. It all happened so long, long ago. We're adults now. Grow up, Jimmy. That's all water under the bridge.

Those were the voices in his head. Maybe they came from Jim. Maybe from his siblings. Maybe from both. Maybe from none of the above. Who could tell? Human brains were mysterious. Especially your own.

So. The upshot was – Luke had a million rules about how to act around him. All of them unwritten. Luke was normal. The rest of humanity was a little suspect. Jim more so than most. Or maybe most of all. This was going to be a long trip.

Fuck.

Fuck. Fuck. Fuck. Fucking hell.

Shit, Jim. Not now. Get it together. Let it go. You don't have to do this now. Let Luke go. Let Teddie go. Let Amy go. Let Lily go. Give them permission to live their lives as they see fit. Let it all go, and give yourself a break while you're doing it.

O.K.?

Fuck.

Fucking hell.

Like being a teenager again.

Fuck.

56
TERMINUS

Dad was dying.

It never changed. Nothing ever changed. Ever. It never did. Shit happened. People died. His brother called. His brother didn't call. His sister got divorced. She didn't tell Jim. Daniel got angry at him. Jim had to figure out why. Nothing changed. That was how it was for Jim. He wanted out. He never got out, but he wanted out.

Dad was dying.

Jim had never gotten over his mom's passing away. Twenty years! Fuck. Still hurt. Do you ask a guy who lost his right leg – when did you get over it? Fuck no. There's a before. And there's an after. After's usually suck.

Death is always about an after. Afters are what the rest of your life is made of. You know what it is? Death? It's an amputation. Death is involuntary surgery. A piece of you that was alive last night, it gets cut off, it turns into meat, not because of something you did, no, but just because, and suddenly a big piece of you is roadkill, it's biohazard waste, it's been disposed of, a piece of you, a living, breathing, blood-filled piece of yourself is transmogrified into toxic garbage and you're different now and your life is different and it's all different and you have to do something about it – that's what everybody says – do something – and you can't do anything – so you don't do anything, except you stumble into work every day and you keep the deposits ticking in, one by one, you keep the joint checking account safely and responsibly and reliably afloat in the blackest of black ink and you keep that credit rating high and you hurt and shuffle and limp because a piece of you is gone, forever.

Gone. Gone missing. Missing.

Missing. That's what death is. That sucks.

Now sucks. You want before. What you get is after. Over and over and over again. Fuck after. Fuck missing.

Mom had been rough. Now, Jim's dad was dying. This time it was dad. Dad. Dad's turn.

Fuck. Fuck. Fuck.

Dad's dying.

Dad's dying.

Yeah. It was true. The words made no sense.

But, he couldn't stop repeating them.

Dad's dying.

They turned into croaking sounds, Then into heavy breathing. He was hyperventilating. It was something to do. It passed the time.

Fuck.

He stared at his chilly toe, exposed on the tiles in the hallway. Felt the heater breathing on him again, it stopped, it started, it stopped, it started. He saw an empty glass sitting next to his toe. What was that doing there? He watched the light hit the glass. The pixilated living room behind him got bright. Then it got dark. Got brighter. Got darker. Bright. Dark. Bright Dark.

It was odd. Having a body. Moving around in this mound of meat hanging on bony girders, burbling with fleshy plumbing. While you were alive you moved around the world, looking out from inside of it. A ghost. Haunting your own body. Then you left. Or it left you. Either way, it was odd. Especially the part about leaving. Leaving everyone else behind. That was the oddest part. Leaving. He couldn't make sense of it. Leaving. Leaving. Nope. All nonsense.

Dad was leaving. Dad. Jim couldn't think. Bright. Dark. Bright. Dark. Dad. Bright. Dark...

He'd had no clue it was going to be like this.

Somebody or something should've warned him.

57
CLICK

Out of the side of his eyes, Jim saw the kitchen clearly. Very clearly. Too clearly. It was strangely shadowless. Bright as the inside of a light bulb.

Jim stood on one foot, then the other. He leaned forward. Peered around the corner.

Where was all that light coming from?

Jim saw a blaze of white and black, glowing in muscular luminescence, pouring out of the refrigerator. Fuck. What was that? He blinked a couple of times. It looked like a… a…

Penguin?

No. Plural.

Penguins?

Yes. More than one. Poking their heads out of the door of Jim's freezer?

Which meant?

What?

It meant the friggin' freezer door was open.

Meat rotting, dollar-draining disasters in the making here folks – emergency! – all hands on deck!

Is it opening by itself now? Shit. Have to fix that. This moment. Right? Shit. Yeah. Right.

He started towards the kitchen. Jim stubbed his toe on a glass sitting on the hallway floor (what was that doing there?) and he shuffled off. The glass ricocheted into the living room, ringing merrily, rolling who-knows-where. Jim paused. He blinked. Wondered why he was pausing and blinking. Then he stumbled on into the light.

58
UNDERWORLD

He texted Daniel at some point. All he could think to say was "Help." Yes, it was drama. But Jim was allowed.

Besides, it was necessary. One word sentences were the highest level of external communications Jim could muster out of his neurons at this juncture. And Jim figured he'd pretty much explained everything to Daniel with those four letters. They were pithy evidence of his current emotional state and managed to make a request, all at the same time, and using only four letters. Jim thought it was pretty fucking impressive. Like condensing an entire coupla-pages-worth of method calls into one line of Regex code. Sweet.

Come to think of it though, condensed shit like that usually pissed off every other programmer who had to work on that code afterwards. They'd curse her/his name long after the proud programmer who was the original condenser had moved on to greater and more glorious feats of disastrous brevity. Well. Fuck. Anyways… Shit. It had seemed a good idea at the time.

What was he doing again? There was a reason he was texting. Right?

As he paused in his typing he pondered – I'm typing on my cell – where did I find this cellphone? Not on its shelf. He'd looked. Then where, Jimmy? That's when Jim forget to press send. The text disappeared into the black hole of Drafts. Then his cellphone disappeared. Again. Jim was left staring at his hands and wondering why he was staring. It didn't occur to him to look in his shirt pocket.

Dad's dying.

Fuck.

Fuck this shit.

Why wasn't Daniel home?

A hour or so later, when Daniel got home from work, Jim had forgotten all about Daniel. He was trying to get the refrigerator door to shut properly. It kept swinging open. Fucking cheap Chinese shit. He pushed the door shut. It closed. Almost. He watched it. Nothing. Then, ever so slightly, the door began to swing out. Slowly. He couldn't think why. O.K., all right, Jim's mind was mud. Not the height of mental clarity at the moment. But why did the fucking frig choose now to break, huh? He didn't need this. Not with dad and all. He needed to fix this once and for all.

O.K.

He'd have to tie it shut somehow. Did they have twine? Or rope? What about a repairman? Replacement parts? Where? What? He squinted his eyes and peered at the small print on the label on the inside of the door as it swung slowly into view again. Were those warnings? Directions? Model Numbers? Was it in Japanese? Nah. Have to be Chinese. No? Yes? Maybe if he took a picture of the label with his cell, he could upload the pic and get this Japanese, no, Chinese shit translated and then he'd…

But where in the fuck was his cellphone?

O.K. No phone. What now?

Jim's toes were freezing. His fingers were freezing. His head hurt. His eyes were so dry his eyelids were stuck to his eyeballs. It was annoying. All right. One more time. How many times had he done this already? A lot, Jimmy-boy. He smiled. Sean. Sean would know how to fix this. Or he'd pretend he knew how. Or… Jim pressed his knuckles to his head. His eyes hurt. His head hurt. Just get through it Jimmy. No complaining. Just do it. Do it. Do it. Do it.

The light clicked on. O.K. That made it easier to see. That was progress. Sort of. He'd done all this before. The light had clicked on before. If the light was on, why was the kitchen so dark all of a sudden? He pushed his reading glasses down his nose to see if he could decipher the miniscule scratchings that apparently were in English (progress!) and may have turned out to be the make and model number of this chrome-covered monstrosity (even more progress!) but that was when he heard the strangest scuffling noises at his feet.

Behind him. Sneaking towards him. In the dark. Mice? Rats? Roaches? They'd have to be fucking large roaches.

Hidden, behind the open door, Jim grabbed a large, melting, half-eaten brick of gelato (it was satisfyingly heavy) right off of the top shelf of the freezer and swung it into the air. He looked down. Of course, his eyeglasses skidded off the end of his nose and hit the floor, spinning under the refrigerator. Shit. His best pair. He peered down, trying to see if any part of his reading glasses might luckily be sticking out in plain sight (yes? no?) and began the lengthy process of getting onto his knees, remembered the rats and stopped in mid-bend. Nope. Not doing it. No rat was going to eat his toes, or his fingers, even if they were frozen. Besides, he was still holding the gelato in one hand. He twisted to the left (something his bum shoulder didn't appreciate) and cocked his arm back ready to fire the gelato at anything that moved.

There was a largish shadow bending towards him. Jim jumped backwards and knocked gallons of frozen veggies onto the rest of the trash scattered on the linoleum of the kitchen floor (how had all that shit got there? – oh yeah – he'd knocked over the garbage pail earlier looking for a screwdriver, and not the liquid kind).

He was shaking his head, looking at this ruin of a kitchen when a hand touched his shoulder. My god! The shadow! He'd forgotten about the shadow! His left knee jerked upwards as he spun around, hit a knob on the stove and Jim got a nice bruise. Bruise number one. With his right leg he tried to kick the shadow, but drop-kicked the granite kitchen counter instead. Great. Fine. Bruise number two. O.K. That didn't work out so well. Shit. Fuck. The refrigerator handle took out his right shin as he fumbled his leg around dancing to keep his balance (bruise number three – Jimmy, you're out!). And Jim stepped on his glasses, causing him to yell and release the gelato which spun out of his hand and splatted into the wall, thankfully missing the kitchen window by millimeters. He hopped on one foot and watched the gelato hang, undulating, flattened on their Spanish glass kitchen tile. It was suspended there for what seemed like hours but must have only been seconds. Jim couldn't help but see his big hand-print proudly impressed into the middle of the squashed brick. Then the brick inched slowly downwards, slowly, slowly, then faster, and faster, then it slid in a long, creamy, high-caloric streak to disappear into the multi-colored, garbage-covered floor far below. At the last possible second, it somersaulted and fell backwards, glopping onto the oven hood, then winking out of sight as it plummeted behind the stove.

"Honey? What did you... What are you... What's that? What do you have sticking out of the freezer? It's a sock. It's one of your socks. This not going to happen. You've got it caught in the hinges. No, I'll get it out. Don't help. No. I said, I don't want your help. Stop. I don't care what you're trying to do, but you're not going to store your socks in the freezer. No. We're not. And I saw all those clothes all over the house! And that dirty glass in the living room. I'm not going to live this way. I'll have to throw out these veggie burgers now. Covered in socks! You know I have to. They're not cheap. And all the broccoli and the Brussel sprouts. And look at the corn. On sale too, at Costco. They're never that cheap. Now it's all defrosted. All ruined. What have you been doing? What were you thinking? And get some underwear on. You know the rules. Naked and kitchen don't mix. I'm not living this way, James. Is that trash on the floor? That's trash. And it's all over the place. We've talked, I thought… I… Honey? Jim? Jimmy? Jimmy? Jimbo? Jumbles? What's wrong? What's going on? Jimmy? Tell me. Talk to me, Jimmy. Jimmy? Jimmy? Why are you crying? Don't cry. You'll have me crying in a second. Oh, Jimmy. What's wrong, Jimbles? What's wrong?"

59
VELOCITY

Daniel did most of the packing.

Scratch that, Daniel did all the packing. After Jim spent ten minutes looking at a shirt drawer trying to find his dress shoes.

Daniel led Jim him out of their bedroom and sat him down on the sagging Italian couch and left him there. On Daniel's side of the couch. He immediately began sinking. Daniel hated that couch. When Daniel sat down on this side of the "red beast" (as they called it), Daniel usually slowly sank out of sight too, as if he were the Titanic post-iceberg and past saving. Jim felt guilty whenever they watched T.V. Couches were expensive. Jim was forcing them to save up for a new one. So Jim saved. And Daniel sank. Neither were happy. Jim supposed that must be what they meant by compromise. Everyone unhappy.

Daniel put Jim's phone on his lap. Jim's butt was, yeah, pretty much touching the floor. Daniel said in an irritated whisper that he'd found the phone in the freezer. Jim glanced at the freeze-dried cell resting on his underwear. He'd managed to put his undies on. He still didn't have pants on though. Oh look! A text was there. A draft text, Before he thought about it, Jim had already hit send. A curious warbling noise went off in the bedroom.

For a few minutes there was a remarkable amount of activity and conversation in Jim and Daniel's house. Daniel took back Jim's cell. For safekeeping, he said.

Jim's brother went curiously silent. Teddie was in an airport in Virginia, then stuck on a plane waiting for a repair part, then waiting for clearance to take off, then she was flying cross-continent on a red-eye, having missed her connection in Dallas. So Teddie was busy. But at least she texted, on occasion. Lily and Amy were reliably silent – yeah, they'd never talk to Jim, not directly at least. Jim assumed, as usual, they'd be texting Teddie like mad. Teddie fired four-word-texts at Jim. Daniel read them. Amy would be there in two days, Lily in four, if she could get away. Jim forgot what Daniel said almost before Daniel had got done speaking. Daniel repeated himself. Jim forgot again. Eventually Daniel gave up. He read the texts silently.

Jim and Daniel drove up from Los Angeles towards Northern California in rainy and soggy silence. He couldn't think of anything to say. Daniel had on this corny 40's golden oldies music. He wanted to get Daniel to turn off the radio. But he kept forgetting to ask.

Daniel kept one hand on the steering wheel. He kept the other on Jim's left thigh. Jim put his left hand on Daniel's right thigh. It completed some essential emotional Daniel-Jim circuit, freed up the Daniel-Jim electricity to flow easily, kept the Daniel-Jim battery efficiently charged and ready. Daniel looked over from time to time at Jim. Jim didn't look back. Daniel kept looking.

Jim stared to his right for so long he got a crick in his neck. He watched the rain outside the car window. As if he'd never seen it before.

It was raining and raining and raining. Not like Southern California at all. Like some Alternate Universe Southern California where the last ice age had never receded and grass stayed green for longer than two months out of the year, and water flowed over the land unnaturally in rivers and lakes. Very odd. Like it was fucking Michigan. Or Minnesota. Or Siberia.

Jim expected to see a tree-trunk sized leg of a wooly mammoth stamp in front of the windshield on the Interstate and stop all traffic. Or at least stop their car. Abruptly. Permanently. He wanted it to happen. Crush the memories out of him. Splat! Squish the hurt as if it were a pimple and watch it squirt out, into open space.

Jim smiled. Of course, he would make sure Daniel would get out of the mammoth-leg-crash, Daniel would survive, injury-free. No woolly death for him. Daniel deserved better than death-by-pachyderm.

Jim didn't actually consider if Daniel would want Jim to be pachydermed to death though.

60
WHATEVER

Daniel did most of the driving.

Scratch that. Daniel did all the driving. It took a few hours. Well, more than a few hours. To be honest, Jim couldn't tell how long it took. Jim spent a lot of time looking at his cellphone. Daniel let him have it back after he turned it off. Jim memorized the scratches on its screen. He hid it under his thigh. He thumbed it open. It woke up. It flashed for a moment between this thighs, then it calmed down. It was silent and quiet. He wondered why no one was calling him. No calls. No texts Nothing. He wondered, he asked himself, why Benny wasn't calling him. Then he'd answer himself. Because Benny hardly knows you, you dumbfuck! Look to your left. Who's driving the car, shit-for-brains? What business do you have thinking of… You're a… You're out of control Jim.

Then he'd stare at his phone. Wonder why no one called him. Wonder what he would say to Benny if Benny called.

He also spent a lot of time breathing. And smelling. The car smelled clean, fresh and hopeful. Daniel's car was always clean, fresh and hopeful. You could perform surgery on those car seats. The outside was preternaturally shiny and scratch-free. It was a perfect car. That was Daniel. He took time to make his life livable. Daniel made life make sense, no matter how much effort and planning it took.

That was a big reason Jim and Daniel worked. Daniel was solid and stable. Jim tended more towards crumbly and broken. Daniel was less good with money. Jim saved and budgeted as if it were 1929. Jim oozed logic and rationality. Daniel ran on heart and emotion. Daniel was hope. Jim was despair. It worked. Even if it sounded as if it were a bad telenovela. And Jim was trying his level best to fuck it up as permanently as he was able. Fucking Jim. Fucking Daniel. Fucking Benny.

Fuck.

So, Daniel was hope?

Yeah, well, Jim didn't want hope now.

To be fucking honest, Jim didn't know what he wanted.

Did Jim want honest? No. Not Jim. He didn't want honest right now.

What do you want, Jimmy?

What is fucking wrong with you?

Jim was looking out the window at stuff he didn't want to see. Jim was listening to music he didn't want to listen to. Everywhere was wet. Everywhere was weeping. Everywhere was wrong and the whole fucking world was weeping and look at Jim.

Jim was dry-eyed.

What the hell?

You really are a self-centered creep, aren't you?

What was fucking wrong with him?

They called around (Daniel called around) and found the name of the suburban hospital with his dad as a new resident. It was late. It was very late. It was early morning of the next day, nearly. They skipped going to the hotel room first.

61
X-CLAMATION

They drove straight into a deserted parking lot, under fog-rainy sulphur arc-lights, and ran inside, some parts stiff, some parts numb, on pins and needles, muscles and tendons complaining from sitting in one position for seven hours too long. They ran hunched over, hunch-backed and puppet-like as if they were two old men. Or maybe they were running that way, hunched over because, yes, they actually were two old men. Old and getting older. They were an Old Married Couple – O.M.C. A living, breathing stereotype. Which just goes to show you, if you wait around long enough, you become every single stupid joke you've ever told. Clichés aren't merely true. They're curses. We're, all of us, cursed. We just won't admit it. If we don't admit it, it's not happening, right? Said the ostrich to the sandbank. No one here but us ostriches. Ha. Ha.

Jim didn't share any of these thoughts with Daniel.

Daniel would have been easy to talk to though, patient, a good listener, he always was. But Jim didn't trust his mouth would work right. And his vocabulary had gone, it had disappeared, it was currently unavailable (in internet-speak). He lunged at words in his head and they'd dart away honking as if Jim were skeet-shooting them. If Jim attempted speech, he'd probably point at the big lights in the parking light and moan. Out loud. That would be accurate, but not effective communication. Besides, Jim didn't feel like moaning now into the fog. So he didn't.

They finally found the room. After any number of false starts down long hallways, shadowy stairwells, darkish, closed spaces, corners inhabited by chuckling machines, walls of bouncing worms made of white light next to grim, disappointed sick persons drowning in chemical smells surrounded by the sounds of shallow, laborious breathing and haunted by retreating, professional footsteps. It was a puzzle. A puzzle of pain. And everywhere they went they could smell disinfectant – a strange, orang-ish scent hanging in protective clouds over everything, slowing them down, making them sneeze.

This night-hospital-world was so perfectly safe, stable, secure and closed, Jim found it impossible to believe morning ever came here. It was a pocket universe. A dimension folded into itself and onto itself and thus entirely and permanently removed from the real world. Jim didn't like it.

Yeah, so the two of them hit a lot of dead ends. They didn't ask for directions. It was the middle of the night, after all. Neither of them wanted to bother any more of the ghostly staff then they had to – pale persons levitating quietly in and out of rooms they skirted past. No questions for them. Questions that might seem demands or even complaints. It was so long after visiting hours they felt a little ridiculous. Maybe they'd be asked to leave. Maybe they'd be escorted out. If they saw a security guard, they ducked down another hallway, well, Jim would suggest it and Daniel, with a puzzled, patient expression in his eyes, would follow. Dozens and dozens of bodies were suffering through these long hospital nights around Jim. It seemed such a private thing. Who did the two of them think they were? Waltzing in and breezing through it. What gave them the right? What did they think they were doing?

The hospital slept. Or worked. Or shifted uneasily in pain and fright. Or stared at the ceiling and waited. Hospitals are great places for waiting. Things happen there. But they take time. The building felt patient and careful and practical to Jim. Disease and death came to everyone, but they came daily here. No, hourly. They came slowly, from a great distance, and you saw them approaching from far, far off, and you learned to be patient.

Jim would go crazy in a place like this, a place that asked, no demanded patience.

They wandered, ducked, slipped, strode.

Jim could tell, he knew in the pit of his stomach, that it was the right room as soon as they walked past the open door. He could tell who was on the bed immediately, from fifteen feet away, those limbs were so familiar to him. The shape of that back. The head. The shoulders. Dad looked so small. His arms were so thin. And his legs. Ah. Dad.

Jim's heart cracked seeing them. He thought it was only a phrase you read in books. Hearts. Cracking. It wasn't. He felt it. It cracked. It had already cracked open when he'd got the phone call. Now it cracked again. Into two more pieces. How much more splitting could Jim's poor heart take?

Yup. Jim's heart cracked more than it already had, which Jim didn't think would be possible, and his heart didn't mend. It never did. It just stayed that way. The rest of his life. It shouldn't have surprised him. But it did.

62
YEARNING

They found Jim's dad in a sack of lamp light, pulled closed, snug and tight by deep-ceilinged shadows, on a raised steel bed.

He was safe. In this sack of light. Around him, smallish lights of various colors, blinking and twittering and snaking about in the gloom were very busy. Keeping dad safe. Inside, under the light, his dad was still. He could've been asleep, arms carelessly outstretched this way and that, resting on clean blankets, under a knot of tubes and wires. Jim listened more closely, and he could make out his father breathing hoarsely, every breath an agony. He was curled in on himself, spine, arms, legs and head arched., as if something had been about to hit him, and he ducked, and he forgot how to straighten up again.

Ah dad! I'm so sorry you're having to go through this.

Within this space, this room, all was soft and calm. Blankets and lights were soft. There was big band music playing. Softly. Was it playing everywhere? He supposed it was good to have music on. Dad liked noise. At home there was a T.V. going in every room in the house. Well, maybe not every room, but it drove Jim bonkers. It made dad feel at home. So Jim never used to say anything. Well, he almost never said anything. Jim was glad of the familiar patter of noise in this cave of a hospital. At least that hadn't changed. Jim and Daniel had stopped in the doorway, halfway in, halfway out. Daniel waited a moment, then put his hand on Jim's shoulder and gently pushed Jim inside.

It was so quiet. Except for the precise pain of each breath, in and out, in and out, from the corner. It was good. It was all good.

One arm had fallen out of the twisted blankets and lay on the sheets exposed. It also was curled in on itself.

Jim could feel Daniel standing behind him. They weren't touching. But he could feel him, every bit of him, outlined in heat and flame behind him. Very much alive. The world was still. The three of them, Jim, Daniel, his father were stock still in a calm center, a tiny piece of stillness, a peace in the middle of everything, in the middle of the night. Jim could feel it. A tight bag of quiet. The stars wheeled about above in all their cold precision. Rain rained. Tides turned. Second hands spun. Here, things had stopped. Nothing was happening. Nothing could happen. It was good.

Daniel gave him another push. Jim walked forward. Daniel followed close behind him. Jim grasped the curled-up hand emerging from the blankets. It was warm. Suddenly, his father gripped him back. Hard. Jim hadn't expected that. But, yeah, it was good too.

His father's eyes didn't open. Jim gripped the hand back. Jim didn't let go. He looked over at Daniel, not speaking, smiling and nodding, motioning with his eyes at the this amazing sight, the hand gripping his. Jim was crying. But that was fine. It was good. It was all good. Daniel sat down on a chair wedged in by the sink. Jim stood next to Daniel and held the hand and stood by the bed and felt the calm everywhere around him sink into his skin.

His father lay, cradled on a pillow, breathing cautiously, but a little more energetically now. His eyes moved under his closed eyelids. Jim found himself breathing in the same rhythm as his father.

They stayed that way for some time. In a gold-white sack of light in the middle of the night, Jim standing, Daniel watching, his father breathing.

Jim stared at his father's hand, gripping his. It was beautiful. Clear pink skin, translucent over hard bone, it was a miracle of fragile unbreakability. That was his father's hand. His father used to look at his hands and ask Jim – how did I end up with an old man's hands? – these aren't my hands. But they were. He'd earned them. Year by year. Jim could feel all five fingers, the bones of his father's fingers, holding onto the bones of his. They weren't going to let go. None of them were. He looked and understood he couldn't tell where his father's hands left off and his own began. And that was fine. They were all the same hands, anyways. The same flesh. They always had been. They still were. They always would be. Nothing about that was going to change. Nothing ever changes.

It was good.

Jim blinked and thought and he was surprised again.

It was good.

He hadn't expected that.

63
CLICK

He closed his eyes, opened them, and turned to say something to Daniel when he was… then he was… he was…

Upside-down.

Falling upwards.

Falling. Falling. Falling.

Falling into a blue, blue bowl of bluer light. Falling and you fall and you never stop falling, grass itching your ears, sweat trickling, tickling your eyes, it hurts, thick smell of black soil spaded over and growing things up your nose, under your fingernails, cicadas moaning, droning summer, summer, all summer long, getting up, lying down, drowning under miles of humid air, a distant thunder, nothing ever changes. Summers simmering. Bright translucent Springs. Gray winters. Slow-burning falls. Summers. Springs. Dirty winters, iced-over and overstaying their welcome. Falls. Summers. Obscene green Springs. Winters. Falls. Summers of swimming pools. Bicycles. Schools. Baseball (Jim hated baseball, what the…) springs, winters, falls, summers, springs, winters… He fell upwards until his face hit a body-sized pit of powdery shit, and he came to a stop and his whole body hurt. Every friggin' piece of it. Bones. Tendons. Muscles. Eyeballs. Ear drums. He had a bizarre feeling of his skin slipping down over new bones, draping, folding, snapping, clicking, fastening neatly into place. It all shifted, he did a quick bounce upward and he was… well… here again. Jim had long scratches down his back, his arms, his legs hurt like a motherfucker. He was lying in snow. What was he doing lying in the fucking snow?

64
ZIP

Jim wrinkled his nose. Damn! That hurt. He sniffled. Stinging pain spread into his cheeks, under his eyes, something with rough edges made grinding sounds when he blinked, not good, not good at all, his fucking face was broken. Shit!

His nose was blocked, stuffed, packed in wet wool, the back of his throat stank with the iron taste of blood – he sneezed – damn! that hurt – yup, his nostrils were full of it, blood everywhere, it was crazy hard to breathe, he had a whopping headache and his legs didn't work, as if he'd misplaced them, as if he'd forgotten to put them on this morning.

It was freezing out. Jim didn't think this kind of freezing was physically possible. Not in Jim's California. Maybe under the ozone hole in Antarctica, but not anyplace Jim would... And, oh yeah, he was fucking upside down.

Yeah, his head hurt. No, that was a pathetic word to use. He didn't remember drinking, but he was sure going to remember this hangover. You know, he'd had it before. It was the last trolley stop before alcohol poisoning. His skull didn't fit anymore. The seams were breaking open, gray matter spurting out. The next day or so wouldn't be very pretty. Daniel wasn't overly sympathetic when Jim got really fucked up. Daniel got pissed. Daniel's wrath was one reason why (besides having your brains scooped out of your body while you were still alive the next day) Jim had stopped doing the alcohol-induced-amnesia bit years ago. Epic, heroic drinking bouts. Yeah. It'd been years. Years, since he'd had a blackout, right? Until now. Apparently. Obviously. Why was he such an asshole? Why now? Why now, Jimmy?

Fuck. Shit. Not again. He had a lot of explaining to do. No Danny boy was not going to be pleased. Not in the slightest. Fuck.

Fuck. Fuck. Fuck.

And it was bright, too fucking bright, man! Fucking hell. Was that a lamp? More like a laser. What a ridiculous amount of light! Who needed that much bright? The mother ship was fucking beaming him up. Where was his dad? Where was Daniel? Everyone was gone. Fuck. It was the middle of the night. And all this light.

He and Daniel must've hit some switch by accident. They'd wake the whole floor up. Must've blinded him. Must've blinded fucking everybody, man! But how did he get drunk? And what was this itchy jacket he was wearing?

He hated wool. He hardly remembered the stuff. Hadn't worn it since he was a kid and his mom got him that heavy blue winter coat. He'd hide it. His mom would find it, she'd punish him, and then he'd be forced to wear it. Yeah, he'd always hated smell of it. And the feel of it. As if he were wearing a boy-shaped cocoon of fiberglass insulation. And this… It was that same… Shit. Not that he could smell anything right now. But he was wearing wool. He'd bet his life on it. Soggy wool. And it was making him itch. And yeah, he was hating it.

He felt hands under his armpits. Then the real pain kicked in. Fuck, did it kick. What was before, what the pain level had been before, well, it had only been an overture, no, a rehearsal for an overture compared to this. This was… Well, … It was… Jim didn't want to think about what this was. He screamed. He wasn't ashamed of it. He did it again. Although he'd never been dropped into a flaming, molten lake of lava and slowly morphed (living) into a cinder, he was sure it was a similar experience to what was now currently happening to him and his body, so screaming seemed the best thing to do. It was appropriate. And it came naturally to Jim. He let loose. Jim screamed like a pro. At least that's what he thought he was doing.

"Zeke, He's kind of moaning, but he's not making any sense"

"Heck, Stan. Look at him. Look at his head. Heck, look at the rest of him."

65
ANGRY

"What are we going to do, Zeke? What are we going to do?"

"Don't pick him up, Stan. We oughtta let go. Yeah. Slowly. Now, first, we pull his legs off the fence. Now his arms. Ah, just look at the rest of him. Nah, Stan. No. This ain't working out so good. What we're needing is something to carry him."

"Like a sled? Where are we gonna get a sled out here?"

"Nah, no sled. I got it. My dad's old horse blanket. Yeah, the one covering the back seat where the bottom's caved in. We can carry him in that."

The voices seemed friendly. But nothing else was. The world started spinning. Spinning and spinning. It wouldn't stop. Jim threw up. He threw up again. Every time he threw up the pain got worse. Every time the pain got worse, he threw up. Did he know these guys? Should he know these guys? Where was Daniel?

"This? Is this what you wanted? It's filthy, Zeke."

"We gotta do something, brother. Any ideas?"

"He's a mess, Zeke. He's a mess. What are we going to do? Yeah, I got his arms. Now what? Hell, he's bleeding all over his jacket."

"Walk slower. Yeah, over here, Stan. Backwards, past the door. Watch out for the seat that has that one spring poking up. Can you ride next to him? Crouch down. Don't let him sleep. I don't know why. Brother, look at his head. That's what they do when you hit your head. You don't let 'em sleep."

Jim didn't remember much for a while.

There was a lot of bumping. Sheets of pain wrapped and tightened around him. There was no end to the pain, there was yards and yards and yards of it. Twisting. Tighter and tighter. He couldn't move it was so tight. He couldn't tell if he was yelling. He couldn't tell if he was crying. Strange scratching noises emanated from deep inside his body. It was wrong. All of it. Wrong. Flames shooting out of his eyeballs. He heard angels moaning. He could see straight up into the heart and bowels of God.

"This is too slow, Zeke. Look, I know a shortcut to St. Luke's."

"St Luke's? I was headed to County Hospital, Stan."

"The County? Why would... oh yeah, we're up north. The other side of the river. You think quick, Zeke. For a quiet guy."

"It's the quiet ones you gotta watch out for, Stan. Don'cha know that?"

"He's looking pale, Zeke. He's not looking so good."

"I'm going as fast as I can, Stan. You wanna drive?"

Every time the gears changed, the car shivered and rocked and Jim's eyeballs dropped out of his head and exploded on his chest. Every time.

He was falling to pieces. The bricks of his body were loose and tumbling. This must be what a wrecked building felt like, sagging into a pile of rubble, it's plumbing painfully exposed and swinging out in the wind. Bam! Bam! Bam! So good to rest for a minute. Just a minute. Why wouldn't they let him fucking rest? Who would want to be awake for this?

"C'mon Paul. Look at me. Who am I, Paul? Tell me who I am?"

Bam! Bam! Bam! Who was Paul? Who owned this face watching him, this impossibly young kid watching him, stretched out over him? They had strong accents. Reminded him of… He felt a hand holding his. That hand holding his was on fire. And Jim's hand was a block of ice. Jim's hand didn't want to move. He couldn't exactly feel the other hand in his. More like he was holding a raw pork chop. Just meat. Hand-shaped meat. Where were his legs? He tried to throw up again, but nothing came up. Why would they be taking him to another hospital? He was in a hospital already for fuck's sake. These guys were crazy. They were going to kill him. Where was Daniel? Where were the professionals? This place was staffed by infants. And all he wanted… All he needed… was rest. Peace and quiet. Some sleep and this hangover would be history. Where was Daniel? It's only a fucking hangover.

"Daniel? What did you do to Daniel?" He was spitting out blood. The words gurgled upward.

"He's asking for someone, Zeke. He's falling asleep too."

"Keep him awake, Stan, It's all we can do, bud."

Jim felt fingers on his cheek, then a hand. It was dead too.

"Paul, you have to listen to me, now. Listen to old Stan. Look at me, Paul. Look at me."

Then there was nothing. Nothing. For a long time, maybe for only a second, maybe for hours and hours, how the fuck would Jim know how long it was? Bumping and bouncing went on forever, then it stopped – completely – and bright white lights hit him hard in his broken face, they flattened him. Then, nothing again. Then, Jim was rolling in the middle of the air, ceilings sweeping backwards over his head, it made him vomit, and then it was more yelling and more lights and something heavy strapped to his face and then it was nothing. And more nothing. A good nothing. A necessary nothing. Finally.

66
BROKE

He woke up in pieces.

Parts of his body were talking to him, other parts were stubbornly silent. Those were the good moments. The not-so-good moments were when everything woke up, all at once, and pain became his best friend, always there, always ready to lend a helping hand, glad to be of service, man, let me torture your other leg now for a change, huh?

Fuck! He opened his gummy eyes. He heard big band music. Well, that was familiar, one constant in his life, lately. He was in some kind of Masterpiece Theater set – all circa-1930's pale green and white colors, heavy-duty deco furniture made out of shiny metal, everywhere he looked, and Jim looked everywhere, he saw third-rate replicas of antiques. Jim himself was strapped into some kind of harness. It had the look of something a horse would wear. It was a cartoon hospital room. Not terribly believable. It looked cheap. Contrived. Jim wasn't impressed.

He peered up at the rings holding up his white, hospital-y cartoon curtain. Evidently purchased from Walmart. Laughable, really. He was wrapped in bandages as if he were a stunt double in Return of the Mummy. Even more laughable. All he could smell was rubbing alcohol. And soap. There were rows of beds, in front, to the left, to the right. People talking. People sleeping. Outside, windows were gray. Bright gray, featureless clouds. Daylight? More cheap set decoration. They couldn't even spring for a normal sky, maybe some fluffy clouds, a bird or two? No. Jim got battleship gray.

He tried to turn his head. The pain slapped him silly. Tears ran down his cheeks. He could hear footsteps and moaning and mumbling all around him. You know, he really didn't want to be here. It took a while, but he fell asleep. He felt hands on his forehead. He woke up. But he couldn't stay awake. It was night. Someone put strong hands under his body and shifted him sideways, then re-positioned him. He smelled alcohol. Heard voices. He dreamed. He woke up. People touched him, mumbled at him. He dreamed. Woke up. Dreamed. It was light. It was dark.

At some point he was staring at the ceiling, trying to piece together an object hierarchy in his head for Finance. The doomed Renormalization Project. Instead of getting red in the face thinking of it, and wanting to hit someone, he was remembering it and enjoying remembering it. That's how he knew he was turning a corner. Maybe he was getting better. Or maybe he was going insane. Jim despised normalization on principle. Messed up your data lakes. But did any one listen to Jim? No.

Yeah, he'd be retired long before they got that project online. Luckily. It was a non-starter. But nobody but nobody said no to George "Jorge" Rodriguez, the new Datacenter V.P. Jim knew. He'd tried. And failed. Just yesterday in fact. Whenever that was. Jim and Jorge had been arguing about architecture again – Jorge liked complicated inheritance and elegant, multiply-layered hierarchies – no one else on the team did. They had to build a middle tier to the database. This project's Team Lead, who was 150 years old and wrote like it, flattened his code every time into pretty much one single method call. Shit, when Jorge had perused that piece of the project, well, let's just say hell hath no fury as a… Yeah, he shit bricks, he…

Jim tried to smile, and pain jumped up and started batting him about, playing with him, daring him to move again. All thoughts of objects and hierarchies dissolved. Jim disappeared again. He was an ocean of pain. He held his breath and counted. A half hour later, a very, very long half-hour later, he was easy again. As long as he didn't move. Or take deep breaths.

At least the alien white-hot light was gone. His eyes weren't melting anymore. But where was Daniel? Daniel. Yeah, where was Daniel? In a heartbeat, Jim was scared shitless. Jim was in a hospital, alone. Daniel would never leave him alone in a hospital. Never. Only one explanation. Daniel was dead. He couldn't be alive. No. Jim couldn't breathe. He didn't want to breathe. He held his breath and blinked a lot, trying to calm down. He heard footsteps, and saw a shadow cross his line of sight. He exhaled.

Daniel.

Finally.

Jim couldn't see him, but he'd know that shadow anywhere.

"Where have you been, Danny?"

Silence.

O.K…

"You know I could've been dead. Besides, there's no cute male nurses to tumble in the sheets with. Guess I'm stuck with you."

The shadow moved closer. Daniel looked old. No, he looked young.

But it wasn't Daniel, was it?

No.

No, it wasn't.

It was his grandfather.

Not Daniel's grandfather. No. It was Jim's grandfather.

Granpa? Granpa Olsen? Looking good, maybe ten, fifteen years younger than Jim. And he had hair. He looked sad. And he looked tired. And he looked angry. His angry look was effective.

Jim tried to scrunch down further into his bandages. Jim had always been a little bit afraid of his grandfather. He was kind of distant. And severe. And very quiet. Pretty much a typical Norwegian Minnesota mystery. Can't ever tell what they're thinking. It was a fact, Jim had never known exactly what granpa thought of him. Very polite people. Yeah. He'd gotten presents every year from his grandparents. Polite. Prompt. Good memories. And when his granpa had died, they'd all gone back for the big funeral. Hundreds of people there. He'd been an important guy in Minnesota, apparently. He'd looked so small, though, lying in his coffin. Right now, he looked... Well... Big. Tall. And alive. Which he could not possibly be. Granpa died forty years ago.

"Daniel?"

Jim tried again.

"Daniel?"

"No. Not Daniel, son."

He looked up at his granpa. He recognized the voice. It was a voice that forced you to look up. Yup. Granpa Olsen.

"Granpa?"

"I'm not that old Paul. It's not funny. This Daniel, and who might that be, Paul? Another hooligan? You're getting too old for this, Paul. You've disappointed me."

Paul was his father's name. Jim opened his mouth to ask him why he thought he looked like Paul, he didn't look anything like his father, but his grandfather wasn't finished with him yet.

"We're glad you're here. We're glad you're safe. But you've worried your mother sick with this prank. Had you thought about that before you did it?"

Jim tried to shake his head, yes or no, he wasn't sure which, but he didn't do it very well.

"And you're not making any sense. Why would a man be a nurse? And why would you tumble in the sheets? I'm not sure I appreciate your humor, young man."

67
CLICK

Paul started falling again. Hit more snow. Kept on falling.

Falling, falling, falling.

How far below him could the ground be?

Paul plummeted. Backwards. Arms and legs flailing. Into black shadows. Into darkness. The darkness swallowed him and ingested him and pushed him deeper. Paul kept on falling.

He felt as if he were a bead on a string. Surrounded by innumerable other beads on other strings. Either he was moving, and the strings were still, or the strings were moving and he was still – he couldn't tell the difference.

Did it make a difference?

Probably not, huh? Since this was only a dream.

The strings all lined up in parallel, the beads lined up on the strings. There was movement everywhere. Lights flashed. Things happened. His bead was a sort of pinkish-purple with twinkling galaxies embedded in it here and there – as if they were flickering raspberry seeds in a heaping dollop of translucent jelly. It made him hungry to look at himself. For a moment he was there, warm, in his own sweetish-purplish light. Then he wasn't. He was yanked over into a yellow-blue blob that winked brightly with multicolored flashes – it was the kind of flashes you'd see if chrome car bumpers came in all kinds of colors and you were driving away from the setting sun and the reflections off of all the other cars going the opposite way were blinding you. Dazzling you. Tempting you. Those kind of flashes. Rainbow searchlights. He didn't remember anything after that.

Except the familiar feeling of bone sliding upwards over skin slipping downwards to meet it. And all the inevitable clicking and snapping and everything coming to rest – kerplop! – in a web of muscles and guts and tendons and nerves.

Then, Paul definitely didn't remember anything after that.
Oh yeah.
Except…
The penguins.
Staring at him.
Again.

68
CRASH

Paul was warm.

Which was odd.

And wrong. Blood warm.

As if you were bathing in blood, naked in the stuff. He was touching someone. He had an old person's hand holding his. Bony. Cold. But the grip was firm, convincing, the hand knew what it was doing. Paul was crying. His face was wet. And he was falling. Backwards. Falling, falling, falling as if he'd stepped one step too far backwards and slipped off a cliff. No. As if he'd tripped on his own shoelaces and was falling on his kiester. He bent his legs, fell backwards. The hand stayed in his. A chair hit the small of his back. Hard. It took his breath away. He struggled to get his lungs working again.

It was very dark. Corny, horror-movie machine noises chirped and wheezed around him. He sensed, in the darkness, and it surprised him, that there was a person, a someone, next to him (a guy?), who slapped both his (strong) hands on Paul's shoulders and started kneading them. Now, Paul had never had a massage. No one had ever touched his shoulders and squeezed him as if he were bread dough, lumpy and needing to be broken up. Paul wasn't sure he liked it. The hands were too strong for a woman. Why was this guy doing this?

He let it go on for a while. Maybe he did need it. Maybe it felt good. Brother! It did feel good. That was the reason he was letting him do it. All his muscles ached. His head hurt. O.K., he generally hurt everywhere. He was tired and he was hurt. He felt as if he were a stretched-and-flattened birthday party balloon the next morning, air leaking out, slipping behind the good horsehair couch in the living room, turning into a rubbery corpse, something you wouldn't find until next spring cleaning.

Yeah, his head was white-hot with pain, it was the worse headache. And, yeah (he touched his face with his free hand, looked at his fingers), Paul was still crying.

He looked at the hand holding his. Ancient. A very old hand. His own hand wasn't all that young either. Veiny, bony, hairy. Kind of lizardy. His fingernails were ridged and claw-like. It was strange. It was wrong.

What happened to his skin? His hand? What horrible disease did he have?

"Jimmy?" Paul felt someone kiss him behind the ear. The kiss felt like family. The voice was an old man's voice he'd never heard before. But no one kissed in his family. Especially guys.

He couldn't get over his hands. He brought the one that wasn't otherwise occupied up to his face again. Turned it over. This way and that. A voice floated over his shoulder.

"Jimbles? You O.K.? Does your hand hurt? What's wrong? It's not your heart again? Is it? Jim? James? Do you have your nitro? Do you feel numb? Where does it hurt?"

Paul had no idea what the correct answers were to any of those questions. You know, brother, he'd had enough. Enough of all this. He tilted his head back and directed his voice backwards.

"Who is Jimbles? Why do you keep calling me that?"

The hand in his hand squeezed his harder, the old man's hand. The voice at his ear sounded upset, all of a sudden.

"This is Daniel, Jim. Daniel." Was Daniel crying too? Paul wiped his eyes and his nose with his space hand. O.K. Did his chest hurt? How could he tell? He felt sick. All over. Of course it hurt. Paul was tired. So this guy was named Daniel. So what? So what was he supposed to do now?

You're confused. You are. You don't have it with you, do you?"

"Have what?"

There was silence behind his ear. Maybe a sniffling sound.

"Who are you, anyways?"

The sniffling was louder. This Daniel guy was definitely crying now.

"Stay there, Jim. I'll find a nurse. They have to have that stuff, someone around here somewhere, they have to, I mean... They'll give me some. They will. They have to. They'll... Stay here,

127

Jimbles. This is a hospital. O.K. Bien. That's what hospitals are for. That's why they're here. That's why... Bien. Calmate Daniel! Stay here, Jimbles. Don't move. I'll be right back. I promise. Stay here. O.K.? Jimbles? O.K.? O.K.?"

Paul, rolling his eyes, nodded a quick yes.

The voice wandered off, out into the outer darkness. Paul was left in this inner darkness. There was hardly any light in this place. Didn't they believe in seeing things clearly? And Paul was left with, who? (or was it whom? – Paul could never remember which was which). Whoever it was, whomever it was, he was old. An old man. An old, old man, curled up in front of him, holding his hand. The old guy was trying to say something. Paul could see him now in the dim light, opening and closing his mouth. It was really hard for him to say it. He couldn't really speak. Machines beeped and hissed. Lights blinked and curled. A fan was blowing warm air onto his face from somewhere out of the shadows. The old man was pointing at his hand. At Paul's hand. Pointing at himself. At Paul. His other hand was curled up too. It looked painful. The old guy tried to say something. He tried one more time. Again. Again. He was motioning towards himself.

69
DICTION

"Eeeooo."

Paul squinted. He leaned forwards. He blew upwards to get the hair out of his eyes, and realized he had no hair up there. He was bald. Leaping lizards! As he was running his hand over his billiard ball head, his heart racing in his chest, the old man kept on talking to him. Paul couldn't think. All my hair is gone. I'm bald. At seventeen!

"Miiieeem."

Paul leaned forward more. He could barely see the old man's eyes. They weren't sleepy, they weren't hesitant. They were very much alive and focused on Paul. He bent his (bald) head closer to the old guy's mouth.

"Oooommmum." The guy didn't have the best breath. But he desperately wanted to say something. Paul leaned back. The hand in his never stopped gripping. If anything it was holding on harder. He had a strong grip, for such an old guy. He leaned in again.

"What? What are you trying to say? I'm sorry. I don't know what you're saying." Paul was still running his hand over his head, desperate to find a little hair, any hair, yeah, he kind of wasn't listening all that hard.

"Mooeeeiiii."

"Eeeooommmm."

"What?"

"Zheeooom.

Paul heard footsteps approaching. Multiple persons. He heard a familiar voice – the Daniel guy – saying something about heart pain and nitro. Paul found he was crying again. Or maybe he'd never stopped. How could he tell? He was still holding the old man's hand in his. He wouldn't let go. Neither would the old man.

"Jeooom"

There was more pointing, mostly at himself. Paul got it. He was trying to tell him something, trying to tell him what? Was he cold? Did he need a nurse? Or was he pointing at his chest? Did it hurt? Or was he saying something else? Or was he saying his name? A name?

"Is he saying Jim?" That was the nurse. She was right behind him.

The head, painfully curled into his chest, but with the eyes looking up at Paul's nodded slowly once. The nods were tiny. Miniature. Then it nodded again. And again.

"You're Jim? Who is Jim?" Paul thought it was a reasonable question.

No one else did. The nurse (her face, her eyes, her eyebrows, all if it broadcasting concern, sadness – was every single person that Paul was going to meet tonight going to be crying?), the nurse started asking Paul (me? – why was she asking me?) a lot of questions that Paul didn't know the answers to. Or he got the wrong answers. How could he get the name of the President wrong? Daniel hugged him. Tighter and tighter. His chest was so compressed he could barely inhale. It felt as if his body was bigger than it had any right to be. He looked down. He was fat. No. Not possible. Not Paul. Paul was always sticks and bones. No more. Paul was a fatso. He was round as a beach ball. They gave him a small white pill to put under his tongue. He didn't want to, but they made him take it. It tasted vaguely sweet. It gave him an instant headache. On top of the headache he already had. The arms wouldn't let go of his chest. The hand wouldn't let go of his hand. It should've felt strange, It should've felt insidious (Paul liked that word), but it didn't. It felt like home. It was home. Paul was home. He was home.

Wait.

If the old guy was Jim, then, the obvious question to ask was: who was he?

He'd thought he was Paul.

But clearly he wasn't.

Who was he?

He was nobody.

Another nurse came in, with a futuristic wheelchair, all contoured black surfaces, brilliant metal and soft, leathery webbing stuff – it was a Flash Gordon flying motorcycle for invalids – Paul didn't complain. They bundled him off to a curtained section of very, very white walls, furniture, more fancy machines. Fancy wood on the wall. Tiny, tiny motion picture screens. Fancy furniture. There was a lot of waiting. Then, there was a lot of sleeping. Interspersed with meaningful glances and meaningful handholding from Daniel and more waiting. He and Daniel had many awkward conversations, often ending with tears in both their eyes. Mostly Paul was very uncomfortable, physically and metaphysically. Here was a long ways from Red River Falls, Minnesota. He knew it. People talked funny. They dressed funny, almost naked sometimes. He didn't know who they were. And he had no idea where "here" was. So, "where" was a problem. He also had no answers to "why", "how" or "what".

Paul wasn't having the best time. So why wasn't Paul scared?

70
EQUALS

Now, Paul wasn't the biggest fan of Science Fiction, but if something Science-Fiction-y was occurring and Paul was a part of it, he wanted to know more about it. Who wouldn't'? He was living a Dick Tracy future-life. What had happened to the planet Earth? And the earthling Paul Olsen?

Slyly, he decided to do some detective work. He tried to bring up certain topics indirectly, tried to talk about his suspicions in round-about ways, but subtlety never got him very far. In fact, subtlety didn't get Paul anywhere. No one slipped up and told him he was on the prison planet Zorgan. No one forgot themselves for a moment and revealed to Paul that all this was, in reality, a dream and he was brain floating in a red cylinder of bubbling water connected to a bunch of wires. Nope. Nobody said much of anything to Paul besides "how are you feeling?", "turn over" and "this won't hurt" – everything a normal Earth hospital staff would communicate to a normal earthling.

Paul couldn't tell if they were too clever for him, or if Paul was acting like an idiot, or... what? The strange thing of it was – Paul wasn't caring much, it didn't matter to him, any which way it might turn out to be. O.K. So. Either Paul was crazy, or the world was crazy, or both, or neither. Those were his choices, right?

He couldn't get excited. He tried. He couldn't. It was only a puzzle. It gave Paul something to think about. It gave him something to do. That was it. It was strange how calm Paul was. It was weird. It was wrong. But he didn't care. He didn't. And no one was telling him anything anyways. He wasn't getting anywhere with all his elaborate detective-ing. He got bored with it all after a while.

To be fair, they never listen to you in a hospital anyways, nurses and doctors, they're very focused creatures, and don't have a lot of time for metaphysics, and so, yes, it all went downhill fast and Paul got a reputation for being not-quite-all-there. They started speaking slowly and loudly around him. They used small words. They repeated themselves. They smiled a lot. The worst was this guy Daniel. He would never let Paul alone.

Which is at it should be, Paul supposed. Just doing their jobs. Or being friendly. O.K. Fine. But, c'mon! brother – even Paul could tell something didn't smell right here, Paul didn't fit in. He wasn't crazy. He didn't fit. They knew it. He knew it. It wasn't a secret. C'mon!

That was as much excitement as he could muster. Which wasn't much, brother. Kinda pathetic.

But because no one would listen to him (or maybe because they did listen to him) Paul was quickly and indelibly gifted with labels that seemed a little extreme and more than a little insulting – even to him, a balding, overweight, prematurely-aged seventeen year old lost in a bad serial SciFi film.

"Possible Stroke", "Partial Paralysis" and "Mental Confusion". These were the only answers Paul ever got.

Paul got released to Daniel's harried care and oversight in less than 24 hours. And Paul for one was glad not to be giving blood and urine anymore to random persons at every hour of the day and night. He was relieved. He breathed easier.

Daniel seemed a little overwhelmed by it all.

No, that wasn't fair to Daniel.

This Daniel guy was careful and deliberate. Almost as diligent as a Minnesotan would be. Paul approved of Daniel, after he'd gotten to know him a bit.

And, yes, they were right, in part. Paul was confused. And he stayed confused. For long time (a long time being another day or two). But eventually Paul got it. His name was James, Jim for short, Jimbles or Jumbles to some (Daniel). He was in California. He had a husband. He was 57 years old. He was 70 plus years in the future. He was his own son.

"Leaping Lizards" as they say!

Yes, Paul didn't know a lot about Science Fiction, he hated Science Fiction – they always brought in very unlikely, very convenient Science Fiction facts, at the end of the book, in the very last couple of pages usually, and saved the hero with a smug neatness that made Paul want to scream,. throw up, rip pages out of encyclopedias and howl at the moon. Who could believe such mush? Not any self-respecting Minnesotan. Not a practical Norwegian. For sure, not Paul Olsen.

Yes.

Well.

That was the old Paul.

This was the new Paul.

Paul could believe. Paul could easily believe such mush and much, much more. I mean, look, brother, he was time-travelling! It was hard for a guy to disbelieve his own eyes. So Paul had a problem.

Why? Because, Paul knew in all those stories, when someone got pushed out of their own time, they always had to find a way to get pushed back into it again. Back into their own time. Always. They had to find a way home. Into their own time. Home. That's what you did. You went home. That was how it worked. Right? It was hard. But you found a way.

That was Paul's problem.

And brother, it was a huge problem.

Paul wanted to get back.

He wanted to go home.

He really did.

So he had to… he ought to… to get back to… he needed to… to what, Paully? All he knew was that he, himself, well, his body – heck! – this was confusing – well, his body, Paul's body, was in a Rehab hospital, Paul was a 90 year old man, in hospice, trying to die reasonably pain-free.

Paul was 90 years old!

Wow!

He'd lived a long time.

He hoped it had been worth it.

That's what you're getting back to Paul, huh? Getting back to die?

71
FREEDOM

This body wasn't so great anyways. Did he always have this headache? Was he always in pain? Did he always have to breathe so hard just walking up a couple of stairs?

This person he was now, this Jim, his son, was lying in his body, while Paul, his father, was lying in Jim's body, his son. No. Wait. It was the other way around, right? Heck! Who could keep it straight?

I'm Jim outside, Paul inside. He's Jim inside, Paul outside. An old, old Paul.

Nope. Didn't help.

And what happened to the Model B and the skiing and the snow and New Year's Day, 1944, huh? What happened to all that? Zeke? Stan? What happened to them? And why, oh why was he, Paul, missing 70 years of his life?

One thing at a time, Paully.

But... I mean, you have to...

One.

Well, still...

One.

O.K. Do one thing. First. Just one thing.

Good. So far so good. But what? What first thing?

Ah. Not so good.

He'd almost had it. Almost. That time. He could nearly touch it, it was so close. Almost... Almost... Then – bam! – it always got all tangled up.

He couldn't remember anything correctly. It was either in the wrong order. Or backwards. Or some of it had to be imaginary. And people told him things. But they weren't any better. They didn't know what they were talking about. They couldn't know what they were talking about. Right? Why would words you wrote down make machines talk? And that was his job? Jim's job? Did that make any sense at all? And the rest? How? Why? When? All good questions. Had Jim been Paul for the last 70 ever-loving years? Had he? He must've been. Paul couldn't remember doing any of it. Well, he could. Almost. It was as if you were seeing it through a window – a winter window – that was fogged – and iced over – battered by a blizzard – in the middle of a very dark and cloud-clogged night with no moon. He could see shapes and shadows.

Except it wasn't his life he was seeing or remembering. It was someone else's. That always got him scared. Someone else's memories inside his head. Must be Jim's. The last thing he remembered clearly was that barbed wire fence slicing him into pieces on New Year's Day. 1944, and him landing not in a snowdrift but in a chair. He always came back to the barbed wire fence. Then the chair. Fence. Chair. Fence Chair. Fence. It gave a guy a headache just thinking about it.

After a while, Paul stopped trying to figure it out. He just ran with the ball. Grabbed the fool thing and ran like heck.

The sex hadn't been nearly as hard to get used to (an understatement) as he'd thought. It was embarrassing how little the male body cared about the way holes were used, when, and by whom. It had been a revelation. A religious experience. Not that he'd tell his Lutheran minister about it back home anytime soon. (See? Paul was certain he'd get back – he had to get back). So, yeah, O.K. he'd been a virgin. He admitted it. Lots of guys were. And he wasn't anymore. Boy, wasn't he a virgin! In fact he was tiring Daniel out. In fact, he was…

"What are you thinking about, Jimbles?"

A voice tunneled out from under the covers, Daniel was biting on his knee.

"A little higher would be nice."

"Don't you ever get tired? What happened to your bad back? Did you have a reverse stroke in your dad's hospital room? Did your entire nervous system get rewired through your genitals by mistake? Huh?"

"Maybe."

"No, really. Jimbles."

"Uh…"

"What happened? Jim? Is your memory still blank? Do you feel different?"

"Jim?"

"You need to talk about it sometime, Jimbles, we need to…"

The hotel room they were in had a very noisy heater. It kicked on. Why would a radiator make such noise? Paul took advantage of that fact and remained silent. He did scoot down further into the sheets, pushing Daniel's face upwards. But Daniel didn't take the hint, kept right on going, his head emerging somewhere in the vicinity of Paul's right armpit. Daniel didn't even pause, he rubbed his head into it, knowing he'd be tickling him in his most vulnerable spot. It must be genetics. His Minnesota body worked the same way. Tickling was torture. It always was. Paul fought back the only way he knew how.

About twenty minutes later, sweaty as all get out and radiating contentment, as they were picking up the pillows all over the room and pulling the blankets on the bed, Paul thought he was pretty lucky. He was tired. But it was such a good tired. Who knew he would be so good at sex? Not Paul Olsen.

72
GROUNDSWELL

They were re-making the bed. Why? Paul didn't know why. The maid (probably a guy-maid, knowing this future time) would be in and make the bed anyways, right? In the morning? At least they did in the movies. But Daniel was cleaning up and Paul felt he should do it to. Besides, Paul was cleaning up because he didn't like making messes and then leaving them for other people to clean up, even if they were getting paid to do it. His son, Jim, must've been the same way, right? Neat. Tidy. Careful. It stood to reason.

Daniel didn't say anything as they put everything back in place. He looked as if he could be a boxer. He was thinking about something, Paul could tell, his forehead was all wrinkled. Daniel had big arms, strong legs, strong fingers, an open, honest face. You know, it was strange. Paul had always thought that guys who liked guys acted like girls. Daniel was the opposite of a girl. And how would a girl act, anyways? Paul didn't know how to act like a girl. Daniel didn't seem to know how to do it either. Maybe Paul couldn't tell the difference. Maybe there wasn't a difference. Maybe... Daniel caught Paul looking at the ceiling and with his own eyebrows wrinkled and thinking.

"Jim? What are you..."

Paul threw a pillow over his shoulder. He heard a satisfying "oomph" from over in the corner. It was kind of loud. Maybe he'd thrown it too hard. Paul pitched on the High School Baseball team. They said he had a good arm. Except... this wasn't his arm, was it? Boy! Why was it so complicated? In fact, his elbow hurt. Ouch! From only one throw! Well, the truth was, all kinds of body parts hurt. All the time. It never stopped. Morning to evening. How did Jim live this way? This body demanded so much attention. He was drooping and slouching, all the darn time, but, yeah, so far, no one seemed to notice a body switch had been made in the Olsen family of bodies. No one had put two and two together. Yet.

And maybe they never would.

Jim wasn't calling the shots anymore.

Paul was.

And Paul needed for it stay that way. Paul didn't want people to start noticing. Not if he could help it. Not until he could make his escape.

"Daniel?"

"Put down the pillow, Jim."

"All right, all right. I promise."

"You promise what?"

"I promise not to.."

"Act like an asshole? You almost broke my nose that time."

"Uh… I wouldn't put it that way."

"How would you put it? And since when do you promise anything? You always say – promises are excuses you make to break your word before you do it – or something similar. Or have you changed your mind?"

"I'm just not feeling well."

That got a moment of silence.

"Jimbles, I'm sorry. I shouldn't be hassling you. I should be supporting you."

"Uh. Yeah. O.K."

"Are you dizzy again?"

"No, Danny, not really."

"I think you are. Your chest doesn't hurt, right? We have plenty of nitro right here in the room. They said you didn't have a heart attack. But I know better. You're acting differently. Don't push yourself, Jimbles.

Here. Lie down.

O.K. Danny. I'm lying down. Now what?

On the bed. Not on the couch. I think I need to relax you. But before you start, this is the last time. The very last time. The last time, this afternoon. I mean it. The last time. You're wearing me out."

"Oh. Yeah. For sure. O.K. I need to lie down. Right now. See? I'm lying down. On the bed. I need to relax. Exactly like you said. I'm lying down and I need to relax."

"I can see that."

"Is that all you can see?"

"I think I'd better get in and examine the uh, relaxation situation, you know, more deeply, go in for a closer look."

"I think you better."

"There. I'm close. I think I need to get closer."

"Uh. Uh, yeah. Good."

"Mmmmff."

"Before I completely lose my mind, can we head over to the hospital this evening?"

"Mmmmpphhhoofffevvvooo…"

"What? Is that a yes?"

"Jimmy – do you want me to talk or do you want me to examine?"

Paul had no answer to that. He didn't need to.

73

HELL

Jim didn't remember much of anything.

O.K. Jim didn't want to remember much of anything.

But, then again, it didn't matter what the fuck Jim wanted, now, did it?

Jim couldn't do any of it anyways. Nope. Not anymore. His body wasn't cooperating. His mind wasn't cooperating. Nobody wanted to work. And, dude, it was work. Fucking torture. Thinking. Movement. He was so tired of everything being such a fucking big deal. Blinking took a lot of planning. Shit.

His left side was a mess. Everything on the left had taken a red eye and was a couple of continents away by now, vacationing somewhere off the coast of Africa. Or on Fiji. With no cell coverage. And no return ticket. Leaving Jim flying solo. Jim's left side had left the building. It was gone. Jim was for fucking sure of that. Jim was on his own.

Tired. Scared. Alone.

So. What else is new?

Yeah, getting from point A to point B up there in his brain was not an option anymore. Nothing was clear. Nothing was easy. There were walls and gaps where there used to be four-lane highways up there, inside his skull, between his ears. Huge hollow spots. Abandoned and vacated neurons. In his broken head, it was now Mad-Max-Post-Apocalyptic mayhem 24-7 – burnt out cities – radioactive deserts – extravagant growths and impenetrable jungles. Wild, lush unexpected things, multiply-headed and variously-footed sprouted where there shouldn't have been anything. And where there should have been plenty of stuff, moving and shaking, there were only these blank, white non-things that looked familiar, but did nothing and absorbed everything and left Jim with no words to say, speechless, and Jim hated it, he hated all of it, and he wasn't going to live this way.

Nope. Not gonna do it.

Yeah. Jim was scared.

Do you understand? It was all backwards. Nothing made sense. And everything made sense. Nothing. Everything. Jim was new, he was a new thing. He was starting over. Not again. Yeah, again. But he was tired. Crazy tired. All the time now. Again. And he was sick. Again. But he needed to get well. And he didn't have the strength. Not this time. Not again. This desolation had happened one too many times. Fuck. Did he? Could he? Could he try and recover? Shit no. Probably not. Not this guy. Not this time. Could he? Would he?

What was he going to do?

And would this headache ever stop?

He paused for a moment. To let the thumping in his cerebellum ratchet down a few notches.

Wait.

What was he thinking about?

What?

He couldn't remember.

See? Mad Max Syndrome.

It was very quiet around this new Jim. He was still curled up, his muscles no longer obeyed him. At least not when he wanted them to. His mind resembled a sponge. It sucked up random impressions of his environment. He danced around inside his head. Rotated around the center of a blast zone. Tip-toed on the edges of his huge brain-crater. His memories cowered in broken caves and corners, along with what was left of Jim, too timid to poke their noses out or their asses out and show themselves in the light of day and risk being seen.

Dude, it was a strange way to live.

And, by the way, where the fuck was he?

He slept a lot. It got darker. It got lighter. At night (was it always night here? – how could he tell?) he'd wake up and couldn't breathe for a moment. All of it, every fucking bit of it, it was all too much.

Sometimes there'd be people. People he probably should know. Women. Men. They'd say his name "dad". Which made no sense. But Jim's whole life was nonsense now. So he didn't care. He didn't pay too much attention. He watched these people. And he slept.

He cried at the slightest opportunity, when a light turned on, when he heard someone talking in the distance. And he laughed. Gently, Quietly. He'd smile to himself when startled by the touch of somebody rotating his rebellious body. It would occur to him – I'm alive, I'm still alive. His emotions felt new, brand-new, just-bought-and-unwrapped new. Life was raw. The welcoming feel of clean sheets, that was new. The fussy, complaining smell of orange disinfectant, that was new. Everything was new, everything was a revelation to Jim. He spent a lot of time staring at the doorway or the ceiling or the wall (all new, all interesting) and let anger (a new emotion) wash through him. As well as sadness (another new emotion). Then he'd be furious. His heart would be pounding, pounding, his face would feel warm and alive. But he couldn't move it. Not very well. But he wanted to. He wanted to yell.

It was... all of it... unfair. Unjust and unfair. All of it. Why? Who knew? Then as quickly as it had come, the excitement would go. And Jim would be left huddled in a quiet corner of himself, bored and wondering what was going to happen next.

Little by little images dripped back into his brain. And he began to piece them together, to understand – the understanding was new – and the pictures in his mind – they made sense – they were new too – and all these things – they frightened him. They made his heart race. They made him want to yell again. At first they were blurs. Then they were crystal clear. That was when Jim wished they were blurs again.

They memories were there. He could see them. He couldn't not see them.

He remembered being in World War II – on a dot of a boat in the infinite Pacific, with a bunch of other 18 year olds – Hawaii – Japan – typhoons – Treasure Island – discharge – he'd gone to college on the G.I. bill at the U of M – Go Golden Gophers – crazy crowded campuses – like being back in the Navy – dating – a couple of jobs – more dating – finally a good position with a Marketing firm in Chicago – meeting his future wife (what was her name? – no fucking clue) skiing down a pass on a mountain in the middle of Colorado – moving to Pasadena – kids (how many? – no idea) – his parents dying – vacations – rough times – alcoholism – recovery – that had been rough – retirement – his wife dying suddenly – diabetes – hospitals – discovering dating again – more deaths – more sickness – falling – strokes – fear – hospitals – rehab – senior apartments – hospitals – living under the thumb of nursing home attendants – strokes – anger – shame – guilt – fear – more anger – Stained underwear. The shame of Depends. Loneliness, the T.V. on all the time, the days rolling by and by and by and by – all in his head – all the memories were there.

Yup.

Memories.

All there.

They just weren't his.

An entire life.

How fucked-up was that?

74
IN-BETWEEN

Jim figured he'd have to be in his 90's to cram that much living into his life. Jim was not 90. Not yet. He'd try to tell the random nurse – I'm not 90 – but then he stopped trying. He couldn't say the words very well, yeah, but even if he could, no one would believe him. Of course they wouldn't. Jim laughed to himself as somebody took some blood from his arm. The nurse jiggled his arm, and Jim was asked a question, but Jim wasn't listening. He was watching the doorway again, his mind (blessedly) numb and featureless, his eyes observing the confident persons passing back and forth, intent on their important tasks, each one of them a miracle of self-confidence and self-sufficiency. They, all of them, each one of them, knew where they were, who they were, and why they were. It was an amazing sight. He couldn't stop watching. And, just to pass the time, he'd try to puzzle out where and who and why he was.

He didn't get very far.

Then… it would come to him – I'm in a hospital. And, no matter how much he hammered it down, strapped it tight, flash-welded it permanently onto his brain, he'd forget it. Again. The fact would disappear. Easily. Happily. Pleasantly. One second the certainty would be there, the next second it'd be gone. It wouldn't even leave a gap where it once was. As if you'd punched a hole in a river with your fist. The hole remained for a breathless second, then the hole filled up with water, then water in the river moved on and you couldn't tell if it was the same water or different water and then, you'd ask yourself – why am I staring at a patch of water?

Why? What? Jim would find himself staring at the ceiling or the door and carefully try to work out the who of Jim and the where of Jim. It was tough work, not for the faint-hearted.

Well.

You know.

It was also something to do.

People would visit. They did things to him, and they didn't do things to him. He'd see familiar faces. The strangest part of this whole experience was, he'd see his own face. Sitting in a chair next to him. The face owned a pair of hands. One of them would be holding his hand. And he'd see his husband standing next to himself, leaning on the wall – what was his name? – what was his fucking name? His husband – Jim remembered the face. Never forget that face. Jim knew. He knew. He knew for certain, who it was. It was Jim's husband.

And he knew, for certain, those weren't his memories either.

Right?

Wrong?

Fucking hell!

No memories or too many memories. It was all wrong. He was a fucking mess. A goddamned catastrophe. No wonder he was in a hospital. If that's where he was. Where was he?

Yeah. A hospital.

He was crying again.

"What's wrong?"

Jim heard a voice, he looked up sharply (which only meant his neck moved very slightly backwards). He tried, by focusing his eyes, to focus his life. What is this? Who am I? It didn't work. It never worked.

It was his face.

He was seeing his face again. It didn't make sense. The familiar hand was in his again. Someone else was here in the room too. So. Two people. And Jim.

"What's wrong? Do you need something?"

It was quasi-night again – at least it was dark, the three of them were in a cone of soft light showering down from over behind Jim's shoulder. Wait. There were five people. Or were there twenty? Numbers were a little vague now. Yeah, there were twenty. Or thirty. At least. Let's just say a hundred. And be done with it. Close enough.

He tried and failed to see what was making the light. Jim didn't do a lot of moving these days. He stared back down at the floor and let his tears run down his cheeks.

"Daniel, could you find the nurse? Maybe get some water?"

"Sure, Jimmy, sure. Back in a second." Footsteps padded off and disappeared.

"You're killing me, don't cry. Please. We'll figure something out."

Jim looked up. He tried to say something. Anything.

"I know, I know. You're seeing your own face, right?"

Jim squinted. One side of his face (the left?) refused to squint. The other did it fine. Why was that?

"Well, so am I. Except my face, your face, my face is really, really old."

Jim continued to squint.

"So, I guess, you're my son."

"And I'm your father. I should introduce myself. I'm Paul. But you already know that. And you're Jim. My son. I sound stupid. That's not what I wanted to say. I... I... I wish I could remember you. But, you and I both know I haven't met you yet. And now, I never will, huh? Except I'm meeting you now. Doesn't make any sense, does it? What did we do? Why did they do this to us? Why did it happen?"

143

75
JOLT

The face above Jim was crying now also. What a mess they were. One fucking mess. A misplaced face mess.

Drops fell on his hands. He couldn't tell if they were his or the other guy's. The drops were warm. Summer rain. What you'd feel on a summer night, thunder and lightning, lightning bugs, mosquitos, the soft sound of neighbors chatting on a screened porch across the street, guys playing catch under the streetlight – had to be real careful not to lose sight of the ball – the ball thwopping the mitt each time, a satisfying sound – the smell of cut grass and maybe the creaking of your rocking chair as you rocked away in the humid darkness and…

Were those his memories? No. Fucking no. Jim didn't remember lightning bugs in Pasadena. Maybe because there weren't any. And they didn't have thunder when he was growing up there either. You didn't get thunderstorms, not in Southern California. He knew fucking that much.

Hell, you didn't even get rain in Southern California. That was a song wasn't it? Was it true? Was anything his? Anything at all? Did he even exist? Did it matter? Jim was going to ask the face above him, but it had kept right on speaking, going on and on and on. It wasn't listening to Jim.

76
KNOCK

"And I guess, we're about to die. That's what the doctor says. This last stroke… You're not going to be able to eat."

Paul stopped. The eyes looked up at him. He couldn't tell if they were listening anymore or not. He sighed. Slogged on.

"We have a couple of weeks maybe. Tops. What am I supposed to do, huh? What am I supposed to be doing? What do you want me to do?"

Jim wanted to look back down at the floor. But he couldn't move all that much. He looked up into his face.

Dead. He was going to be dead. Did he feel relief? Yes. He did. His hands were very wet now. Jim didn't care. It had an end. Everything had an end, and this did too. He was ready. Well, as ready as he'd ever be. Wait, he needed to remember this. Remember. Remember. You're dying. Remember.

What was he trying to remember again?

"Jim?"

"Jim?"

"Look, we'll figure something out, O.K.? Jim?"

"Why are you calling him Jim?" That was a new voice. He felt his hand let go. He let it slide down onto his fuzzy blanket. He felt warm. He felt calm. Suddenly Jim was very sleepy. Sleep was good. Sleep was Jim's best friend nowadays. Jim threw open his figurative arms and figuratively bear-hugged sleep and wouldn't let go of it. That worked. He was falling. Deeper. Deeper yet. As if from the bottom of a well, he heard the voices, murmuring. That was fine. That was O.K.

"You called him Jim."

"Uh, yeah, uh, I don't know."

"Or are you talking to yourself again, Jimmy?"

"Uh, do I do that often?"

"You used to."

"Then, yeah, that's what I'm doing."

"You can't fool me, Jimbles, I know you like the back of my hand. You're up to something. I know you."

"I bet you don't."

"I can see it. In your eyes. You could never lie to me. Those blue bedroom eyes always tell me the truth. You'd think after 38 years you'd…"

"I'd what?"

"Have it your way. But I'm sure. I'm sure you'll tell me. When you're ready."

"Uh…"

"Are you ready yet?"

"How about now?"

"Or now?"

"Daniel, have I ever told you, you're a pain in the neck?"

"You'll have to tell me sometime, Jimbo. Sooner or later."

"Shhh. We should get going, Daniel. I think he's asleep."

"That's not stopping me."

"I didn't think it would."

77
LIE

Amy and Teddie came back into the room. They'd got some dinner. They were talking in low voices. Luke came in right behind them with his wife and his oldest boy, Jordan. So far, Paul had gotten by, not talking much, nodding a lot. Daniel had said something about his heart and everyone had seemed to give him space and leave him be. Which was fine by Paul. But it was getting a little crowded tonight.

Amy and Teddie had thick pulp paperbacks in their purses. Luke's wife had crocheting, which she got down to immediately. Luke and son had matching tablets and matching earphones. They were slapping those tablet things like crazy. They'd told Daniel it was a "game" whatever that meant. It seemed as if Luke and Jordan had to be playing in the same game, but on different tablet things, since they both grunted, in testosterone-driven unison, every 10 seconds or so. They were both big guys. They took up a decent amount of space in the small hospital room. It was as if Paul and Daniel were trying to squeeze, shoulder to shoulder, into a room with two bull moose in rut. Teddie and Amy were now completely lost in their books. All you could hear was breathing, snorting, thwapping, needle-clicking and page-turning. Eventually Paul and Daniel looked at each other, looked at Jim's dad asleep in his bed and gave up. Paul and Daniel tip-toed out of the hospital room, holding hands, Daniel leading the way.

Paul's head was wanting to explode. His brain was not a happy brain. It was very unhappy. It made Paul unhappy.

Paul had a pocketful of aspirin in his pocket at all times now. He downed a few more, chewing them, as he didn't have any water. They made their way down another long, white hospital corridor in the long, white hospital maze. He'd done it so much, the pills, he was starting to like it – the taste of raw aspirin – kind of a minty, lemony battery acid. Yeah, it was an acquired taste.

The crunchy aspirin dulled the effect of the pain gerbils boring through his eyeballs into his cranium every day and tunneling out the other side of his skull after they ran for a while doing the hamster-wheel thing on loops of his optic nerve. They ran the wheel, to tighten the pain, to run the wheel, to tighten the pain, to run the wheel, to tighten the pain... Just his luck, pain-gerbils with a work ethic.

And they were cheerful pain-gerbils. Happy in their work. Good for Paul, the aspirin made the gerbils sloppy and sleepy. They forgot to run when Paul ate mouthfuls of the stuff. It helped. Sort of. Kind of. Well, he hoped it was helping.

Of course, whenever Paul cut himself now, he bled heroically. Paul had also taken to carrying a styptic pencil. And Band-Aids. He was a walking drug store and a mass of cuts and bruises – a lot of them in the exact shape of some of Daniel's teeth. But he wasn't about to prevent Daniel from making his appointed rounds around this new body of Paul's. Sometimes Paul felt guilty. Someone else was going to have to clean up all these wounds and bumps – scab and bandage and wait and heal. Right? It wasn't his body. Maybe he ought to take better care of it. Maybe he should be more careful. It was all very complicated. In fact, it gave him a headache to think about it.

"Jim, do you want me… to… drive? No, I guess not."

"You guessed right."

Driving one of these shiny, new, strangely-hued automobiles – machines that resembled a beetle you'd pry out of a rotting log during an expedition into the uncharted Brazilian rain forest – well, driving one of these insect-shaped, clown-colored cars intimidated Paul. For about five minutes. Now he wouldn't let Daniel drive anywhere. Nope. Paul was always the chauffeur. These future-cars! No clutch, lots of music, plenty of heat, deep seats – why didn't people live in these things and get rid of their houses?

On second thought, they'd have to live in their cars, with the sarcastically stratospheric prices of everything. It was a joke. A thousand dollars for a candy bar. A million dollars for a house. You could work all day and never make enough to buy a cup of coffee. Paul let Daniel handle all the buying and selling.

Other things were confusing to Paul as well. Daniel said Paul worked as a programmer. Paul was afraid to ask any more about it. Programmer. What was it? Did he hire dancing girls? Did he produce a radio show? Did he write the skits? Did he act in them? What was he going to do when he had to start doing whatever the heck it was this Jim-guy did, again? What? What, Paully? Then as he found out more about Jim's life – Paul asked less and less. Writing special words to make machines work? Daniel called it some kind of science. Paul called it black magic. How was Paul going to make black magic work? How?

No time to think about that now. Have to get home. He squinted. Sometimes the pain was so bad he couldn't see. O.K. Yeah. Maybe he shouldn't be driving.

Who was he kidding? He loved this car.

"What are you thinking about, Jim? Your head, it's bad isn't it? I'm sorry Jimbles."

Paul felt hands on his shoulders. It felt good. He hoped he wouldn't bruise too much this time. It was raining again. Paul liked the rain. It made him feel real. Thunderstorms, summer afternoons, Minnesota summer afternoons, getting caught under bucketfuls of warm water, waterfalls of the stuff, drain spouts erupting as if they were fire hoses, streets flooding, splashing through warm water while more poured down onto your wet skin, every inch of your skin alive, it was...

"What are you thinking about?" Fingers were digging into the muscles on his shoulder blades. That felt good. If Paul could only relax, only for a second, the headache would be gone, that's all he needed, only a second of rest, a second of feeling normal, a vacation from this constant fear, this hiding, this lying, this cheating. He didn't want to lie anymore. No. Not anymore.

"So what are you thinking, Jimbles?"

"Yeah, right there. Up a little. Perfect. About home."

"What about home?"

"Over to the left. Yeah. Yeah, up a little. Down. There. Right there. You got it. Oh, man! You got it. I don't know. I miss the thunderstorms. I guess. I miss the river. I miss the lakes. I miss, I don't know, the smell of green things getting greener, trees as big as hills, fields as big as lakes, shucking corn on the cob on the back stoop, sitting on the porch and talking, reading by the light of the hall light at midnight when you're not supposed to. You don't miss all that, until you don't have it anymore, you know? Then you realize. That's what's important. Not all the..."

"Hey!"

"What gives?"

"Why'd you stop?"

78
MONSTER

Paul took his eye off the road for a moment, looked sideways at Daniel. Daniel had stopped working on his neck.

"You've been wild lately. In bed. Insisting on driving all the time. Eating like a teenager who didn't just have his gall bladder removed. And what do you know about lakes? You hate the water. I can't even get you into a pair of swimming trunks, or even lie around a hotel pool. And when did you ever shuck corn? Do you even know how to shuck?"

"How could a person not know how to shuck?"

"You hate corn. You say it gets stuck in your teeth."

"I do? Since when? How hard can it be to eat corn? It's supposed to get stuck in your teeth. It's corn. That's ridiculous."

"It is?"

"Isn't it?"

"You tell me. What's up, Jim?"

"Tell you what?"

"Are you going to stop answering me with a question every time I get serious?"

"So you're serious? Stop! O.K. You're hurting the driver. Not the best plan, brother."

"Are you going to answer? You're not Jim."

"I'm not? Wow! You're not even hitting me. You must be serious."

"No, I'm Daniel. Stop it. I mean it. Now, you tell me, who the hell are you?"

"Why would you think I'm not Jim?"

"You're doing the question thing again. Stop it. I've known Jim for almost 40 years. Give me a break."

"Maybe you do. Maybe you don't. Maybe I've changed. What? You're not going to respond? Is that head-shaking meant to mean I should pull over? We're almost back to the hotel. Oh. Guess we're not going back to the hotel yet. O.K. No talking. Silence. I'm parking. There. The car's stopped. All you can hear is the rain on the roof. It that what you wanted? Still not talking? No, don't cry.

Stop it. That's not fair. I can't do this. I can't do it if you're crying. Stop it. Stop."

"Where's Jim?"

"I'm right here."

"No, you're not."

"I'm sort of right here. Stop crying. It doesn't make it any easier."

"I can't stop. I don't want to stop. I don't want to make it easy. Just tell me, sort-of-Jim, what's been going on since we got here. I think I have the right. Tell me. I have the right to know."

"Yup. I guess you do."

"So, there is something to tell me? Pinche Jim. I knew it. I knew it. Are you seeing someone? Is that it? Some alchoholic mid-life crisis? Are you going to leave me?"

"Daniel! No. No. Not that. Why would you think that?"

"Well, things have been… you know… well, what am I supposed to think?"

"Uh…"

"What's going on, James?"

"So… well… I mean…"

"That's it. That's enough. Not another word. Until you tell me the truth. You've never lied to me before. Well, almost never. So, are you… are you… trying to tell me you've had some kind of… I don't know… personality change? Some, what do they call it, psychotic break?"

"Uh, not exactly. I mean, I don't know. Well, I do know, at least I think I do. But not for sure. I'm…"

"Are you possessed?"

"Uh…"

"You're not gay anymore?"

"I'm not what?"

"Just tell me. We can get through it. We always have. Just tell me. Tell me, please. Do I have to beg you? When did you get so cruel?"

"You don't have to beg."

"O.K."

Paul sucked in a huge amount of oxygen. That was a mistake. His head blossomed into a bonfire of pain. He reached for his aspirin pocket. A hand stopped his hand on the way down.

"Tell me."

"Tell you what?"

"Don't start with the questions again. You know what. What do you know? Or think you know? Tell me something. Tell me anything."

"I'm not Jim."

Daniel closed his eyes and sank back into his seat. The entire car filled with the sound of tiny hammers, raindrops trying to beat their way through the roof and pummel the two of them into submission. Paul hoped they succeeded. He wanted some good external pummeling for a change. His insides were an emotional puree at the moment. He hated the feeling.

For a long time, the rain-hammers were the only sound in the front seat. That and two middle-aged men breathing. Paul closed his eyes as he chewed on another aspirin. The acid was probably eating his teeth down to nubs. Well, not his teeth. His son's teeth. Someone's teeth. Teeth were going to be eaten.

"So, you know who you aren't. Do you know who you are?"

"Yes."

"And are you going to tell me?"

"Well. You're not going to believe me."

There was more silence. Paul didn't want to talk, ever again. But he supposed, he had to. Right? It was the right thing to do. That's what you did if you were a Minnesotan. You did the right thing. Even if you were not going to enjoy it. Paul was not going to enjoy this. He knew it. Brother! Did he know it!

"I'm still waiting. If you hadn't noticed."

"I'm Paul. Paul Olsen."

"Is that another personality? Because you used to be Jim Olsen."

"No. Not another personality. I'm Jim's father."

"Oh."

"And that man in the nursing home is Jim."

"Oh. So you're a 90 year old man?"

"No. I'm 17. I don't know why my body's 90. I was skiing and…"

"Skiing?"

"Well, not down a hill, behind a model B. Stan and Zeke were along."

"Were they?"

"Well, of course they were."

"Of course, why wouldn't they be?"

"Daniel, you're not helping. We're all going into the Army, well, I'm going into the Navy, but, anyways, all of us are leaving in a few months when we graduate and we wanted to have some fun first."

"That makes sense. I'd want to have some fun first before I went into the Army. Or the Navy. If I were seventeen. And I had skis."

"You're taking this well."

"I think I'm just taking it. What else can I do? I'm married to a man who is having a psychotic break. That, or bodies have been switched and my husband is dying and I'm sleeping with my father-in-law."

"Oh yeah, about that...let's..."

"Let's just not talk about it."

"O.K. Fine with me. Sounds good. Yes. Let's do that. Right."

Silence filled the car for a few minutes. Paul didn't want to break the silence. He didn't know how. The rain beat and beat on the top of the car. It was as if they were sitting inside a drum. It didn't help Paul's headache any.

"So, by going into the Navy, you mean World War II?"

"Yeah. That's what I mean."

"Let's get back to the hospital, you."

"Why?"

"Drive."

"Daniel, it's almost midnight. Isn't it kind of late?"

Silence.

"Daniel, isn't it late?"

"It is late."

More silence.

"But..."

"But... What? Sort-of-Jim-Paul-whoever-you are, I want to see Jim. He must be frightened. Scared out of his fucking mind. I would be. If I were him. If all this is true. He needs me. Now."

Now it was Paul's turn to be silent.

"You're not fooling with me, Jim, I mean Paul? Please tell me, you're not kidding. Or tell me you're kidding. Tell me that. Tell me anything. I'll believe you. Anything."

Paul only shook his head. Daniel blinked a lot. He looked away.

Daniel looked a bit wild. His eyes were shining. He was smiling with his lips, but the rest of his face wasn't smiling. It was a little frightening.

Paul's head was throbbing. He held his breath. It helped a little, but not much. Maybe if he held his breath for forever, he'd be totally out of pain. Yeah. Brother! Now, that was an idea. Except that, this wasn't his body. Not his body to abuse. Not his body to commit suicide with. What happened when you offed yourself wearing someone else's body? Did you stay off? Or did you pop back on again, somewhere else? Who would you ask? Who would know? Man! His head hurt.

"Hospital? Please?"

"Oh. O.K. Sure, Daniel."

He punched the side of the steering wheel, then the dash (what was he looking for? – oh yeah – no key, Paul, no key) he punched the start button instead, the whole shiny Flash Gordon future-vehicle purred and chimed its obedience to him and came to life and Paul backed up, staring carefully at the tiny motion picture screen which showed him what was behind his car in the puddle-filled parking lot. The rain made it bright and flashy – as if it were an MGM movie of a rainy parking lot. Well, the picture was streaky. This car was kinda beat up. But it was preternaturally clean (Paul liked the word "preternatural" – he'd won a spelling bee with it three years ago). And couldn't these future-citizens twist their necks around and look behind them? Did they have to have movies of their rear ends in order to get through their lives? Guess not. Guess so. Too much work for them, this rotating your head on your spine. No wonder this body was so fat.

Paul glanced up at Daniel. He was staring straight ahead. Daniel was too quiet. Paul didn't know what to do. He put his hand on Daniel's. Daniel jerked it away. Guess there wasn't going to be any wild bed-gymnastics back in the hotel this night, huh, brother?

"Just drive. Whoever you are."

"I can do that." And he did. His head was splitting. He squinted. He jerked the car into drive. Nope. No gymnastics. Probably not ever again. Why wouldn't his head stop hurting? What was he going to do at the hospital? Paul was thoroughly and unquestionably tired. He needed a vacation. From all this. And everything. And soon.

153

79
NEAR

Paul and Daniel got to the hospital after midnight. All the doors were locked and closed. A security guard had to escort them over to the room. It was all the same. It was the white, familiar maze. It was dark. The same humming noises and chirps and flashes of light squiggling across Flash Gordon stage props. Men and women working in odd-colored pajamas. All the same.

The room was calm, no whispering. All the Olsens had left for the night. Just an old man and a radio playing and a light over both of them. Everything was still. As if it were all waiting for Paul and Daniel. Waiting for them to make their entrance.

Daniel glared at Paul, pushed past him as they got to the familiar door and sat down (in the only chair in the room) next to the old man in the bed. Daniel didn't look at Paul at all. Daniel stared at the body in the bed. frowning. He grabbed the one hand lying curled and open over the covers.

The old guy opened one eye, startled, and with a quick birdlike blink fastened onto Daniel's face. Half his face relaxed into a smile. That was the most it had moved the whole time Paul had known it.

"Aaaeeewll"

"It's me Jimbles. It's me."

The half-smile got bigger.

"What kind of a mess did you get yourself into now?"

Eyebrows (one of them at least) went up in a comic strip version of a face registering something like "what can I say? – you know me."

"Yeah, yeah. And I suppose you expect me to get you out of this mess, as usual."

A light nod.

"Typical."

Daniel was crying. The guy in the bed had been crying for some time now.

Paul said "coffee?" and without waiting for an answer, left the room. He didn't come back for quite a while.

80
OVERPASS

Paul slept on the couch that night. Sometime in the long middle of the night he woke up. It was some noise in his dream, a wheezy machinelike gasping, it jerked him upwards, and had him sitting straight up on the couch and he found himself white-knuckled, hyperventilating, heart-hammering-awake, wide awake. He tried to see through the darkness. There wasn't much to see. It was murky and shadowed everywhere he searched.

Except for one place.

He was being watched, he knew it. For one second, his headache was gone. Then, when Paul wasn't looking, the headache pounced on him again and dug its claws in. As he was doing his usual grimacing, he felt eyes staring at the back of his neck. He turned his head. A shadow was sitting cross-legged, Indian-style in a chair opposite Paul. He could barely make it out in the puddle of light falling from the ridiculously tiny lamp shining out of a long, metal worm thing drooping off the wall. Who made light bulbs that small? In worms? And why? Who would be comforted by a light like that? A worm-light? Who?

The shadow had hands. Something was in them. For a moment Paul had no idea when or where he was. He was swimming in strange shapes, wrong colors, odd chemical smells, nothing familiar like wood or furniture polish or soap. This was some kind of laboratory. He was an experiment. The shadow moved. Paul yelled.

The shadow froze. Wait a second, that was Daniel. Which meant he was, where? He couldn't think. Daniel sipped from the thing in his hands. He never took his eyes off of Paul.

"How long have you been sitting there, Daniel?"

"Long enough. So was this your plan?"

He had no idea what Daniel was talking about.

"Silence won't help you, whoever you are. I'm betting you can't even program a computer. You need me. Obviously, or you'll be homeless."

Paul didn't have a home. So he was already homeless. If that's what Daniel meant. Words were slippery in the future. They slid sideways before you could properly get a grip on them. Paul was homeless. Paul couldn't think of anything to say about that. This was going to be a one-sided conversation by the looks of it.

"So you switch bodies? Do you?

"Daniel…"

"You do that so you don't have to die? Is that the idea?

"I… What do you want me to say?"

"Don't start. How could you sleep with me?"

Things began to come back to Paul. He was starting to wake up.

"Is that coffee? What time is it?"

"Get it yourself. There's one more cup."

Wrapping and tying his blanket around his waist (why? Daniel had a perfect idea what Paul looked like nude – close up and nude – but Paul did it anyway), Paul bumped his shin against an unlikely orange cube in the middle of the floor. It left a dent. Worms and cubes. He'd never get used to this place.

"Could I have some light?"

"Get it yourself."

Paul, rubbing his indented shin, had had enough.

"Look, Daniel."

"Yeah?"

"I don't know why you think what you think, but I'm not who you think I am."

"Who do I think you are?"

"Some kind of burglar. Some kind of thief. A kind of, I don't know, soul-stealer. I don't know."

"And you're really just a victim, like the rest of us?"

"Something like that, yeah."

"So how do you do it?"

"Stop it, Daniel, just stop it."

"That's what I want to do – stop it. So how'd it happen?"

"Heck. I don't know. Don't you think I want to know? I didn't do a thing. Honest Injun."

"So, it just happened? All by itself?"

"All by itself, Daniel. How do you think it happened?"

"I don't know. I wasn't there. Just get everything back to the way it was and I'll be happy."

"But you were there. It happened right there. Right in the hospital room."

"Are you blaming me?"

"Maybe I need to get back there. Maybe I need to…"

"I... I need you gone. I think you're going to have to leave."

"Why? What? What are you saying? Why would you say that?"

"I don't have to have reasons. You don't know what happened. You can't make it right. You lie. You hurt people. You take advantage of people. I don't want you around me."

"I'm Jim's father. I'm Paul. I'm only 17. What do expect from me? It's not fair. Why do you hate me so much?"

"Because I do. Deal with it. I need to get back to the hospital. My husband is dying. You shouldn't be here when I get back."

Daniel began tossing pieces of clothing onto the bed. He went into the bathroom. Paul heard water running. He threw some clothes on. He jerked the drapes open. It was morning, mid-morning, late morning. He didn't know. Some kind of morning. He scoured the hotel room, and finally found the keys to the car in Daniel's jeans on the bed. The keys that weren't really keys but were a black plastic blob of machiney-things. Paul hated the future. Nothing was what it seemed.

He thought for a moment. But only a moment. He sprinted down the hotel corridor, dodging carts piled with towels and cleaning supplies and women speaking in another language. The car roared to life. He only had to stop twice at gas stations to get directions to the hospital. He didn't have much time If he had any time at all. Did he? Didn't he? He had no idea what he was doing.

81
PRESSURE

Yup. Paul had no idea what he was going to do.

But he was in a hurry to do it.

He ran down hallways. He bumped into people. He pulled doors open with a bang and impatiently waited on doors that insisted on opening themselves.

He got to the hospital room. It was empty.

He looked everywhere. He looked in the bathroom. He even looked in the cupboards and went through the drawers in the little table in the room.

It was an empty room.

No. No, this wasn't happening. No. He hadn't had a chance to say goodbye. He hadn't had any time at all. And now he was trapped here.

He moved a chair into the middle of the door where he could see down the hallway both ways. Then he sat down. Ah! Good. Good to stay still. He heard the machines going. Talking all around him. There was a fan running. He didn't know what to do. He held his head in his hands. His skull was splitting open from the inside out. He chomped some aspirin. Gulped some water. He couldn't think. So tired. Can't just give up. Just needed to think. To think for a minute. Just a minute. Just some rest. He was asleep in no time, head flopped backwards, drooling and snoring.

"Sir?"

"Sir?"

"Please? Sir?"

Someone was pushing on his shoulder.

"Sir? Could you move? We have to get this gurney past you. Thanks."

Paul woke up to a small crowd of people in the room. There was Jim, on a metal table with wheels. If anything he was more twisted than before. His eyes were closed. There were two guys – a nurse, and another nurse. It looked like two of his "sisters" were there, hovering in the background. They were typing on their hands. Something future people did a lot. There were also two angry eyes behind everybody, immediately behind the nurse. That would be Daniel.

Paul stood up, knocking the chair across the slick linoleum floor, and scrunched against the wall. Everyone squeezed past him. There was a fair amount of fidgeting and fumbling around with the various wires and tubes going every which way and then everyone squeezed out, the sisters included who told Daniel they had a lot of phone calls to make. Everyone was ignoring Paul. Which was fine. Well, everyone except Daniel. Daniel remained, looking at Paul. He was standing there, just standing there, staring, holding his right hand out, palm up, waiting. If stares were nails, Paul would have been securely fastened to the wall.

Paul dropped the keys into Daniel's hand. Daniel wordlessly pocketed them and made a motion with his head for Paul to leave. Daniel sat down in the chair by the bed. He took the hand by the bed in his again. He waited.

Daniel looked up. He looked at Paul. It wasn't a pleasant look.

"Nope. Not going, Daniel."

"I'll call the nurses, whoever-you-are."

"Look."

"No you look."

"If you know what's good for you, Daniel, you'll listen. For once. You are the most stubborn person I've ever met."

"Are you threatening me, Mister-I'm-only-seventeen-years-old? Because if you are… And who are you calling stubborn?"

"Look."

"Stop saying that."

"O.K. O.K., let's just, well, let's just try something. Besides, I think Jim wants your attention."

They both looked down. Jim was staring at both of them. His eyes alert, despite the melted look of one side of his face.

"And my name's Paul. Not whoever-you-are."

"Paul?"

"Yes."

"You're Paul? Really Paul? Mr. Olsen? You know, I knew you for a long time. I've was at every one of your Christmases for the last 38 years. At your house. Before your wide died. And after your wife died. I knew you for a long time. You know, I liked you. I liked you a lot. I miss you. I miss our long morning conversations before Jim woke up. You used to make me eggs benedict. Your own special recipe. You were very good to me."

Paul didn't know what to say to that.

"O.K. What are we going to do Paul?"

"We're going to try something."

"We're going to try something?"

"To try and reverse the whole thing."

"So you did do it – you do know how all this shit happened."

"No. Daniel, I don't."

"Then why?"

"Look. Do you have a better idea?"

"There's no talking to you."

"Or you either. So… are we even?"

"Uh, I guess. I don't want to be even though. I just want to be done."

82
QUELL

"Wait a second." Paul ducked out and grabbed a chair from the hallway.

"Move over, let me sit down. Here, give me Jim's hand."

"You know what you're doing?"

"I have no idea what I'm doing."

Paul sat down, took Jim's hand in his and looked into his eyes.

Daniel had the other hand. Jim watched them both.

Paul sat back. Then he leaned forward. He looked into Jim's eyes. What had he been doing? Right when he woke up sitting in this chair? What was the first thing he remembered in this crazy future world? What was it? Jim looked back and forth between the two of them. Paul closed his eyes and concentrated, gripping Jim's fragile, spotted hands in his.

Nothing.

He didn't feel a thing. Nothing was happening?

"You know, it's not going to be easy, Paul."

"What? What are you talking about, Daniel?" Paul looked over at Daniel, annoyed. "What? Reversing this? I know it won't be easy."

"No. Not this. Your life. You worked hard your whole life. You started out with a great job. But by time you retired, you were barely making ends meet."

"Why are you telling me this?"

"And your marriage wasn't the happiest. In fact, Jim used to say you should never have gotten married. You and your wife were such different people. I don't know. I liked both of you a lot. I loved you. But you fought constantly. Cats and dogs. Your whole life."

"What are you trying to do, Daniel"

"And then when you lost your wife – that was really hard for a couple of years. You were lost. Then things were better. But you got sick. The diabetes got worse. There were a lot of bad days."

"What are you trying to say?"

"I'm not saying anything. I'm just telling you. The life you're going back to, it wasn't the easiest."

"Well…"

"Maybe you're here, not because of what you did. Maybe it's not you. Maybe you're here because of something someone else did."

"What do you mean?"

Jim gripped Paul's hand harder. He could feel it. The pressure increased. His hands were so fragile, so cold.

"Maybe Jim did it."

"How would Jim know anything about body-switching?"

"I don't know. I don't know why or how any of this happened in your lives. I don't know why or how anything ever happens in my own life. Does anyone know? Really know? I don't think so. Life is strange. Things happen. You deal with it. You move on. But…"

"O.K. What are you saying?"

"Well, if you'd stop interrupting, you'd find out. Talk about stubborn."

"I'm not stubborn."

"Sure. Sure you're not."

"I'm not."

"O.K., you're not. Man! I can see where Jim gets that bullheadedness now. It's crystal clear. O.K. Think about it. Maybe it, this, this thing – whatever this thing is – is staying this way because Jim's wanting to give you a second chance. What a mess. That would be something that… I mean…. well, I could see Jim pulling a crazy stunt like this. Once he saw you here in this bed. You know, Jim just doesn't think. He gets that from you, he says. He's impulsive. Goes off half-cocked. I end up having to pick up the pieces. Only this time I can't. Maybe he wished you here. And this time Jim messed up and there's nothing I can do to fix it. Nothing. I've always been afraid this would happen. Pinche Jim."

Paul looked down at the eyes staring back up at him.

"You don't need to do this, Jim."

Paul squeezed Jim's hand.

"If you're doing anything. Stop it. Let me go. I'm not your responsibility."

Paul looked over at Daniel.

"I think you have your hands full right here."

One of the machines started blinking rapidly. Then it started to make a whining sound.

"Let go."

Jim shook his head on the bed. It wasn't much of a shake. But Daniel and Paul could see it.

"Whatever's ahead of me, it's what I chose. Or what I choose. I want those choices. Even the bad ones. I get to make those choices, not you."

Another one of the machines went off. It was a sort of electric scream. It wanted attention. Right now.

"Let go."

"I don't want more life."

"Let go of me, Jim. Let go."

"I'd better get a nurse, Paul. This doesn't sound good."

Paul looked down at Jim.

"We'll see each other again. No matter what, I'll come and find you. You aren't getting rid of me as easily as that."

It looked as if Jim were trying to smile.

"Let go. Give me a chance. Trust me."

Something else started screaming. It started low, and it rose in pitch, higher and higher. And then Paul was tumbling downwards. He fell. Lower and lower. His stomach did flip-flops. He wanted to throw up. It wasn't fun. He wished someone would take the vise off of his head and let it crack open once and for all. His head was killing him. And, oh yeah, his body was flapping in the wind, looking for a new set of bones to slip onto.

83

REBOUND

Zeke's face hung over his as if it were a zeppelin, a Zeke-elin. It was big and blotchy and it bobbed up and down and it was all Paul could see.

"Don't move, buddy. No. Don't even try. You're all broken up. Stan's on the other side of the bed. Nah. No moving. Don't. Don't look. You never listen, do you, brother? Boy! Did we get in trouble, huh? But it was worth it, right? You're O.K., huh? Right? Doc says you'll be fine. Right? O.K. You can talk now, dummy. Say something."

There was light streaming in a window. He was in a hospital room. A normal hospital room. No robots. No electric lights squirming and wriggling in the dark. No machines screaming or whispering to themselves. No people mumbling to themselves and petting their teensy-weensy phones. A Minnesota hospital room. Clean sheets. Spotless walls. Winter sunlight. And his two best friends.

So, he was going to live to be 90, huh? He was going to survive the war. He was going to get married, have kids, live in California?

Not bad, brother, not bad.

That's a lot of living to do.

Man, was he dizzy! He felt himself revolving, going around and around, faster and faster. Where was Zeke? Where was Stan? Where was Jim? Where was Daniel? This couldn't be right. This couldn't be… He spun around a couple of more times and then he conked out. Cold.

When he woke up, he was in the hospital – again? – the first time? – he couldn't remember – he couldn't tell what was real and what was this strange dream he'd had. Dad and mom said he'd talked a lot under the anesthetic. Then for a while he'd been awake, but still not talking sense. How did he feel now?

So, yeah, Paul was pretty messed up. Stitches and casts. But he was calm. And he couldn't stop smiling.

He couldn't wait to meet Jim. Sure, he couldn't wait. Now, he only needed to remember who the heck Jim was.

84
SUDDENLY

Machines beeping, Daniel came running into the room, followed by a very business-like nurse with flaming red hair, who moved to the other side of the bed. It seemed as if he, the nurse, wanted to scoot everyone out of the room. The guy who stole Jim's body wouldn't leave though. They didn't force him. Daniel stayed too. The fake Jim was holding Jim's father's hand. His father looked peaceful. Calm. Daniel was not. He stood next to the fake Jim, who looked sad and pathetic, and Daniel almost felt sorry for him. Almost.

Daniel looked at this person next to him out of the side of his eyes and he frowned.

"So that's it? You're stuck?"

"Yup. And so are you. Stuck with me."

"And why would I…"

"Because" said Jim, and he kissed Daniel. Daniel knew that particular type of kiss. It was very familiar.

"Huh! It's you."

"It's me."

"It's you."

"You already said that."

"What happened to your…"

"I have no idea. Shit happens."

"Yes it does."

"Good shit. Bad shit."

"Less talking. More kissing."

"Uh, excuse me. Excuse me, are you a member of Mr. Olsen's family?" It was the nurse with the red hair. The cute guy. Jim nodded. A doctor came into the room. She was quiet, but business-like. The three of them made room for her. There was a period of hushed discussion between the nurse and the doctor. In the interim, Amy and Teddie piled back into the room. They were whispering back and forth as they entered. They looked up, looked inside, stopped in their tracks.

"He's gone. He had a DNR, is that right? We could get a team in here to resuscitate, but we'd need to do it right away."

He was looking at Jim. The sisters were looking at Jim. Daniel was looking at Jim. Jim blushed. Jim didn't let go of his father's hand.

"No. No, he wouldn't want that. He didn't want to be resuscitated. He was ready. We both were ready. In the end. I don't think I know what the end means anymore. The end. It makes no sense. The end. Nope. Only words."

Jim looked at Daniel. Daniel shook his head. No. He didn't know either. They both looked back at the nurse and the doctor.

The doctor seemed to take that as a "no". And they were right. Jim watched his sisters step back out of the room. They were on their cells immediately. Jim and Daniel stood and stared at the wall. The doctor waited a moment then nodded.

The doctor and the nurse got busy. There seemed to be a lot of dictation going on. And a lot of careful tucking and folding.

85
TESTICLES

The nurse and the doctor worked around Jim for the most part. Sometimes, though, they had to get in closer to the bed, or they had to disconnect some hose or wire Jim was standing next to. That's where Daniel came into the picture. Daniel moved Jim about, as necessary, as if Jim were a piece of furniture. Getting him conveniently out of the way, repositioning him by the chair, moving him towards the window, moving him back towards the bed. Daniel was happy to do it and happy to keep a constant eye on Jim. Jim, for his part, wasn't noticing a thing.

Jim was in a cloud.

Blurry vision. Have to blink. Didn't help. Jim checked his cell. Ran his eyes up and down the screen. Tapped his thumb and flipped screens and still, he didn't see a thing. Not a single friggin' thing. What did he want to see? What?

Both Daniel's hands gripped Jim's upper right arm. Daniel held on as if Jim were slipping off the side of a ship. Slipping away and into the icy, black waters-of-no-return below. Not gonna happen. Not if Daniel had any say about it. Daniel wasn't letting go of Jim any time soon.

Jim continued blinking and tapping until some random neuron fired, and then another, and another and a realization bubbled up out of Jim's subconscious that Jim was holding his cell phone. He looked at it, recognizing it for the first time. The call log was scrolling past. Jim had it spinning as if it were a slot machine in Las Vegas. He spun it backwards until he came to the first entry, spun it forwards until he came to the last entry, spun it backwards…

All right. What are you looking for, Jimmy?

He spun it back to the top.

What do we have here?

Tons of work calls. He scrolled right past them. Two thumb flicks. And lots of texts. There were ten or so from Benny alone.

Benny.

Shit. Fuck. What are you going to do, Jim?

He glanced out of the side of his eyes over at Daniel. Daniel was smiling at Jim's ear. He leaned into Jim's neck. What was

Daniel thinking? He was holding onto Jim's arm. He wasn't letting go.

Benny. Well… Daniel probably knew, right?

And what if he didn't?

Well, nothing had changed, had it?

Had it?

Daniel was still here.

Jim was still here.

Sticking around. That counted for something. Despite Jim's whining and complaining, Jim had stuck around.

That was something. Something he could point to and say – I did that – that's real. Right? Right?

And Daniel was sticking around. Right?

There was a lot of good sticking around going on around here, around Jim.

Right?

Yeah?

And?

So? What are you going to do, Jim?

Jim leaned back into Daniel's neck. That seemed the best thing to do. And also, Jim didn't want to let go of his dad's hand. He'd grabbed it the last time Daniel had sashayed him away from the window back towards the bed.

The doctor and the nurse continued their mysterious errands. Daniel and Jim continued to stand in the middle of them all.

86
UNDERSTOOD

The nurse worked around Jim standing there, once again. The doctor put her hand on Jim's shoulder on her way out. The two sisters cornered the doctor as soon as she started down the hallway. Their voices disappeared into the normal, general background fuss and uproar of the hospital.

Daniel kept saying "You're back. You're back."

The nurse thought it an odd thing to say to someone who had just lost their father. At first he thought Daniel was talking to him.

The nurse didn't respond though. He knew. He nodded. He understood that no one honestly expected him to answer, even if they were saying something to him. He was used to people spouting nonsense, talking to themselves, talking to God out loud. Huge, important things happened to people around him every single day. Normal, nondescript stuff happened too. But you didn't remember that as much. It was the strange, wonderful, horrible, terrifying, ecstatic stuff that caught your attention. Every time. Every single day. And it happened. All the time. You saw it. Huge transitions. You got used to it. I mean what else could you do? What choice did you have? None. You didn't get a choice.

He moved on to his work station to begin his final report on Mr. Olsen, start the transfer to the morgue and leave those guys alone with their relative for as long as they needed. Yeah, as long as they wanted. Everybody said goodbye in different ways. You let people do what they needed to do. It wasn't hard. Most of the time. Although sometimes it was really hard. Yeah. But these two seemed to be taking it pretty well, though, better than usual. They'd probably be O.K. Sure. They'd be O.K.

87
VIRULENT

Paul got out of the hospital pretty quickly considering. Made it into the Navy. Made it out alive. He started college, finished, got a job, got married, then he got sad. Paul couldn't shake it.

He remembered this feeling. From when he was a teenager. The hurting-so-bad-you-forgot-who-you-were feeling.

His job turned out to be a dead-end. For some reason he wasn't surprised. His marriage wasn't the best. That didn't surprise him either. He was beat. He started drinking. O.K. that didn't work out so well. Then, he was ready to call it quits. He'd had enough. It was Paul 0, Life 1. He'd lost. They didn't have any kids yet. Which was a blessing, right? His exit would be simple and quick. The house was worth something, though, huh? It wasn't paid off, not by a long shot, but it had a tidy amount of equity. Susan would have a head start finding another guy. Maybe the next one would understand what she wanted. Paul sure didn't know, did he? She was still young. It wouldn't be the end of the world. Everyone could still be happy. There could still be a happy ending. Right?

In the shadows of the garage, Paul could barely spot his band saw on the table he'd made for it. The walls were covered with tools, and although you couldn't precisely see much of them, he knew they were there. They were polished and organized and hung on pegboard with neat outlines in magic marker of their shape for easy retrieval and easy storage. All the screw jars were labelled. Even the scrap lumber was sorted. Paul was proud of his little workshop. It would be someone else's soon.

But, yeah, the exhaust was getting pretty thick, brother. He was in their new Plymouth Fury III with the windows down, and he'd been running the motor for five minutes. He'd been coughing non-stop for three. He was starting to feel sleepy. That was fast, huh? Faster than he'd expected. But that was good, too, right?

He felt a familiar click in the back of his neck. It took him a second to realize what it was.

<cough>

No. <cough>

Nope. Not doing it <cough><cough> again. No.

I'm not. <cough>

He saw penguins marching in from the right.

<cough><cough>

Ah. C'mon, guys!

<cough><cough><cough>

Then he felt his body slipping off his bones. He was falling, faster and faster, face forward, down and down and down and down, he saw comets shooting past and the moon and then he saw the stars hurl past him in the sky – an odd sky – a sky black as midnight – cold but filled with light, a solid light, as if Paul were burrowing to the center of the Antarctic Ice Sheet – and he felt summers piling on winters piling on summers piling on winters piling on summers piling on...

With a thump he landed.

Face down.

His mouth filled with blood.

He broke his nose on a pane of glass in front of his face.

That sure got his attention.

That and the fact that Paul's breath had been knocked right out of him.

He struggled for a long time to get air back into his lungs. He really didn't think he was going to make it.

88
WHIRLYGIGS

Paul tried to move but he couldn't. Blood was puddling on the glass in front of his face.

A pleasant female voice (patient, official) with a strong accent kept announcing his oxygen something-or-other. And saying the name Lela. Who was she? Lela? And why would she be so curious about Paul's oxygen? The numbers kept going down. The voice was sounding unhappier and unhappier. Paul couldn't understand half the words. The voice plainly barely spoke American English. Probably Chinese. Or Vietnamese. Paul listened. Paul kept bleeding onto the glass.

He felt strangely heavy in the upper ribcage area. He squirmed his arms about (he was in some kind of plastic bandage – wrapped over 100% of his body – it tickled and it pulled on him whenever he shifted his body) and as he tried to free himself from whatever was pressing down on his lungs he was shocked to discover he had breasts on his chest. They were attached to him. It was his own flesh. Which meant… He squirmed some more. Yup. Stuff was missing down-under. Important stuff.

The voice kept chiding him about oxygen.

Paul kept bleeding.

Paul looked up.

He shouldn't have. Yeah, it was very hard to move his neck, painful in fact, but mostly he shouldn't have because he didn't end up liking what he saw.

The sun was going down. Way far away. At the opening of a canyon. He was in a canyon. The sun was a pale gold-white color. It was a wimpy sun, a pinprick of a sun. The lower part of the sky was a brilliant, dark blue. The blue ringed the horizon then faded as you went upwards. At least what he could see of it did that. The rest of the sky was red. Reddish. You couldn't really see a lot of sky as a matter of fact. He thought he could see stars coming out behind him. O.K. He wasn't at all sure about these new sky-color-schemes. The sky was turning out to be pretty much a mystery to Paul. He was on the bottom of a canyon for cripes sakes!

The ground under his body was red. He was lying at the base of a cliff. It was a big honker of a cliff. He must've fallen off, huh? Why was he still alive? He'd made a little impact crater in the dust. The dust was still settling. In graceful, balletic puffs.

Rows of numbers and symbols scrolled across his view. More collected on either side of his face. Strange mini-movies played here and there. A circle with two dots inside of it, on the left side was outlined in bright red. It looked important. It looked military. More numbers that looked as if they might be latitude and longitude were under it. There was this tiny map. He could see an X on it, it was green, and little (red) arrows with dots puffing out behind them were making their way towards the X.

O.K.

Fine.

If he was the X, did he want to wait for the arrows?

Or if he was the X, did he want to run away from the arrows?

All right, Universe. Which is it?

He'd already figured out he was on Mars. Or a red planet. If not The Red Planet. He wasn't on earth, he was sure of that. Well. Almost sure. And he was a woman. Yes. That was true. And it probably wasn't 1971 anymore. That's when he saw, of course, the giraffes.

"They never did talk, you know."

And the penguins, riding their backs.

"It was the pikas, all the time. Ventriloquism."

Paul realized it wasn't the penguins talking, it was a row of little balls of fur to his right. Bouncing slowly in the evening light. Must be the pikas.

"You can call me Fred," said a voice high above his head. That was a penguin. He could recognize a penguin's voice anywhere.

"Call him Fred," said another voice. Plainly another penguin.

"They never stop, do they?" said one of the bouncing furballs.

Paul spit out a bit of broken tooth and ran his tongue over the rest and found all the other broken parts. There were quite a few. He cleared out his mouth. What came out of his mouth went on this faceplate. He coughed. That hurt. More liquids dribbled onto the old faceplate. It was rapidly becoming opaque. Paul blinked and tried to breathe. He coughed again. The official voice was getting frantic. It started repeating numbers two and three times a second.

"O.K. Fred," said Paul. Paul found he had a high, pleasant, feminine voice – probably a soprano if he (well, she) were singing in a choir, maybe St. Francis choir back home. He had a strange accent too. Not unpleasant. Just strange.

"He got it," said a distinctly penguin-like voice. It was familiar. It sounded astonished. A little stunned. Maybe a little disappointed.

"You're Fred. That's your name. I get it."

"Yes, he's got it. Well, almost all of it."

"How many more times do we have to do this little party game? How many times do I have to die?

"Paul!" "Paul!" "We lied." "The giraffe's really do talk," A chorus of little voices skipped and leaped slowly up and down around his/her head. Paul could hardly hear the penguins now for the squealing and the chirping and the dancing and prancing in front of his faceplate. They were trying to distract him. Acting like kids, little kids. What the…

"Ignore them. They hate that" said a voice from high up. That was a new voice. It was deep. And echoey. As if it had a very long neck from which its voice had to be constructed.

Paul took a deep breath and spoke into his faceplate.

"O.K., O.K., Look, I'll be a good boy. Just let Lela here or whoever she is die in peace. Or recover in peace. Get me out of here. I'll get out of the garage, promise. Cross my heart and hope to die."

"Now he's got it." A penguin voice. And, yup, once again, the penguin was depressed. It was unhappy. What was it with these guys? There was just no pleasing these penguins. No matter what he did..

The oxygen voice was almost hysterical at this point. Yeah, Paul was having a heck of a time trying to get enough air in his lungs to talk, let alone live. The voice had a point. A definite point. Paul should do something. And soon. And Paul was listening. And if he could've done anything, if there was something for him to do, for darned sure, Paul would've done it. But. There wasn't anything, was there? Paul was out of options. And Paul was out of luck.

He could hear the penguins discussing something in murmurs and sighs above his head. The little balls of fur were preserving a sullen silence as they bounced. Facing him. It was eerie. The beady little pika eyes never left his bloodied faceplate.

"Guys?" <cough><cough>

"Guys!" <cough> "I hope the arrows are," <cough> "coming to help her. What I should do?" <cough> "I want to help."

<cough> "I should do something... for Lela... something... I should... I..."

But he was slipping back. All the flesh coming undone. Sliding off and slipping upwards. As he floated up faster and faster he passed impossibly long legs and a pert mouth and gorgeous eyes adorned with eyelashes the size of Japanese fans. Paul heard a deep-ish voice.

"Yes, we talk. When there's something to say."

89
X-TRA

And then the red planet became a red dot, which rapidly became a twinkling red star, and then there was a lot of black and then a blue marble hoved into view and a gray marble next to it, and they waltzed in front of Paul's eyes for a bit and before he knew it Paul was clicking back onto and into a familiar body with a familiar set of bones. He'd barely slipped and snapped into place when he was coughing, and Susan was frantically fanning the air in the car with a newspaper she'd pulled from the trash, while she pulled on his arm, trying to drag him out of the driver's seat of the Fury III. She wasn't a big woman. She hadn't pulled him very far. The car wasn't running anymore. The garage door was up. She was crying. He could see his tools again. There wasn't a penguin in sight. He crawled on all fours out into the inevitable, cheerful California sunlight.

He collapsed against the decorative brick siding on their ranch style house. He pushed his feet through the small bush he'd recently planted by the corner of the garage and closed his eyes. He could smell hot brick and stucco. He could hear the freeway in the distance. He concentrated on his breathing. It was taking a lot of concentration. He was so sleepy. Susan didn't say anything. She didn't demand. She didn't fall to pieces. She wasn't crying, not anymore, but she held him. Paul had never seen her like that before.

Maybe it was time to have kids. Yeah. He was thinking, maybe four. No, five. None of them would be called Fred. He was sure of that. He wasn't sure why. But he was sure. He did like the name James though, for some reason. Fine name, that. James. Jim. The first boy they'd have to name after Susan's grandfather, Luke, they'd already decided on that, Susan got first choice, that was fine by Paul. But the next son, he was going to be Paul's to name. So, Jim it was.

It seemed important to remember that. Again, he wasn't sure why. But he closed his eyes and repeated the name over and over to himself as he sat in that oven of a sun and whooped and barked his lungs out and put his arm around Susan's shoulders.

Jim.

Jim.

Jim.

Jim.

Jim.

90
WHY

Well, that's the way Paul wanted to remember his life.

But it wasn't that simple. It never had been. And it wasn't going to be now. Not this time. Not ever. Nice try, Paully.

91
ZERO

Paul didn't "return" for a year or so. As he found out later.

His wife pulled a body out of the garage, but the person inside the body she pulled out was Lela. That was a shock. To Paul's wife. And to Lela.

Then Paul had come back. Suddenly. Unexpectedly.

"Paul. No more of those stories. We have to eat."

"Amy wants a little more."

"I don't think it's Amy that wants more."

"What did you say, Susan?"

"Nothing. Your food's getting cold. You heard the dinner bell."

Paul lowered his voice and tried to speak faster.

"So, Amy, Lela was the great-great-great granddaughter of Paul and a famous areo-engineer on the Great Circle Trans Mars Rail Project."

"You mean the 3rd Great Circle Trans Mars Rail Project, daddy?"

"Yeah. You're right. It was the third. What a memory! You're a very intelligent girl, did I ever tell you that?"

"Every day. And you're Paul. I know, I know. Tell me more about Lela."

"No, Paul's only a guy in the story. He has the same name as me. Stop rolling your eyes. It's true. O.K. Moving on. More about Lela. Why do you want to know so much about her? Maybe because that's your middle name, right? Right? Hey there!. No pulling on my arms. You're getting strong. You'll pull one right off one of these days, if I don't civilize you some. That's right, civilize. It means... O.K. O.K. All right. Lela. Here goes. Lela got caught in the fighting between the Federal Martian Guards and, yes, the G-Group (you're right – the biggest mega-corp on Mars) during the Wars of Independence. Both G-Group and the Feds were building the rail system. But only one could own it."

"Why? I don't know. That's just the way it was. No one wanted to have only a part of it. Everyone wanted everything, all of it."

"Yeah, it was stupid. You're right. People should share."

"So, At one point, an act of sabotage (sabotage is... oh, you already know what sabotage is – guess you've heard this story before, huh?) so, a bomb blew Lela's body into the air in an explosion and she fell – all the way from the top of the Land's End canyon down to the bottom. It took a long time to fall. You fall slower there. Land's End is called... right! Valles Marineris – the... – yup, right again – biggest canyon in the Solar System. How'd you know all that? Did I ever tell you you're a very intelligent girl? Every day?"

"C'mon you two. Last call. Now. You hear me? I'm not saying it again, Paul! Paul?"

"You want to finish the story yourself, Amy?"

"Oh daddy. Can't you tell it quick? I like it better when you tell it. You make better voices. Ah. C'mon... Please? Please? But you have to promise you won't laugh, O.K? You're nodding yes, right? O.K. So, Lela shouldn't have lived after she fell. But all the dust clouds that happened after the sabotage got the attention of a mining bot and Lela was pulled into an emergency medpod. The G-Group medteam found the medpod, and Lela was safe. Before any more bombs could drop on her. The G-Group lost the war,

Earth and Jupiter made everybody be friends again. Mars broke up into pieces. Lela left G-Group and she worked for some of the pieces called the Mars Commonwealths. G-Group was mad and threw a moon down at Mars, and it hurt a lot of people, especially in the capital city, but luckily, Lela got out before the moon could hurt her. Hey! All right. I'm going. I'm going. Ah, mom… I was almost done."

Paul and Amy were being pushed by two strong arms into the kitchen and through that into the dining room. The other four kids were already there, eating (or not eating – they ate like birds, unless they were having waffles – the Olsens had a lot of waffle dinners) and little Jimmy was dropping his mashed peas on the cat under the table. The dog was licking them off the floor. And off the cat. The kids were chopping their pork chops into smaller and smaller pieces. Everyone had a job at dinner time. It was a system. There were rules. It worked.

Susan whispered at Paul as she passed.

"You promised. No more stories."

Susan missed Lela. Susan missed being listened to. There'd been a lot more conversation back and forth and a lot more "paying attention" and "talking it over" before Lela made her exit, and Paul made his new entrance. Apparently. Susan brought that up occasionally. Occasionally being every other day. Paul didn't know how to respond to that. So, mostly he didn't.

Paul pushed his chair back and winked at Amy. Amy didn't see. She was busy cutting up her pork chops. Susan grilled them (the pork chops) mercilessly when it was pork chop night, until each one of them were pretty much what you would nail on to the bottom of a good pair of working shoes. Leather, in other words. No child of hers was ever going to get worms from food she was responsible for. If they ate most of their pork chops, and their mashed potatoes, they got huge dollops of homemade applesauce from the enormous bowl in the middle of the table. Everyone was working diligently, eyes peering over their plates at the translucent amber mounds of sugary cinnamon goodness just out of reach in front of them.

Susan had also made steamed artichokes, with strained butter for dipping (for the adults). The kids thought their parents were a little off, eating weeds, and in public. Paul didn't have the heart to tell Susan he hated artichokes. Apparently Lela had loved them.

He'd have to tell her soon, right?

92
ANTIDOTE

Paul never told the kids that Lela didn't make it out of the capital city. She was there when it vaporized. As the blast hit and Lela/Paul was blinded, and then a tsunami of fire rolled over him/her and she/he was flame-broiled, and then cinderized and then efficiently dispersed by a nuclear hurricane into the thin Martian atmosphere, while all that was going on, Paul saw familiar shapes outlined in the glare of the explosion as the moon fragment hit.

There was this classic nuclear bomb flash on the Martian horizon. Then there were these even more classic shapes not ten feet away.

They were, of course, penguin-shaped.

And surprisingly, they looked happy.

And yeah, as usual, happy penguins were always a bad sign for Paul.

Darn.

There was the routine, quick, body-slip-n-click, and Paul popped back into his family's life in 1972. Lela was dead on Mars in the future. Paul was alive on Earth in the present. Death and click. Then and here. That's the way it worked for Paul. He wasn't complaining. He just wasn't happy.

Paul was not surprised to find his wife and kids had been happier with Lela than they had been with him. Paul decided to turn over a new leaf. He was a new Paul. It took him a while. He worked hard at it. But before another year was over, Susan and Paul were as miserable as they had ever been before. Probably more so.

No wonder the penguins were happy.

This wasn't working out. Not at all. But Paul was trapped.

Susan loved the kids. Paul loved the kids. But Susan and Paul were more of an economic life-support system for their growing family than they were partners marching bravely into their own futures, arm in arm, now weren't they? O.K. It was true. Things weren't turning out the way Paul had envisioned it when he'd met

Susan years ago. This wasn't the life he'd signed up for. And, to be absolutely honest, it wasn't the life Susan had signed up for either. Was it? No. It wasn't. What person in his right mind would sign up for a life like this?

And Paul was having serious doubts about the rest of his life again. He was sad. And getting sadder. And you know… It never hurts – if you've already punched yourself in the face a dozen times and fallen, writhing on the floor in agony – it never hurts to kick yourself in the groin too as hard as you can and as often as you can, just to get the point across, again and again (that it hurts) solidly and thoroughly, and ensure that you never forget, and that the hurt never stops. Yeah. It works. It's evidence-based. It's a proven technique. Backed by research. It invariably gets the point across. Hurting hurts.

And hurting a guy while he was down, Paul was good at that, especially if the guy he was hurting was himself.

93
BEING

Yeah, Paul was nothing, if not consistent.

Paul went through the same cycle, depression, suicide, bouncing into ever-more-distant futures, he did it many, many times, after the kids grew up. Susan never got used to it. It was tough on her, having to get to know new people, Paul admitted it. It'd be tough on anybody. Heck, it was tough on Paul.

New lives. New personalities. It was strange and exciting. Then it was just strange. Then it just was.

Susan passed. Then Paul was alone. That was an eye-opener. Paul realized how much he'd needed her. Man! Did he realize it! He was still depressed. But now he was alone. And depressed. He dated a little. He was a little less alone. But he was still depressed.

The cycle continued. And so did Paul's life. And Paul's life, well, it wasn't a life exactly, was it? But it was better than nothing, right? The snapping? The clicking? The slipping? It was something, right? Not nothing?

Sometimes life is really good. Most times it isn't. Paul ploughed on through all of it. All the goodness. All the strangeness. All the in-between. He got on with it. He was a Minnesotan. That's what

Minnesotans did. They got on with it.

94
CODA

As he got older, Paul didn't think he got any wiser.

He looked in the mirror, and instead of seeing wisdom beaming out from his aged face, Paul saw wrinkles. Crinkling wrinkles. Skin blotched wrinkles. Crevassing wrinkles. Sagging wrinkles. Wrinkles on wrinkles. A lot of wrinkles.

And he saw more than wrinkles. Paul saw long nose hairs. Longer ear hairs. Eyes red-rimmed, runny, bloodshot and distracted. Scaly skin cancers.

And Paul saw other stuff staring back at him in his eyes. Odd stuff. Strange stuff. Familiar foolish hopes. Unrealistic trust. Hugely un-met expectations.

Strange stuff. His stuff.

But not buckets of wisdom, no.

Actually, it was soothing. Encouraging even. There was still a little residue of seventeen-year-old smeared here and there in Paul's life, in Paul's body. There was a lot of experience and learning, yeah, of course. And lots of scars. Scars all over the place. But there was also the leftovers. Hopes, trusts, expectations. A little in the corners. A bit in the closets. Tiny amounts forgotten behind the couch. The seventeen-year-old was still there, despite everything life had dumped on and over his head. He was there. If you looked for him. With all his imperfections and irrationalities. If you looked, you saw him.

Paul liked that. Paul looked. And he saw.

The minute before he'd had his last stroke, Paul had been shaving. Nothing unusual about that. Paul did it a lot. He liked to be clean. However, the older Paul got, the more shaving changed. Lately, shaving resembled de-needling a cactus. His facial hair was tough. You could make sewing needles out of the stuff if you wanted – the gray hairs were short but indestructible. And the skin – Paul's skin had deep wrinkles to shave into and over (as he'd already pointed out) – you had to grimace and smile, pull and stretch, you could probably get two faces-worth of skin off of Paul's head if you needed to, there was so much extra skin sagging around up there now.

So, yeah, Paul's was the face of a cactus, an ancient Saguaro, most likely. If Saguaro's had faces. Which they didn't. Paul had been to Arizona many times. Saguaro's were faceless, right? Anyways, Paul was shaving, and as shaving always took a while with his new electric shaver, no matter how speedy the commercials said it should be (it wasn't, how could endless repetitive scraping ever be called speedy?), regardless, shaving left Paul with lots of time to kill. Getting himself cleaned and polished took time, and Paul had the time, and he put it to good use. He used it. For thinking.

He was in his rehab apartment in his overly-roomy bathroom that had been built for wheelchair whirling and spinning and wheel-in, rolling showers. It was very white. The light was very bright. The fan motor was very loud and powerful. The toilet was powered by a turbine engine (Paul swore you had to have a pilot's license to sit on it). Paul's rehab place did not believe in fooling around when it came bathrooms. These bathrooms meant business. No doubt about that. Not places to relax in. No. They were places to roll up your sleeves in and get some serious work done in.

Luckily, Paul still could get around on his own two feet. No wheelchairs. No canes. Except when he was in the hospital. And that hadn't happened for months. Not bad for a 90 year old, nearly 91, huh? He'd been wondering how he'd made it this far, after his crazy life, after all the crazy jumping about he'd done and the places he'd been and the people he'd been and he'd asked himself – why am I still here?

And then it hit him. He stopped shaving for a moment.

His left hand felt a little weak. He was starting to get a headache. He moved the razor to his right hand.

I am still here.

I chose to be here.

Through it all.

That's why I'm still here.

I'm still here because I'm still here.

I stuck around.

I did it.

I'm still here.

And I've changed.

I've changed since I've been here.

I've changed because I've been here.

He was feeling dizzy, so he sat down on the toilet.

He was dizzy and he was hot and he thought, remember this, Paul. Remember. You should remember this. Remember.

You know what I should remember? I should remember to lie down. I'm so hot. So tired. So nice, just to lie down on those cool white tiles. Lie down on the floor. So good. They'd feel good to rest my face on. Cool. Smooth. So good. So nice.

So he did.

One of the caretakers found him a couple of hours later, when she returned his laundry and went into the bathroom to hang up his towels and also went in wondering (a little grumpily) why Paul left the lights on (again) when he clearly wasn't using the room.

They ambulanced him to a hospital. They put him in a room with one cozy light. They played Big Band music to cheer him up when he was awake and when he was asleep. They played music all the time. His favorites. They were right. It made a difference. It cheered him up. His son visited him there one night with his husband. He remembered. He remembered that. He ended up remembering a lot of things.

0
AFTER

You know the feeling. It's a bad feeling.

Being.

It's confusing.

Then it gets worse.

Being.

Pleasures land on your front doorstep in fat, juicy parcels, so reliably, one after another, you don't even bother unwrapping them, let alone pick them up. Then, one day, you find steaming piles of pain and boredom deposited instead, and you wish you'd owned a different doorstep and you wonder, you have to ask – is there a reason behind all this?

Being.

There's no sense to it. What's the cause and effect of it? Where's the justice in it? How do its rewards and punishments work? And why? You ask why. Nobody gives you an answer.

There's no neat system of pluses and minuses. No equals sign giving you what you deserve. No tools. None that you can see. Or use. You end up un-asking the questions.

Being.

As long as you're here, and you are still here, maybe while you're asking and un-asking these questions, maybe you can practice something else. A new skill. A pastime. A kind of hobby. Like… Maybe… Love. It's something to do. As long as you're here. And you're still here. Who knows? Maybe questions weren't the reason we were here. Or answers.

It's confusing.

Being.

You know the feeling. It's a bad feeling.

But not all the time.

ABOUT THE AUTHOR

Anders lives a quiet life which is getting quieter on the edge of the continent in California.

He sees life, increasingly, as a race against time. It's not a race he can win. So he's stopped trying. The important thing to remember is that all of us are going to lose that race. It makes you look at people differently. We're all on the Titanic together. We're all going under, we're all going to lose. The race was always fixed. Always. It's freeing. Freedom is freeing (unsurprisingly). It's giving yourself permission to be happy, right now, right this very minute, no postponing, no procrastinating. Freedom. Now.

But you have to give yourself permission. You have to say it's O.K. It doesn't happen by itself, not very often.

Then you have to find something to do with all the new energy you've decided to give yourself. Learning to love the people in front of you better – that's always a good hobby. But you come up with one of your own. Make the time remaining meaningful, be it one day, one decade or six decades.

Freedom. It's powerful. And it's frightening. It's the reason the band kept on playing as the Titanic sank. They were free women and men. They were free by choice. They chose it. No one could take that away from them. And no one ever did. They made it their own. That's the hard part – choosing. Or even knowing you have the ability or right to choose. Once you know, it gets harder not know it, even harder to forget it. Freedom. It's addictive.

And it's insane. There are hundreds of different things we have no control over in our lives. It's true. Freedom is freely choosing the uncontrollable, making it your choice, and letting it go. Then getting on with doing what you really wanted to do all along. It's crazy, right? To think you're free? It's insane. Go insane. Do it. For yourself. For everyone around you. Choose to consider yourself free.

Or not. You're free to choose. You have been free all along.